Kiss
the
morning
star

Kiss the morning star

by elissa janine hoole

SKYSCAPE

SKYSCAPE

We're grateful for permission to reprint 360 words from *The Dharma Bums* as well as 18 haiku from *Book of Haikus, Desolation Angels,* and *Some of the Dharma* by Jack Kerouac:

For *Book of Haikus*: Reprinted by permission of SLL/Sterling Lord Literistic, Inc. Copyright by the Estate of Stella Kerouac, John Sampas, Literary Representative, 2003.

For *Desolation Angels*: Reprinted by permission of SLL/Sterling Lord Literistic, Inc. Copyright 1965 by Jack Kerouac, renewed 1993 by Jan Kerouac, renewed 1995 by Joyce Johnson.

For *The Dharma Bums*: Reprinted by permission of SLL/Sterling Lord Literistic, Inc. Copyright by John Sampas, Literary Representative of the Estate of Jack Kerouac; Lohn Lash, Executor of the estate of Jan Kerouac; Nancy Bump; and Anthony M. Sampas, 1958.

For *Some of the Dharma*: Reprinted by permission of SLL/Sterling Lord Literistic, Inc. Copyright by the Estate of Stella Kerouac, John Sampas, Literary Representative, 1997.

Library of Congress Cataloging-in-Publication Data
Hoole, Elissa Janine.
  Kiss the morning star / by Elissa Janine Hoole. — 1st ed.
     p. cm.
  Summary: The summer after high school graduation and one year after her mother's tragic death, Anna and her longtime best friend Kat set out on a road trip across the country, armed with camping supplies and a copy of Jack Kerouac's *Dharma Bums*, determined to be open to anything that comes their way.
  ISBN 9781477816660 (paperback) — ISBN 978-0-7614-6271-2 (ebook)
  [1. Self-realization—Fiction. 2. Coming of age—Fiction. 3. Grief—Fiction. 4. Love—Fiction. 5. Voyages and travels—Fiction. 6. Lesbians—Fiction.] I. Title.
  PZ7.H7667Ki 2012   [Fic]—dc23   2011042177

Book design by Sonia Chaghatzbanian
Cover photograph by Digital Vision/Thomas Barwick/Getty Images
Editor: Melanie Kroupa

First edition

To my favorite road trip companion,
from your scribbling navigator,
with love

—e.j.h.

Kiss *the* morning star

1

The dog yawned
and almost swallowed
My Dharma
—Jack Kerouac

It's strange how a plan can unfold sometimes—an umbrella shooting up at the touch of a button and extending out in all directions quickly, effortlessly. In so many ways, this journey is exactly the wrong thing to do. I mean, what kind of daughter leaves her grieving father and takes off across the country for no reason, or no reason she can say out loud? But I look at Katy beside me—I see her clutching that book like always, the bright flash of her blue toenails on the dash—and I can't help but smile.

It comes over me in a rush, as we pull into a spot at Camden State Park, the sun setting in an impressive fiery red ball behind our campsite.

The light. Red like the iron ore dust that settled on the sills of the shabby apartment where I abandoned my father. I can still hear the trains rattling through the thin walls of my bedroom at night, the whistle growing so loud and then fading, into the distance. I can still see his pale face at the window, the small motion of his hand, waving good-bye—a sorrow-laden blessing.

A feeling. Real feelings, rushing over me like the strands of the retro bead curtain in Katy's basement, each one familiar and fleeting, clacking together softly in my wake. It's the first time in forever I'm actually interested in what comes next—or even in what happens now.

She would not shut up about the rucksack revolution. I have no idea how many times Katy read that passage to me, how many times she begged me to do something exciting with our last summer together—something besides shuttling coffee to little old ladies and phony hipster teens at the Village Inn. Something besides taking care of my father.

I never believed we'd really go. I mean, how could I leave? There was my dad, lying on that sunken Goodwill bed, no longer able to sway me with his golden voice, staring bleakly into the dusk. The ever-present tumbler of whiskey leaving rings on the hardwood floor.

But the idea was so tempting—a way to escape. I thought of the stacks of college applications lying untouched in their envelopes on the kitchen counter. My lack of a boyfriend, my persistent virginity. The fact that I don't believe in God anymore.

"Just listen to this, Anna." Kat forced her dad's battered copy of *The Dharma Bums* into my hands. She's been spouting the words of Jack Kerouac at me since April, when Mr. Griffin made us do these research projects about catalysts of social change. Kat's dad suggested we study this crazy group of writers from back in the fifties and sixties called the beatniks. Kerouac was his favorite, and he dragged out all his old, raggedy books from college, including this one. Kat quoted it from memory.

". . . I see a vision of a great rucksack revolution thousands or even millions of young Americans wandering around with rucksacks, going up to mountains to pray, making children laugh and old men glad, making young girls happy and old girls happier, all of 'em Zen lunatics who go about writing poems that happen to appear in their heads for no reason . . . ." Her voice resonated with excitement.

"See? Doesn't that sound perfect?"

Perfect. Yes, perfect for Katy, who must think I'm still the girl she knew a year ago. The girl who cared. The girl who dared.

I shrugged, the noncommittal gesture that I have adopted as my main method of communication. "Well, it sounds pretty, but I mean, what's the point of it?" I closed the Kerouac book and handed it back. "So we take off on some 'rucksack revolution,' for what? I don't think I've got any spontaneous poetry in my head, and I *know* I don't have any more prayers."

"Anna babe, your whole life is a prayer." Kat tapped the cover of *The Dharma Bums*. "And Jack here. He can show you the poetry." She flipped through the pages, not like she was looking for something specific, but more like she just wanted to feel the words running through her fingers. She was so excited, so filled with hope, like she could change the world. I think I used to feel that way, at times. But it's hard to remember. Before.

"Yeah, right," I said. "A prayer to something I don't believe in."

Kat's hands froze. "What are you talking about, Anna babe? Of course you believe. In God?"

"Whatever."

"No whatevers! You can't just whatever *God!*"

"Well, if God *is* real, he whatevers *me* all the time. Look, maybe there is a God, and maybe there isn't. But I'll tell you what I *don't* believe in anymore. I don't believe in God's love."

The thing is, I'm not even sure that's true. I mean, it was true when I said it, but thoughts like that are shifty; it's impossible to pin them down.

Kat wrapped her hands around her hair, pulling it into pigtails the way she always does when she's thinking. "Well, there you go. We'll leave right after graduation."

"Katy, stop it with the dharma bum crap. We're not doing this. I told you. There's no point."

Kat shook her head. "Oh, we're going. The *point* is to find proof of God's love," she said, and then laughed. "And who knows? Maybe we'll even get laid."

Reasons Why This Dharma Bum Business Is Crazy Talk

- *What the hell is a rucksack revolution, anyway?*
- *No matter what Katy says, there's no way I'm getting laid. I'm probably going to be a virgin for the rest of my life.*
- *What if things have changed too much? I've barely talked to Katy—to anyone—in the last eight months. Awkward silence on a road trip is . . . awkward.*
- *Jack Kerouac—what I know about him isn't making this seem less crazy—didn't he drink himself to death?*
- *What will my dad do if I leave? What will he do if I stay?*
- *What will I do if I stay?*

But on the Other Hand

- *What if it's not crazy? What if it's exactly what I need?*
- *What if?*

2

The summer chair
rocking by itself
In the blizzard
—Jack Kerouac

She was always singing, though not always in tune. Hymns, of course, but also show tunes—she belted them out brave and funny while she worked in the garden, her long hair gathered up in a silk scarf, smelling of jasmine.

They sang together, all that summer the year I turned twelve, the year we moved to Sterling Creek and my parents built their church, their dream. They were happy.

We were happy.

My father's voice slid neatly under hers, under the sound of saws and hammers. It was almost like the church—and our home in the parsonage upstairs—was held together by the sound of their voices. So it shouldn't be a surprise, I guess, that my father's voice disappeared along with those walls, along with the dreams they built together.

There is a clump of dead thing on the road in front of us; its muddy brown fur lifts softly in the prairie wind. A gruesome flash of ravens as we pass.

"I'm making a new category for ones like that. The ones I can't identify." Kat makes a tally mark on the back cover of my spiral notebook. Her hands are already tanned a rich gold, even though we've only been on the road for two days.

"I think that one had a collar." I can't help shuddering a little, even though I'm joking. Death is always harder when it's fresh.

Kat laughs. "Collared Critters! Another great category for the Roadkill Count." She scribbles something with my purple pen. "I'll put it next to "Possibly a Hitchhiker.""

I settle back against the driver's seat, my right arm outstretched to rest on top of the gearshift. The sun slanting through the windshield makes me squint. "This was a good idea, Kat. *Is* good." And it is. I've been still so long, cooped up with my empty-shell self—it feels strange to be moving, entirely present in space and time. With Katy back in my life (or me back in hers) and the road ahead, for once the world doesn't feel too heavy, too crushingly real for me to bear.

Kat turns down the music. "So my dad sat me down for his 'Think Carefully About Your Future' talk," she says, imitating her dad's serious tone. I smile, picturing his worried brows knitted together above the smudged tortoiseshell glasses he has worn since we were kids.

"He was all, 'Young lady, you had better think about this very carefully. A degree in commercial art or design will allow you the income you need, the *stability* you need, to be able to create your *other* art.'" Kat laughs, but there's a catch in her voice. "*Ugh*, the way he said that, like fine art is somehow dirty or . . . I don't know, shameful. My secret pornographic life."

"Well, I guess . . . I can see his point, Kat. And with so many options for digital media . . . " I'm treading carefully here, stealing a sideways look to make sure it's all right, that my long stretch of silence is forgiven. I'm still trying to find my way back inside this friendship, to the freedom I used to have with her. "I mean, starving artists and all."

Kat sighs, pushing back against the seat. "I know, Anna. I *know*. The sensible part of me knows. But graphic art? What the hell? Why would I want to spend my *life* designing blog headers or . . . advertisements? Whatever. Art should be important. Art should . . . *change things.*"

I nod, but I'm not sure I understand what she's getting at. Can art really change things? I remember when we painted that mural on the ceiling of her bedroom two years ago, the beehive with the bees dancing. It was interesting, lying on Kat's electric blue bedspread looking up at all that geometry, but did it change us?

"You don't believe me," she says.

"You know I'm not artistic." I'm not musical, graceful, or athletic, either. I basically have no skills. "At least you know what you want to do with your life." A lurch of panic in my chest. Maybe I should have enrolled in the community college after all. This road trip won't last forever.

"What happened to social work?"

"Katy Kat, that was from when we were like thirteen." That was from before I became the kind of kid who *needed* a social worker.

"So is that nickname," she says, slapping the back of my notebook with the palm of her hand. "I'm not a child anymore. From this moment on, I shall be called Katherine."

"Katy." I've missed her. I've missed this old playful tone that has crept into my voice, the way my eyes are drawn away from the road, drawn to her.

She waggles her eyebrows until those stupid sunglasses she wears slide down her nose, revealing the deep blue of her eyes, which are turning toward serious. "Anna babe, you can call me anything you want, as long as you keep talking." Her fingers tap again on the cover of my journal. "What about writing? You're always scribbling in your journals. Remember those stories you used to write for me, the ones we used to make into sexy mad libs? Two body parts, one liquid, an adverb, and a past-tense verb." She laughs loudly, her head thrown back against the seat.

I feel my face heat up. "Those were so gross."

"But seriously, Anna. Maybe you could write a book or something."

"Whatever. I don't write books. I write . . . I don't know." I feel suddenly anxious about my notebook in her hands. I want to take it back, but that would only make her curious. "I write stupid stuff—feelings and memories and junk. Nothing anyone would want to read."

"Well, maybe you need to have something to write about. Maybe Kerouac is right, and you'll have spontaneous poems just . . . leaking out of you. Words dripping out all over the place." Kat giggles. "That sounds kind of fun, you know."

Yeah, right. Poetry. "Sounds messy," I say.

"Maybe it would do you good to get a little messy, Anna babe. Lose a bit of that perfect control you've got going on."

"Whatever, Kat." I roll my eyes. "Let's hear a poem from you, how about? We'll have a contest. A Haiku to South Dakota Contest." The moment the idea spills out of my mouth, I'm certain that I can't do it, can't say a poem out loud, even to Kat. I watch the newly green fields flash past, fenced into tidy rectangles—varied shades of green, yellow, and brown.

"Haiku? Okay, wait. Five-seven-five? Or is it the other way around? For syllables."

This is way too complicated. "I have no idea. Maybe? I think so."

"Let's make them Jack Kerouac–style, in the spirit of our road trip," says Kat. "No rules. A short poem in three lines. An image, but no tricks, no . . . artifice."

"I don't even know what artifice is."

"Yeah, well, then you probably won't use any." She laughs, and the sound of it crinkles in my chest like a candy wrapper in a quiet room. I want more.

My own laugh sounds forced, and I let it die quickly. It seems an insult to Katy's happiness, but at least I'm trying.

"Okay . . . okay . . . let me think," says Kat. "A Haiku to South Dakota." She falls quiet, gazing out the passenger window.

"Here it is." She turns to face the front, crosses her feet underneath her on the seat, and clasps her hands in front of her.

> *Sundappled mare, snapping mouthfuls*
> *of grass. Tail whips her*
> *Stomping hind leg.*

Kat smiles as she finishes, points at the hillside dotted with horses. "Your turn," she says.

I steer the car around a particularly fresh bit of roadkill. "I think you'd better mark that one as a 'Former Flyer.' Lots of feathers." Oh, *nice*, Anna. This is how I respond to her poem? "That was pretty, Kat. I liked it."

"You're stalling."

I shrug. "I'm not a poet."

"C'mon. It was your idea."

"I know, Katy, but . . . I told you, there's no poetry in me. I write . . . lists." I have about a million lists for this trip alone: Things to Do Before Careening Toward the Unknown (At a Safe and Legal Speed); Things We Cannot Leave Without; Ways to Convince Dad That Driving Off into the Unknown Is a Very Good Idea.

"Perfect," says Kat. "Make a list of what you see. C'mon, Anna, you're always scribbling in that journal. I know you've got more than lists in there." She pauses, holding my notebook with both hands as though she will open it and look inside, and then she sets it down on the console between us. I exhale my relief.

When she speaks again, her voice is resigned, wistful. "You used to share things with me."

The sky has grown darker, a royal blue that stands out in stark contrast to the pale white stone formations up ahead. I shift in my seat, a series of satisfying crackles making their way down my spine. "Look, Katy! The Badlands!"

It's crazy. Like the prairie has sort of belched itself up along one ragged edge and then beyond that the world is an alien landscape—a rocky, spiny, sharp world made of hot sun and shadows like creases neatly pressed across the face of the rocks.

Kat sighs, but she doesn't push it. "That's amazing," she says. "I want to get right in the middle of that place and camp there tonight, with nothing but that creepy shit all around me." She nods. "Don't people find God in the desert or whatever, like in Bible stories?"

"God knows where to find *me*." I pull the car into a picnic area by the side of the road, and we get out and peer over the edge into the chasm of craters and craggy peaks. "But this might be a good place to hide."

The sun bakes us into the pavement. I lean against a rock formation, position my face into what I hope is the kind of cheerful expression typically seen in people's vacation photos, and Katy snaps my picture with my phone.

"I can send that to my dad," I say.

Maybe then he'll love me again, I don't say.

"Is he coming to terms with this?" Kat hands the phone back.

I shrug and keep my eyes on my screen. "He's texting me the things he's getting out of bed for, and I'm supposed to send him . . . what I'm learning, I guess." I hate thinking of it, of the heaviness that clung to him when I told him I was leaving. "He . . . he asked me to bring him his Bible." I glance at Kat's profile, soft against the sharp contrast of the boulders behind her.

Kat nods. "Do you think he'll ever . . . "

I duck my head, pulling my sunglasses back down over my eyes. "Who knows." To be honest, I don't really care if he goes back to preaching, if he would only start living again. Still, his interest in his Bible and in our dharma bum project is a pretty significant change already. A glimmer of the man with the golden voice, the father I revered for most of my life. The father I left behind. I slide my finger over the phone and stick it in my pocket. "Let's find a place to camp before it gets dark."

"There. Right there." Kat points at a spot on the map, completely surrounded by the Badlands. "Sage Creek Campground."

I take a good look at the map, thinking about that formidable landscape. There is no way I want to go into that craziness unprepared. "Primitive," I say, reading the campground designation. "That means we'd better haul in water."

"Look at you, all taking charge." She slips her goofy sunglasses up onto her head and winks at me.

I roll my eyes, but a smile slips through my defenses. "You're trying to get me to cook dinner tonight, that's all."

I check through our supplies quickly, my clipboard in hand, and then we fill a five-gallon plastic jug with water from a spigot near the ranger station at the park entrance. "I guess we're all set. Do you want to drive?" I toss the keys a couple of times in my hand, hoping Kat will tell me to keep them. "Maybe we'll see some buffalo."

"You drive, and then *I'll* cook dinner," says Kat, climbing back into the passenger seat.

The road is thin and dusty. It's a rough ride, and I drive slowly along the rocky gravel track. The sun is getting lower, and still the road snakes around the outcroppings of bright rock, following closely along the lip of a deep chasm in places.

"Anna, what time is it, anyway?" Kat gazes out the passenger window, searching for buffalo. The clock display in Kat's car has never worked.

"I don't know. Seven maybe?"

"So what happens if we get all the way out there, and there isn't a spot for us to camp?" Kat plucks at her toes with one hand, looking out the window.

"I don't know. There's no time for us to drive to the

campground, find out there aren't any spots, then get back to that bigger campground by dark."

"So do you think maybe we should go stay at the bigger campground?"

I shrug. I sort of hate changing plans once I'm settled on a direction. "You're the one who wanted to camp right in the middle of all this, weren't you?"

Kat tilts her head, and I see her hands go up to her hair and then float back down uncertainly. She hardly ever looks uncertain, which is another part of what I've missed about her.

"Yeah, you're right. I guess. . . . I guess I haven't ever really done anything like this before. Wow, am I actually nervous?" She laughs, pulls her knees in closer to her chest and wraps her arms around them. "I never get nervous."

True. "The map says some people don't even pitch a tent out here, Kat. They sleep right out under the stars."

"I bet there will be a ton of stars. But what about . . . buffalo, or . . . ?"

"Prairie dogs!" I push the brake down so hard that the car rocks to a stop. I point out the window. "Look!"

There are prairie dogs everywhere, as far as we can see—prairie dogs standing up straight as sentinels and prairie dogs peeking out of tunnels—prairie dogs poking up from the horizon and right beside the road.

"It's the Roberts Prairie Dog Town," says Kat, reading off the map. "Cute. They kind of look like they might bite a leg off, though, to be honest."

A smile tugs at my face. "I don't see any buffalo."

"American bison," reads Kat. "Which means buffalo, really."

"I guess this is it." The road circles a grassy field, dotted with pale wooden picnic tables, each with a slatted wooden roof. A dusty trail leads to a pair of outhouses. "I hope we'll be able to find a spot away from the biffy," I say.

It's a joke. We're the only people at the Sage Creek

Campground. I park at the far end of the field, taking a moment to marvel at the beauty—those eerie hills rising up out of the prairie all over the place. "Tent or no tent?" I look for Kat, but she has already taken off—a whirl of cartwheels across the grass.

"Run with me, Anna babe! Shake off that driving!" She veers back toward the car, where I'm trying to unload the trunk and get everything organized. Kat swoops in and grabs me by the arm. "Fly with me!" She drags me away.

"Katy, stop! I want to get the camp set up before dark." I look back at our stuff, lying on the ground by the car.

"Fly with me, or else! Fly or die!" Kat shrieks loudly, hauling me across the field. "FLY OR DIE!" Her eyes are closed, her feet bare and skipping across the grass. I look down.

"Kat!" I'm slightly out of breath, my own feet heavy in my stiff new hiking boots. "Watch out for—"

But Kat's foot disappears into a prairie dog hole, and we both tumble to the ground. Her face goes pale, and for a moment I'm certain that this is it. The end of our road trip. She's broken her leg or something, and we'll have to go back home. It surprises me how much it bothers me. How disappointed I feel.

Kat hops, with my help, all the way over to our picnic table. By the time we get there, her face has some color again. She insists that she's fine, but she holds a plastic bag full of ice from the cooler against her foot while I set up camp.

For the first five minutes or so, I'm silent, unpacking gear from the car and stacking it on the picnic table. Okay, so maybe I set down our plastic tub of kitchen stuff a little more forcefully than necessary. Maybe I kick the bag of tent stakes with a little more zeal than it deserves when it slips out of my hands and lands on the ground. So maybe I'm a little pissed.

"What if you had broken your leg?" I snap at last, my voice grating against the quiet of the campground.

Immediately I want to slap myself; I sound so lame.

Kat bursts out laughing. "You're worse than my mom," she says.

I sulk to keep from smiling. "It's not *that* funny." I pull the stoves and fuel bottles from their sacks and slam them down on the picnic table in front of Kat. "There you go, Miss Katy Kat, Bringer of Hilarity to Sage Creek. I believe you said you would make me some dinner."

"Hey! I'm an invalid!" She groans for effect.

"You're full of shit is what you are."

"Do you need me to get soap for that mouth?"

I smile, but then I hear the sound of tires crunching along the Sage Creek Rim Road, the distant roar of an engine. At the horizon, a low cloud of dust rises behind a big black SUV. Something about the way it approaches—fast and reckless—makes my stomach plunge. "We've got company."

Kat slides off the table and attaches the two cookstoves to the fuel bottles. "Well, so we do," she says, keeping her voice light. "Let's hope they're well-behaved company."

I focus on my clipboard for a moment and then get back to work, pulling the tent, ground cloth, poles, and stakes out of the trunk and fishing around for the hammer in my little red toolbox. I move around the tent, pounding in stakes, keeping my eye on the black truck, which has parked at the opposite end of the field. I count five men. I tighten my grip on the hammer as they pile out of the vehicle and start spreading out across the grass. I don't need to be afraid of these guys.

Kat has her attention fixed on them—wary but calm. She sets up the stoves without too much trouble at all for a first-timer, and she puts two pans of water on to heat. "I'm going to make us some coffee."

I finish with the tent and check the time on my phone. "Went up faster tonight than last night."

"You're such a geek," says Kat.

"You'll thank me for being a geek if we ever need to get this tent up in the middle of a rainstorm."

"Yeah, okay. I'll watch from the car."

"You can't cook in the car."

"What makes you think I'm cooking in a rainstorm?" Kat starts the rice and pours boiling water into the coffee filters.

I watch the men set up camp. Why do five people have to be so loud? Two of them are splitting up a huge pile of wooden pallets, ostensibly to make a campfire. They jump on the pallets to break them up, shouting and cursing as they splinter.

"These boys have been drinking," says Kat, pouring lentils into the other pan. She hands me a steaming cup of coffee, which I slurp, instantly burning my tongue and the roof of my mouth.

"Whatever happens, stay calm. Don't say a word," says Kat.

"What do you mean, don't say a word? So I can't even talk now?" I scowl and set my coffee down on the picnic table. I don't want to talk to these creeps, but why does she get to decide who talks?

"Anna." Kat's voice is terse, and I look up to see that three of the guys are moving across the grass, weaving a little as they approach.

The hammer. It feels solid in my grip, heavy and powerful. I can feel the muscles across my arm and shoulder, still poised for action after pounding in the stakes of the tent.

The men advance, bringing their cloud of noise with them—a sing-songy, taunting kind of noise that blurs together in my ears. "Good evening, fair maidens!" shouts the one in the middle, raising his beer. "Would ye care for some beer 'round our fire?"

The other two guys laugh in a vaguely lecherous way.

I don't really mean to speak, but I'm still annoyed by

Katy, telling me to keep my mouth shut. "We're trying to get our camp set up before the light is gone, but thanks." I keep my tone polite.

The men move right up and around Kat's car, edging in toward our picnic table. I step closer to Kat without taking my eyes off them. Just the way the air moves ahead of them makes my skin crawl.

"C'mon, join the party!" This from the guy on the left. His teeth are a mess. I imagine his breath and cannot keep the look of disgust from my face.

"What? Aren't we good enough for you girls?"

"We're busy," says Kat. "We said no thank you."

Something flashes across the face of the man in the center, and I follow his eyes over to Katy, who looks exactly as she looked a moment ago when I watched her stirring lentils except that now she has a gun in her hand.

The other two spot it. All of them, it is clear, fully believe that Kat would put a bullet through them. My heart races, and I wonder if it's true, if Kat would really shoot someone. I mean, I've known her since seventh grade, but seeing her there with a gun in her hand—she's like a complete stranger.

"Excuse me, miss," says the man in the middle, once again raising his beer. "We was hoping to trade you some firewood for some water." He nods to the guy on his left, who drops a bundle of pallets next to our picnic tables. "We . . . uh . . . *neglected* to read the signs saying there was no water up here. If we could trouble you for some water, you'll see no more of us, I promise." He places a couple of bottles of beer on the picnic table, moving slowly with his eyes on Kat.

The man on the right holds out two water bottles, and I fill them from our five-gallon jug. "It's good to be prepared before you head out into the wilderness," I say. "You never know what you'll run into out here."

They slink away from our camp, and Kat calmly cooks our food, as though nothing unusual has happened. I try to concentrate on building a fire, even though the lack of a campfire grate makes me worry that it's against the rules. Like it matters when you consider how the freaking *gun* is against the rules.

"Dude, what the *hell*?" I whisper, when we're settled with our dinner in front of the crackling pallets. "What's with the gun? Don't tell me it's loaded!"

Kat scoops up a forkful of rice and lentils and holds it poised in front of her mouth. "Hell of a lot of good it's going to do me unloaded," she says.

"Katy! Oh my God! You could have shot them!"

"I never shoot people when they're well behaved. Beer?" She opens one of the bottles left by the men and holds it out to me.

I wrinkle my nose but take the bottle. "*God*, they could at least drink decent beer."

"I know, right?" Kat sits in one of our new camp chairs and leans back, tipping up the beer while she looks into our campfire. Her face is thoughtful. "I wanna go find a buffalo," she says.

A buffalo. No thanks. "I don't want to get anywhere near a buffalo. Have you ever seen how huge they are?" I hold out my arms. "Their heads are bigger than this."

"Maybe we could find a *baby* buffalo."

"Yeah, with an overprotective mama. So, Katy? What's with the gun, hey? 'Cause that was pretty crazy, you know?" I take a gulp of my beer, making a face. At least it's cold.

"Those assholes." Kat shrugs. "They won't give us any trouble now. We're all going to act civilized-like."

"Kat. The gun. What the fuck?"

Kat laughs. "Yeah, well, actually, the gun is stolen, and I used it to kill three cops back in Minnesota." She takes another swig of her beer.

I glare at her. She laughs.

"It was my grandpa's gun, Anna. His service revolver when he was a cop. He gave it to me three months before he died, but he taught me to shoot it when I was like ten. I'm a good shot. Or at least, I was when I was ten." She flexes, Rosie-the-Riveter–style, and grins at me. "I may be flighty, but I can fight, too."

"And it was loaded."

"*Is* loaded. Don't worry about it, Anna."

I shiver, even though the night is comfortable. I can't get used to the idea of Katy having secrets from me, things I don't know. All at once the sheer distance of the last eight months stretches out between us. The drunk guys have been quiet since their visit, but I can still sense them, like a scent on the wind almost, or like tremors in the earth— making me uneasy.

"Well, there you go," says Kat, nodding. "Nothing happened. First proof of God's love."

"Shut up, Katy. You can't prove *something* when *nothing* happens. That's like, saying something is true just because nobody argues against it. Ridiculous."

"Okay, all right. But still. Nothing happened."

"So if we had been attacked by those guys, would that be proof that God hates us?"

Kat pulls her hair into pigtails and twirls them around in her hands, right behind her ears. "Oh, Anna, I don't know. You know I always sucked at math. I barely graduated. True story."

"You are such a liar!" I throw the pack towel at Kat and miss. "This isn't a math problem. It's completely irrational. I don't even know why we're here."

"I know why I'm here. Sure, it's Kerouac and art and God and whatever else. But you know what? I'm here because of the way you look right now." Kat points at me with the mouth of her beer bottle. "Look at you," she says. "You're awesome at this."

I force my face into a scowl. "You keep saying that."

"'Cause it's true. You're, like, happier than I've seen you in forever. We get out here in the middle of nowhere, and instantly you're all saving the day with a big jug of water and the perfect little stoves and these comfy chairs . . . I mean, you put all this thought into everything. You're actually . . ." She stops talking.

"I'm actually what?" I take a drink. Actually good at something?

"Actually fun again," says Kat, her voice hard to discern over the crackling of the wood combusting at our feet.

"Oh." I can taste the sour hops from my last swig of beer. Of course. I'm actually fun again.

"I mean, you're not as fun as, say . . . Pop Rocks or illegal fireworks, or . . . oh, Anna babe, I know you're trying. I mean, nobody is expected to be fun after . . . aw, don't cry. Or . . . cry, if that will help."

My whole body shakes, and I think I might be sobbing, except my eyes are dry; my mouth turns up at the corners and laughter rushes out—not any kind of laugh that has come out of me in forever. It comes from so deep within that I can feel the tremors of its origin, the path as it ripples up through my chest and explodes out of my mouth.

I am a little drunk. My cheeks burn.

"Let's go for a walk," I say, standing up beside the fire. "Let's go find a buffalo!"

Reasons Why Katy Packing a Pistol Freaks Me Out

- *It's a LOADED GUN. That's the definition of insane. Okay, maybe not, but like, it's close. So many headlines! Words like "Accidental Shooting," "Teenager Slain," and "Critical Condition" jump to mind, followed by "Psychopath," "Shooting Spree," and "Death Toll."*
- *It's a LOADED GUN. Where has it been all this time? Where is it RIGHT NOW?*
- *It's a LOADED GUN. When the hell did Katy start carrying a gun, and when the hell was she going to TELL ME about it???!?*
- *What else has changed?*

3

The moon,
the falling star
—Look elsewhere
—Jack Kerouac

It would not be fair to say that the fire stole my faith, since in truth it has been slipping away from me all my life, flipping between my fingers like a shiny little minnow—such a far cry from the trophy salmon that dangled from my father's fist.

I witnessed no epic battles between my father and his faith— no desperate dives, no fishing poles bent double with exertion. It came to him so easily. My father reached out his hand, and the fish swam happily to him. Although I long for his pride—for the ring of approval in his golden voice—again and again my own hands come up from the water empty.

My thumb creeps toward the switch on the side of my flashlight, but I don't turn it on. My heart hammers in my chest. I feel something, something like excitement, and it's almost like when we were kids—one of our secret late-night adventures in the dark. I press my eyes tightly closed for a moment as we walk, willing them to adjust. I see the bright campfire flames outlined on my eyelids.

"Don't even say one word. Just try it," Kat whispers, as soon as we're out of sight of the drunk guy camp, behind some scrubby clumps of shadowy vegetation.

"What is this?" Kat slips a small metal object into my hands.

She passes me her lighter, which my fingers recognize in the dark. The last time I used one, though . . . my stomach lurches. "Smoke it," Katy says.

It's a pipe. "Oh," I say. "No, I don't think I can do drugs." I know. I'm that lame.

Kat's face slips into a smile. "It's not *drugs*. It's just pot, Anna. Smoke it. It will be fine."

But I shake my head, stubborn and speechless, darkness hiding the stain on my cheeks, and I hear the tiniest puff of breath from her nose.

"Control freak," she whispers, but then she takes the pipe from my hand, squeezing my fingers as she does. "You should lighten up a little, Anna babe."

"Why didn't you ever tell me about this?" She doesn't cough at all.

Kat dumps the bowl into the palm of her hand and then brushes it onto the ground. "You've been hard to talk to." She tucks the weed back into her satchel and takes my hand. It's funny how she can do that, how she can touch people like that—like it's nothing. Is it nothing? My hand feels heavy and awkward clasped in hers. We trek across the field, heading toward what I hope is the road.

"Let's stay up all night," Kat whispers. "Let's wait for the moon to kiss the morning star."

There are so many stars. I tip my head back and smile into the night.

The tall grass brushes against me, tickles my hands as I walk. I'm still wearing my new waterproof hikers; I like their sturdy weight and stiffness of sole. I like their soft impact against the earth below, the way they connect me here, to this night. To this moment.

The night smells of prairie grass, some early wildflow-ers—I stop dead in my tracks as I notice the way the smell of the air has changed from daylight to night. "Kat," I say, inhaling deeply. "I can *smell* darkness."

Her grin by starlight is beautiful. She glows. I stare,

my mouth falling open to speak, but it's like I forget what speech is. I can't stop looking at her.

"Smells amazing, Anna."

It does. A laugh bursts out of me—*burst* is the perfect word, like the way flavor will burst out of a handful of ripe blueberries tossed in your mouth—and I bury my face in my sleeve to stifle the noise.

"Are you sure you're not stoned?" She laughs, too.

But I frown, peering into the dim space in front of us. "Are there snakes here? Like, you know. Ones that bite and stuff?" I've been reading a guidebook about animals in the American West, and I search my memory for the little colored maps showing rattlesnake territory. The tall grass could be crawling with danger. I see a headline: *Teen Hikers Found Paralyzed by Deadly Venom—One Carrying Loaded Handgun.*

Kat shrugs. "I'm not afraid of snakes. I like them, the way they move, like a Slinky with attitude. And their sweet little tongues, darting out." She pokes her forked fingers at me.

"But the poisonous ones, Kat. You're wearing flip-flops." I think of her little shiny toenails, imagining two huge holes in them, dripping with venom. "And your ankle . . ."

"Anna. *I'm not afraid of the goddamn snakes.*" Still, her voice has a thread of uncertainty that is new.

"Aw, don't be mad at me, Katy. I'm not trying to be obnoxious, I swear." I turn around and attempt to skip backward, facing Kat.

Kat smiles. "I'm not mad."

I have about a second to be happy before Kat's face is plastered with fear, and she lurches forward and grabs me with both hands. "But you," she says, breathless, "are about to step off a fucking cliff." I spin around, her arms tight around me.

It's true. Two more steps—a step and a half, even—and I would have gone skidding off the edge and into a deep black hole, a steep, rocky abyss. I breathe, breathe. All I can do. My heart . . . I think I see sparks.

"Holy shit," I say at last, when I've got the breathing thing down. I can feel Kat's pulse in her grip on my arm.

"That would have sucked," says Kat.

For some reason this understatement sets us off giggling, adrenaline releasing in waves as we cling to each other.

I hear a sound from behind us. A *big* sound.

"Kat!" The air in my lungs hisses out in a terrified whisper. "Buffalo!"

I can't see much of it—a large dark splotch of steaming breath and glinting eyes and a sort of shaggy, heavy kind of presence there in the darkness. We hold very still, clinging together, shaking with fear and shock and leftover laughter.

The bison snorts a little, takes a step toward us. I feel Kat tense, sense her hand moving to the small of her back. What is she . . . *no*. No, she's not.

"You keep a gun in your *Yoga* pants?"

The buffalo, hearing my voice, stamps a couple of times, and moves a few paces closer to us. Oh shit. Not good. The beast is agitated, nervous. It's so huge. I can feel the void yawning behind us, the edge of the cliff at my heels, and the panic stutters in my chest, tightens around all my organs as the buffalo clomps ever closer.

Kat moves; I can't let go of her, and suddenly the air beside us explodes, the flash searing across my retinas. The gun. Oh god, she *shot* it! The sound of the gunshot is so crisp and *immediate*. And loud. I'm blind, my ears are ringing, and I can't move for fear of the buffalo and the cliff. So instead, I scream.

The poor animal, nervous to begin with and then faced with the sudden explosion of sound and flame only a few feet away, turns tail and gallops or whatever it is that buffalo do when they are hauling ass to get away—and runs across the field. Straight toward the camp of the creepy guys.

It's remarkably loud when it crashes into their tent, stomps across their firewood, and flings their camp chairs to the side with its massive head. I wait, tense and terrified, for the sound of someone injured, but the men are reacting with a combination of shouting, swearing, and laughing.

"Uh, Kat?" My voice is quiet in the darkness.

"Yeah?"

"It's not . . . exactly . . . *legal* to shoot at a buffalo, is it?"

"I didn't shoot at it. I shot into the ground. Just to scare it."

"But still." I tug at the sleeves of my fleece. "Is it legal to shoot at the *ground*?"

Kat laughs. "It's complicated."

"Meaning?"

"Meaning not exactly." Kat takes my hand again, the hand I have finally successfully removed from its death grip on her forearm. "Look. They're coming."

It's true; the men are moving toward us, their flashlights bobbing ahead of them, sweeping in wide arcs as they search the darkness.

"That was a gunshot," says one of them, loud as can be. "You see anything?"

Kat pulls me along the edge of the ridge. "They know it was us," she whispers. We scurry along with our bodies stooped down in the shadow, hoping to flank the group of men.

"Hey!" shouts one of the men, his voice thick. "Little girls like you shouldn't be playing with guns!" The flashlight beams dance over the edge of the cliff, but we're able to slip behind them and sprint back to our own camp.

"Let's get out of here," Kat says, tossing things into the trunk. "They probably didn't notice too many details about our car. They were already wasted when they got here."

We shove all of our stuff into the car as quickly as we can. My fingers fumble with the plastic clips that hold the tent fabric to the poles, and I'm glad that I practiced pitching and striking this tent. Who's the geek now? With each action, my thoughts grow clearer.

"They're coming back!" Kat hisses. She jumps into the driver's seat and starts the car, and I run to open the passenger side door.

"The fire!" It's down to embers, but still. "We're not even supposed to have open fires!"

"Anna. Get in the car. The fire is fine."

"But . . . leave no trace . . ." I've also been reading a guidebook to wilderness camping.

"We can't leave no trace *and* get away from these freaks. Now get in, babe."

I almost climb in, but then I glance over at the picnic table. "Katy, the *stoves!*"

Our two shiny new camp stoves, still attached to their fuel bottles, are sitting neatly on the picnic table. Without them, we're screwed. "Anna, they're coming!"

The flashlight beams are flickering over our camp now; it must be obvious that we've packed up. "Hey, girls!" shouts one of them. "Hey, little gunslingers!"

"Oh, laaaaaaaaaaaaadies! Where are you gooooing?" This one calls out in a falsetto voice that dissolves into rough laughter.

"Don't leave now! The party just started!"

"Get in the car right now," hisses Kat.

I leave my door ajar and run over to the picnic table. I can't abandon the stoves. I scoop them up in my arms and start running back to the car, but before I reach it, a man steps in front of me. His headlamp is aimed right in my face, so all I can see is a dark shape, and then his hands are grabbing me, wrapping around me, pulling me roughly toward him. I'm not afraid, oddly enough. I feel strong, ready to fight. His hands are on my ass and in my hair; his fingers curl into the base of my ponytail and grip hard.

"Get the fuck away from me!" The jumble of camp

stoves and fuel bottles in my arms is just awkward enough to give the man some trouble as I shove hard against his chest. I grip one stove in my right hand, lift my knee toward the man's groin, and swing the stove at him. The heavy canister of white gas, still tethered to the stove by a thick metal tube, connects solidly with the man's forehead, and his headlamp drops to the ground. He goes down after it, clutching his balls.

I slam the car door shut behind me. "Move!" I shout, hitting the lock. "Get us out of here!"

Kat is already squealing out of the spot, tires spinning in the dust. "I told you to get in the car, Anna, are you crazy? You could have gotten killed or raped or worse for a stupid stove and some plastic fucking forks!" She shifts as she swears, whipping the car around and pressing the gas pedal to the floor. I grip the dashboard with one hand, the stove-weapon with the other.

"Do you think I killed him?" I think of the solid crack of metal on skull, the way the man had dropped to the ground.

"We can hope," says Kat.

The car lurches over the bumpy grass toward the gravel, throwing me halfway across the seat. Kat flips on the headlights, and there, directly in our path, are two of the men. In the instant I see their faces illuminated by the headlights, they look dazed; their eyes seem unable to focus on the oncoming car. "Shit!" says Kat, and she snaps off the lights again, swerving to one side. "They'd better get the hell out of the—"

A thud—the car bounces as though running over a curb.

"Katy, stop!" I scramble in my seat, turning to see if I can catch a glimpse of the men behind us, but it's too dark in the shadow of the ridge. Ahead of us, the moon faintly illuminates the path of the road, and I pull my seat belt tight across my lap as we speed away.

4

The low yellow
moon above the
Quiet lamplit house
—Jack Kerouac

Wait, that's not true, what I said about faith, about how I never had any. Or it is, but it's not the whole truth. I couldn't catch and hold my father's faith—the competing columns of virtues and sins, rewards, and punishments. The Holy Bible According to Pastor Jake. But that doesn't mean I believed in nothing.

I used to believe in so many things—elves and leprechauns, virgins riding unicorns. I trusted that the world was made up of people who were generally good, though they may have lost their way temporarily. The faith my mother gave me—the words she whispered when she said good night, the idea that gave me hope for the two of us even when we fought bitterly over trivial things, as mothers and daughters do, I guess—was her belief in love, a love so unconditional we could barely scratch at the edges of comprehending it.

"A clod of dirt," says Kat, scooping a forkful of pie into her mouth. "Slight possibility of a prairie dog."

I want to believe her, I do. But that image . . . those guys with their slack-jawed faces and terror in their stupid eyes. The thud. Seriously, the *thud.*

"What if we killed them all? What if I killed the first guy and then you killed those other two?" I fold my legs underneath me on the bench and wrap my shaking arms around them, tugging on my sleeves. If I can hold myself tightly enough, maybe I won't fall apart. We are in so much trouble. The gun, the guys . . . the shaking escalates. My teeth chatter. Kat's hand reaches out and touches my cheek. Her touch is light, but her voice is firm.

"Anna. We did not kill anyone. We didn't hit either one of those men. I'm telling you, there was a huge mound of dirt; I saw it before I turned off the headlights."

"Why in the hell did you turn off the headlights, anyway?" I close my eyes tightly, but the images play again on the backs of my eyelids.

"They were frozen," Kat says. "Like deer, I guess. Mesmerized by the lights. I turned them off so they could get their asses out of the way." She licks her fork. "And they did, Anna, I promise. We didn't kill anyone." Her tone drifts toward curt. "Can you just try to trust me for once?"

I try, but I'm not convinced. "Well, what about the guy I brained with the fuel can?" I clench my right hand; it's like I can still feel the impact. My right hand of death.

"You didn't kill him. But I bet he's going to have some headache when he wakes up. Also, nice job with the knee to the balls. With any luck you did permanent damage."

"But . . ."

"*Anna.*" Kat grabs my phone. "Should I call the cops? We're not that far away. I'm sure the police can be here to arrest us within a half hour. Forty minutes, tops." She dials a 9, then a 1. "If that's what you need me to do, I'll dial this last number. I'll tell them everything, but seriously, show me a little faith."

I take the phone and end the call, looking around the diner to make sure nobody witnessed the spectacle. "Don't be stupid. Of course I don't want . . ." I trail off, not sure exactly what I want. I know I don't want to end our trip, not yet. Still, the headlines rise up in my brain—*Drugged-Up Teens Kill Three in Hit and Run: Police Say Illegal Firearms Involved.*

"So let's make a plan." I take out a map from my backpack and spread it out on the table. I don't handle uncertainty very well. Kat slides into the booth next to me—to see the map better, I suppose—but instead she puts her head on my shoulder and sort of burrows her face into my neck. My cheeks grow warm, and I pull away, embarrassed.

"So here we are." I point at South Dakota, trying to make this fact expand enough to push all the other thoughts out of my brain. "We can go down to Nebraska or keep on west into Wyoming, I guess." I trace my fingers along the corresponding routes.

"Do you want to do any of these touristy things? Mount Rushmore? Devil's Tower?" says Kat, pointing at the map.

"Well, we could pretend to be in *Close Encounters of the Third Kind*." It makes me smile to think of that movie, one of my mom's favorites. She loved alien flicks.

"I suppose it would be sort of cool to see it. Even though it seems hopelessly cliché," says Kat, "but who knows? Maybe God is in the clichés."

I roll my eyes, but this whole thing . . . it's just a road trip. God is not a real variable in this equation. Or if he is, where would we even look? My brain reels. "I need to make a list. WHERE TO FIND GOD'S LOVE." I take out my journal and open to a clean page, writing the title neatly across the top. "So where do we start?"

Kat doesn't even hesitate. It's like she was waiting for me to ask. How far behind am I, anyway? I fiddle with the rubber grippy thing on the end of my purple pen and write down what she says.

"Art. Creative stuff. You know, he's the Great Creator or whatever. We should try to catch a few concerts and visit galleries and make a point of talking to people. Put that down, too. People." She sips her coffee.

"And Nature," I say, adding to the list. Katy's not all that crazy about my backpacking idea, despite her fondness for Kerouac's "rucksack revolution." I love the idea of getting way out in the wilderness, nobody around for miles and miles. I don't even really know where this longing comes from; it's just that ever since the fire and everything, I've had this urge. You know when you step in the mud with boots on, and there's that satisfying sound? A *squilsh*, my mom used to call it—the way it tugs at your boot when you try to lift your foot, but not in a scary way like you might lose your boot forever—that nice little tug that reminds you you're solid. That's how I imagine it would feel to sit in the middle of the woods and close my eyes and do nothing but breathe and listen and let myself *squilsh* right into the world. Solid but not scary. Alone but not lonely. Missing but not lost.

I doodle in the margin. "What else?" I pretend like I'm thinking about the question, but really I'm just sitting there, taking up space. It's how I spent all of my senior year of high school.

"Drugs."

"For serious?" I write it down, but I have to fight this ridiculous urge to cover what I'm writing with my other hand, like when you're taking a quiz next to someone with wandering eyes.

Kat nods. "Acid, peyote, mushrooms. Stuff like that. It would be an adventure."

Adventure indeed. Is it the kind of adventure I'm ready for? I'm not sure. "Okay, I wrote that. And?"

"Church?"

"As if I haven't had enough of that to last me all my life," I say, but I write it down on the page. "Oh, and meditation. Prayer, I guess."

"Sex."

I wish the sound of the word wouldn't make me blush. "You think so?"

"It's at least as possible as finding God in a tree. I don't even really *like* trees, you know. Unless they have Christmas lights on them."

Our waitress comes to clear away the dishes and top off

our coffee. She smiles at the map spread out on the table in front of us. "Are you on a trip?" she says.

Kat nods. "Excuse me," she says, "but if I asked you where a person could look to find God, what would be the first thing that comes to mind, for you?"

The waitress shakes her head a little, her brown pony-tail flipping back and forth merrily. She bites her lip. "Well, gosh, I guess I'd have to say old people."

"Old people?"

She smiles. "Yeah, like, you know. I volunteer at a nursing home in the summers. I go in and read and talk to them, play cards, learn how to crochet, you know. Just be a friend. And every time I go there, I learn so much about life. Old people are all full of God, I think." She laughs. "More coffee? I can get your check, but I'm not trying to rush you out of here or anything. Take all the time you want."

Kat nods. "Thanks. Old people. Cool." She turns to me. "Write that down."

I write it down, but I really don't see the point of any of this. I mean, so we go looking for God in all these places, but really, it's not like we're going to prove anything. It's not like people haven't spent entire lifetimes looking for divinity. And sure, some of them claim to have found it, but they can't prove they're right. I go back to studying the map.

Kat snaps her fingers. "Hey! Let's let Jack tell us where we should go next," she says. "What if we just, like, flip through the book and stick our finger in it to see where we should go next?"

I nod. "Bibliomancy."

"What?"

"It's when you use a book to divine the future. Usually you use a sacred book, I think, like the Bible maybe."

Kat laughs. "And Anna sucks the whimsical right out of my idea."

"I'm gifted like that." She's teasing, but she's right. I haven't been very much fun this year. But I'm trying. I mean, I'm here, aren't I? I pull *The Dharma Bums* out of my backpack and study the faded cover. I can't quite imagine Kat's dad reading a book like this, even in college. He's so practical, so solid and secular—the complete opposite of this mystical, Buddhist poet guy.

"Okay, just point to something," says Kat, grabbing the book out of my hands. The pages fan back and forth between her fingers.

I stick my finger into the book and squint at the words I'm touching. "What if it's not a place?" I'm pointing to one of those long exuberant passages about enlightenment or something. The kind that makes Kat squeal and me roll my eyes. This book is full of them.

"Read it anyway. Maybe it will tell us what to do."

"Well, okay." I'm still doubtful. "It says, 'What does it mean that I am in this endless universe, thinking that I'm a man sitting under the stars on the terrace of the earth, but actually empty and awake throughout the emptiness and awakedness of everything? It means that I'm empty and awake, that I *know* I'm empty, awake, and that there's no difference between me and anything else.'"

I sip my coffee, tasting the silence that follows. In my reluctant head, thoughts hum like mosquitoes.

"Well, I guess the meaning of that is obvious," says Kat. "It is?"

"Well, I mean, what it's telling us to do is obvious."

"Oh?" I hold Katy's gaze, the sparkle of her deep blue eyes. "Would you care to enlighten me?"

"It's zen. I can't *give* you the answer."

"Yeah, because once again, you're full of shit." I slap at the mosquito-thoughts with an impatient movement of my hand, which I try to disguise by smoothing out the map. "I am empty and awake." For an instant the words fall into place—for a moment I *am* empty and awake. A laugh bubbles up.

I'm about to speak, to tell Katy everything I now

understand with perfect clarity, but of course it all vanishes; once again, the ideas are nothing but a vaguely annoying hum in the cavern of my vacant skull. But sitting here—sipping coffee with Kat—our future is any one of a thousand crazy lines snaking off in all directions. Maybe that's enough.

I pull out my phone and text my father. I think of how I felt on the road, like I was solid and real for once. *Maybe it's enough just to move.* I send it. I can be all zen and stuff, too. Maybe my dad could journey along with me, if he'd only get out of that damn bed.

"You looked like your old self for a minute there." Kat frowns, looking up from the map and into my face. "Your eyes," she whispers. There is a long silence.

"What?" I shift uncomfortably in the booth, my bare legs sticking to the vinyl seat. "What is it?"

Kat shakes her head. "I don't know. Your eyes were happy. You . . . do you ever forget about it, like I did just now?"

"Forget about it?"

Kat takes my hand, squeezes it a little. "You look like her, you know. Especially lately, the way you've been wearing those little scarves to pull your hair back."

The scarves. I tug at the back of my kerchief with my free hand as a memory surfaces—from maybe my sophomore year—our faces side by side in a mirror. My mother's eyes, with that strange reproachful look she sometimes wore.

"Your hair could be so stunning if you'd take care of it," she had said, as she smoothed her hands over my frizzy mop, trying to twist it up into something sophisticated. "Here, what if we wrap one of my scarves"—she plucked a green silk from the basket where she kept them—"and you know your hair will get darker, more auburn like mine. It will be less . . ." She wrinkled up her nose and put her face beside mine in the mirror, leaving the distasteful adjective to my imagination. "See? You could be so pretty, Anna Banana."

"*Whatever.*" I jerk my hand away from Kat. My memories of my mother are all kneaded through with that twisted chest feeling, the one that makes it hard to breathe.

Kat stares down at her empty fingers. "I guess I can see why you'd be angry at God." Her voice is quiet, thoughtful.

"I'm *not* angry, Kat." My tone is about twice as bitter as I would like it to be. I fiddle with the empty creamer container for a moment, waiting out the silence that follows. A silence that is unrelenting.

I mean, okay, maybe she's a little bit right. I'm pretty pissed, to be honest. But not . . . not at God. I'm pissed at those kids for messing around with fire underneath our stairs. I'm pissed at myself for acting like I did that night, for not waking up in time to change what happened. And one more thing. My face burns. "I'm pissed at my dad for sleeping in his study that night. For not getting her out." I grab for my coffee cup, and the lukewarm coffee sloshes out on my hand. Kat hands me a napkin in silence.

I laugh, but this time there's no joy in it. "I didn't really realize that." I mean, I knew I was mad at myself, but not him. "He's so crushed by all this. What kind of a monster am I to be angry with him?" Tears slide out of my eyes, and I stab at them furiously with the coffee-sodden napkin. I can't believe I'm crying, right in the middle of this stupid greasy spoon.

"Anna babe, you're no monster." Kat reaches out and brushes her fingers across my cheek. I can't help it; I push her hand out of the way and try to cover my eyes with both hands, but she won't leave me alone. "Anna, stop hiding from me." Her fingers close around my wrist, and she pulls my hand to her mouth. She kisses two of my fingertips, softly, her eyes closed. Then she places my hand on her cheek, holding it there with both of her own hands, looking intently at me from behind the dark curtain of her hair.

I am helpless, helpless. "Not hiding." My lips form the words, but the sound is missing.

Tears well up. I want to brush them away, but she has my hand. The other one has fallen to my lap, clutching a soggy napkin.

I can't look away. Helpless.

Kat's cheek is warm and damp; her hands are soft. Did she just *kiss* my fingers? My heart is squeezed between two plates of glass, like it's being squished into a microscope slide. Still it manages to quicken its pace.

"Where're you gals headed?"

The sound of his voice startles me, first because it is so amazingly warm and rich that I mistake it for my father's voice, and then because it is coming from directly behind me. Kat and I both spin around to see the owner of the voice, and our knees collide forcibly beneath the table. Pain jolts through me, and I'm not sure how much of it comes from my knees and how much comes from the realization that I am further away from my father right now than I have ever been.

Then, leaning in to rub our knees, Kat and I collide: her forehead and my nose. The tears, already primed, spring up again as pain rockets through my sinuses. We're a pathetic slapstick routine.

"Oh. Oh, dear," says the man behind us, leaning awkwardly over the back of his booth, a napkin in his hand. "You've got a little bit of a bloody nose there, darlin'. No, don't lean back; the blood will run down your throat."

I take the napkin and hold it to my nose, pinching the bridge with one hand while the stranger peers at me with worried eyes. For the briefest of moments I recognize the echo of my father's eyes, back when he still climbed my attic stairs to find out if I was all right. I scowl at the man.

"I'm so terribly sorry to startle you gals like that," he says. He wrings his hands apologetically, and I notice he wears a smooth gold wedding band on his left hand. I think of the woman who wears the matching band. I wonder if she sings with him. I wonder if she smells of jasmine.

He nods toward our table. "I'm Lucas Shepherd. Pastor Shepherd, if you'd like. I have a parish here in town, a little country church."

A pastor. I nod politely at the man and turn back to my own table, hoping he'll take the hint. I don't want to talk to anyone right now, least of all some prying-stranger version of my own father.

"Wow, that's kind of coincidental that you're a pastor," says Kat.

Oh, god, Katy, not now.

"See, Anna and I—I'm Katherine, by the way—we're on a trip. A pilgrimage, if you will, with a religious purpose." She turns to Anna. "Right, Anna babe?"

I shake my head, looking back and forth from Kat to this Pastor Shepherd guy, a strange knot forming in my stomach. "We're on a road trip, that's all." I feel panicky.

But Kat is still smiling and nodding her head at something the man has just said. "Yes, yes," she says, nodding some more, "Anna's dad is a pastor, too, back in Minnesota. And we're seeking out proof. Of God. Well, of his love." She hits my shoulder lightly. "Show him. Show him the list. Maybe he'll have some ideas for us."

This is embarrassing. "Really, it's just a road trip." And I'm not showing him this list. Is Katy crazy? It's full of drugs and sex.

Pastor Shepherd's eyes are a warm caramel color, and they seem to grow brighter as his smile widens, revealing a charmingly crooked set of teeth and a lopsided pair of dimples. "Well, now," he says, drawing out the syllables like music, "it's mighty coincidental that we should meet just now. Or, not really coincidental, you know." He gives us a conspiratorial wink and then casts his eyes toward the ceiling. "I don't believe in coincidences."

I tug at Kat's sleeve, but she doesn't look at me. What's she getting at, anyway? I try to figure out what it is about this guy that makes me so nervous, makes me feel like ditching the bill and running off. There is nothing outwardly scary about him; he appears to be a kind and genuine person—the kind of person I have to grudgingly admit might have something to offer us—some wisdom for a couple of dharma bums. He's not icky, not like a molester or a murderer. But still I feel danger, something unsettling about him.

Kat has the Kerouac book out, now, and she reads the rucksack revolution passage to him. I wait for the man's eyes to harden, for him to warn us of the sins we could encounter in such books. But he nods, his eyes full of that warmth, and he listens to Kat's enthusiastic monologue with a patient smile.

At last Kat stops for breath, and Pastor Shepherd speaks up. "I just know it was no accident that we met here this evening."

"How's the sermon coming, Pastor Shepherd?" Our waitress beams as she fills his coffee cup.

"I was struggling a bit, Dana," he says, "but I think it's coming together now."

She includes us in her smile. "If you girls are looking for God, well, you've found one of His people, right here. I don't know how many sermons have been written in that booth, but it's got to be quite a few."

"Well, Jack's pie is the best inspiration," he says, handing her his plate and fork. "You tell him that, now." He clasps his hands together, and I worry for a minute that he might ask us to pray right there in the diner, making a big show of it. I hate praying in public.

"Say, are you girls moving on this very evening, or are you staying here in town?" He looks concerned. "It's awfully late to be out there on the road now."

"We're heading out," I say.

"We could stay," says Kat.

"Excellent!" says Pastor Shepherd. "My wife and I would love to have you stay with us. We have a guest room that nobody uses since our sons went off to college. You'll have to put up with a bit of a mess, as we've been packing all week for a little road trip of our own, though."

"Oh?" says Kat. "Where are you headed?"

Pastor Shepherd smiles broadly as he slides out of his booth. He picks up his check and then casually snags ours as well. "No, no, I insist," he says, in answer to our protests. "My Bible study group is heading down to Mexico with several other congregations in Wyoming and Utah for a missionary trip. We're going to be laying the foundation for a new church in a village in the mountains. We leave the day after tomorrow, in fact."

"That sounds amazing," says Kat.

I follow them out of the diner, feeling far from home, but I know I'm not missing the dusty train tracks and the stale room where my father lies staring at the ceiling. Home doesn't exist anymore. Either that or I haven't found it yet.

Reasons My Mother Would Support
This Rucksack Revolution

- *She sang hymns with my father, but alone she belted out Janis Joplin's "Me and Bobbie McGee."*
- *At church, she was known for her taste in shoes, but outside of church, she was barefoot most of the time.*
- *She would worry about my father, but Mom had a little streak of tough love in her for both of us, and she said my dad was prone to babying me. Was I babying him in his grief?*
- *She loved everything about Katy.*
- *She believed in silly things like possibility—she described meeting my father as an act of fate.*
- *When she told stories of my daring feats as a child, she always seemed a little proud, even as she clutched me closer, the reflex motion of her hand on her heart balanced by the shine in her eyes.*

5

Wooden house
raw gray—
Pink light in the window
—Jack Kerouac

I don't have nightmares about it, not exactly. I don't dream about
flames or fire engines or the pale, shocked faces of my neighbors.
The night my mom died and my home burned to the ground is
surreal and terrifying in my memory—I recall tiny things like
the feeling of the frosty grass on my bare feet and the smell of
the oxygen mask, but I forget the big things like how I broke my
bedroom window or who called 911 or when was the first time I
realized my mom wasn't beside me.

Instead my dreams are filled with images of classrooms,
where I am surrounded by robots who speak to me in unintel-
ligible beeping. Or sometimes I dream of Katy, doing my homework for me like she did in real life after the fire. When she hands
me the page, it's covered from top to bottom with neat, red tally
marks. Sometimes I try to count them. What do they stand for?
Probably it's how many times I kept her at a distance when I
should have shared. Like best friends do.

She tried. All those months she tried; she stopped by with
her armloads of books and drawings she made for me, an old
guitar she bought at a thrift store, her face full of complexity. I
answered the door, stood and shuffled my feet, until finally she
retreated, walking away from our red dust apartment and the
train tracks and the sadness.

"Katy?" I listen in the dark. Kat doesn't answer, but I can hear more of the soft sounds that woke me. "Are you crying?"

She only sniffles. "Go back to sleep."

"I wasn't sleeping." Tiny movements on the mattress— she *is* crying. Kat never cries. "Um, are you okay?" I find Kat's shoulder and pat it awkwardly. Her back is to me; she's coiled into herself. My hand feels stiff and stupid on her back. I've never been good at this, at touching other people. Kat is the hugger—the hand-holder, the comforter. I give encouragement best in the form of . . . oh, I don't know. I mean, nothing I did worked for my dad.

Except. The text he sent back.

Woke before the sun today. Called Gran with birds singing in the backyard.

"Nothing's wrong," whispers Kat. She rolls, trapping my arm underneath her, burrowing her head into my shoulder. "I dunno," she says. "It's been a weird couple of days so far." True, that.

I feel my heart compressed again, fluttering madly behind glass, this time more like a panicky fly trapped in a window. "Did we hit one of those guys, Kat? Really, you can tell me. I can take it. Did we kill someone?" I can't take it. I wish she had called the police from that diner, I really do.

Kat starts to shake again, but this time she's laughing. Hard. She props up her head on her hand, still on top of my arm—close to me, so close. "Anna, how many times do I have to tell you? It was a chunk of dirt." She can't even go on for a moment because she's laughing so hard. I feel like an idiot. "There was a little bump in the road, that's all. I saw it before I turned off the lights, silly. It wasn't a person, I promise."

Quickly—so quickly I have no time to respond—Kat leans in and kisses me. She tastes of toothpaste and tears. "You're so cute, Anna babe," she says, pulling away. "I'm sorry I woke you with my stupid crying. I . . . maybe I'm homesick."

Just like that, her breathing settles, falling into the slow rhythm of sleep, or nearly so. For a while I lie awake in the Shepherd's guest room, one hand on the bed beside me, feeling the warm spot where Kat had been, and the other softly resting on my own mouth. Finally, giving my fingers a little kiss—the kiss I did not return—I let my hand fall away, and I think for the first time in years about Meggie Dempsey's twelfth birthday party, where Katy and I were the only girls to choose Dare instead of Truth.

"All right, we're saving the Dares for last," Meggie announced after Katy chose, and then all the other girls went around and chose Truth. One by one, they shared secrets about the boys they liked and whether or not they had their period yet. All the while, Katy sat smiling and waiting, her dark eyes moving from girl to girl. Finally it was my turn.

"Dare." It was Katy's eyes that made me say it, dark and blue and *interesting*. I wanted her to be my best friend.

All the girls moved their heads in close, smothering giggles behind their hands. They huddled around the little table at the front of the camper, peeking at us over their shoulders, rocking with laughter.

Katy touched my arm, her hand warm and reassuring. "Don't worry. It's almost always food-related," she said. "We'll have to touch something gross or eat something gross. Or both." We were all sleeping in a small travel trailer in Meggie's backyard. I was the new girl, transplanted just in time for middle school. The girl whose father was building a church—and some weird church at that.

The girls broke out of their huddle, and Meggie stepped out in front of the table. I instinctively drew my knees in toward my chest, clutching my Strawberry Shortcake pajama pants. I hadn't quite figured out which of the girls could be trusted and which were like venomous snakes, their mouths ready to hiss with gossip and lies.

Meggie smiled, her braces laced with hot pink bands,

her hair in two bright blond pigtails, dripping in glitter. "Gravel Pit!" she said, like it was Disneyland. I glanced at Katy, who smiled back.

"We're sneaking out," Kat said. "Mischief and mayhem."

Sneaking out of the camper was a Dare in and of itself. The little trailer was parked in the yard with the door in plain view of Meggie's parents' bedroom window. I could see their television from inside the camper. I slipped my feet into my shoes and wiped my palms on the legs of my pajamas.

"Katy goes first," said Meggie, pointing toward the floor at the back, toward a small cupboard next to the bathroom door. Kat didn't hesitate. She opened the cabinet, wriggled in headfirst, and made a little bit of noise—some thuds and a clank or two—and then the sound of a door opening to the outside.

"There's an access panel that hooks up with this cabinet," explained the girl beside me. "You have to sort of wiggle down until you're through it."

All of the girls disappeared through the cabinet, and I was last. Taking a deep breath, I dove down through the crawl space, my arms swimming in front of me, my chest scraping along the linoleum flooring as I squirmed my way through the access panel and then into the arms of the girls who were waiting to catch me. They giggled, pressing their hands over their mouths—all of them softly glowing with the moonlight shining on their pastel pajamas. We tiptoed in a wavering line through the little thicket of trees that separated Meggie's yard from the road.

Beyond the trees, the moonlight was bright enough to see, and we spread out, gravel crunching beneath our shoes. I walked beside Katy, sticking close in the unfamiliar shadows.

A loud hoot sounded suddenly from the woods, and I jumped and grabbed for Kat's arm. She shrieked, and all six of us were nearly lost to the cataclysms of giggling that followed. I was passing the first test—becoming one of them.

"An owl, just an owl," somebody whispered, between giggles.

The gravel pit was eerie in the moonlight, a landscape alien to begin with and only made more strange by shifting shadows as the clouds passed over the moon. We pressed in close to one another, our giggles fallen into soft whispers and occasional urgent hisses to "wait up!" I wrapped my arms around myself and tried not to stumble on the loose rocks as we made our way up over the first hill and down again, out of view of the deserted road.

Meggie directed us to a flat area, and we all gathered in a tight little circle, our knees touching, the cool gravel seeping through our thin pajamas.

Silence settled around us. I thought of the owl; I wondered about omens. I seemed to remember reading something about owls being a sign of death, and I shivered, goose bumps rising along the nape of my neck and chasing each other down my spine and arms. As one, we pushed in closer together, gathering our courage.

"Before we do the Dares," said Meggie, theatrically drawing out her words in a low, husky voice, "we'll share communion." She giggled a little, then pulled out her dad's silver pocket flask and sloshed it from side to side so we could all hear the liquid inside. "Everyone drinks on the first round," she commanded.

Surely the rest of the girls could hear my heartbeat as the blood reverberated in my ears. Meggie tipped up the flask—I watched her throat bob twice in the moonlight— then passed it to her right, to a tiny girl named Naomi, who shook her head quickly with fear plastered across her pinched white face.

"Come on, Naomi, just a little sip. Don't be like that." Meggie hardly bothered putting any muscle into the command. She knew Naomi would comply.

Sure enough, the girl lifted the glinting metal flask to her thin lips and grimaced as she took a drink. She didn't make a sound, but clamped her other hand over her mouth instantly and shoved the flask toward the girl to her right.

"That's not good enough," said Meggie, pointing her

finger imperiously at Naomi. "Next time around you have to go twice."

Naomi looked terrified, peeking out from behind her hand, but each of the girls in the circle after her drank from the flask—if not eagerly, then stoically—as though their honor depended upon putting on a good show. Only Katy sat easily to my left, all smiles. She tipped the flask back without the slightest pause, and I watched her swallow several times before bringing the flask down again. She handed the cold silver bottle to me while whispering, "It's watered down, anyway."

The flask felt heavy and oddly satisfying in the palm of my hand. I ran my thumb over an inscription on the side and brought the flask to my mouth, the slight metallic odor reaching my nostrils a moment before the sour scent of the whiskey. I could feel the pulse jumping in my throat. Could they see it? Katy put her hand on my knee, and the touch gave me courage. I tipped the flask back and felt a rush of liquid pour into my mouth. I gulped twice and lowered the flask, suddenly aware of the slow heat spreading down to my belly in a wave. I coughed as a flicker of heat shot up into my sinuses, but only a little, and I handed the flask back to Meggie, to my right.

Meggie Dempsey locked eyes with me for a long moment, then turned to the others again and smiled widely, sealing my acceptance into the circle. "Now. The Dare."

She sat up extra straight, her platinum pigtails looming above the rest of the circle. "We *dare* you two to kiss each other," she said, triumph in her voice. "Right on the lips."

"Not just a kiss. You have to make out," spoke up one of the others. I couldn't remember her name, but her bangs hung in her eyes.

Meggie shot the girl a withering look. "Longer than a minute," she said.

I felt my cheeks burning. Was it the whiskey or the thought of making out with Katy—with a girl? With anyone. Did a first kiss count if it's another girl, or is that like practice?

"No tongue," said Meggie, giggling. "That would be gross."

I blinked, kneeling across from Kat, my cheeks growing even warmer at the thought of tongues. Tiny, pea-sized pebbles dug into my knees. I shrugged. "Why not?" I said, forcing my voice to sound confident. "It's just a kiss."

Before I could even take a breath, Kat leaned in—her hair a dark shroud that hung around us. She was warm; she was close. Her hand came up to my face, cupping my chin but also obscuring the view of our mouths. "Just pretend," she whispered quietly, her mouth millimeters away from mine, her breath hot and tasting of whiskey. We held the pose, as close as if we were really kissing but without touching, while the girls giggled and shrieked around us. My heart nearly leapt out of my chest. I felt Kat's closeness as though I were a moon in her orbit. I was drawn close—closer, made bold by the thought of her interesting blue eyes.

I moved suddenly, pressing my lips against Katy's mouth, and we both gasped with the contact. The warmth that was still floating in my belly spread up my chest, and then my lips burned with their own daring, and I pulled away. My first kiss.

There was a moment of silence between us, our bodies still close enough to share the same atmosphere, and then we drew apart quickly with a spill of nervous giggles. The circle of girls dissolved into laughter, too, and my heart fluttered away like a small, frightened bird inside my chest.

Mrs. Shepherd raps lightly on our door with offers of pancakes, eggs, and hot showers. I have to pry myself out of the blissful warm water, wondering when the next shower will come. At the breakfast table, I watch Pastor Shepherd. His hope and faith radiate out from him as he talks; it flows between him and his wife—a sun and his reflecting moon. It makes me wistful and wary.

"If you girls are looking for proof of God's amazing love, what you should do is join up with us," he says, leaning forward in his chair. His voice ripples with excitement at this idea.

"Join you?" Kat leans toward him. I cross my arms over my chest and try desperately to avoid rolling my eyes. There's no way. I know church people. I know how kind they are, how eager to help. I know how they gossip, how they keep a tally inside their heads on everyone.

"Darling, what makes you think these young girls would want to join up with a bunch of old folks on a mission trip?" Angela Shepherd pats her husband's hand.

He beams at her. "They're on a pilgrimage, dear. They're seeking evidence of God's love, and who better to show them that evidence than our wonderful parishioners? What better way to learn the lessons of love than by leaning their weight into a shovel in the mountains of Mexico?"

Kat is nodding. She is actually nodding.

No way. They have been very kind, hospitable, but there is no way that I am getting on a bus and going to Mexico with them. No freaking way.

"I'm sorry." I hate speaking up like this, but someone has to, or I'm afraid we'll end up bouncing along some dusty Mexican road singing rounds of "Jesus Loves Me" while I struggle to keep from vomiting. "That doesn't seem fair. I mean, obviously Katy . . . *Katherine* and I haven't done any of the fund-raising or the other preparation."

It isn't enough. He's still looking at me with that . . . that *fervor* in his eyes.

"I mean, it's been super cool to meet you guys, and Pastor Shepherd, you've already taught us a ton about God's love just by—" I wave my hand to indicate the delicious break-fast, the conversation, their home.

Lucas Shepherd nods several times, seriously, his hands

folded in front of him. "I understand, Anna, if you're not ready to serve. Though I feel, in my heart"—here he places one hand against his chest, the picture of sincerity— "that we met you two young ladies for a reason. In any case, I hope our paths will cross again someday." He spears one more piece of bacon off his plate and then ambles away from the table.

Not ready to serve? His words are slippery somehow, reminding me of television church, the ministers with the sharp white teeth smiling while the operators stand by to take your Visa number. Did people think that way about my father? No. Not Pastor Jake Marshall. A few months ago, I could conjure up a memory of his presence—the sincerity of his voice—to reassure myself, but now it all gets mixed up in my head with the shadow he has become since my mother's death. I pull my phone out of my bag and quickly text him again. *What will become of your church?* I need to jolt him out of this grief coma before he forgets who he was.

Kat follows me back into the guest room, and I lean down, pulling the bottom sheet tight on my corner of the bed. "How about grabbing that other side and flipping up the bedspread?"

Kat nods and smoothes out her side. "I'm sorry about last night," she says, so quietly that I almost miss it underneath the rustling of the comforter.

"Sorry?" Sorry for crying? For . . . for kissing me? My heart skips.

"For crying and . . . stuff."

I tuck the spread around the pillows and frown. I busy my hands with straightening out an invisible wrinkle. "You don't have to be sorry. I mean, I cry all the time." There's more I want to say—the words rise up in my mouth but remain trapped there, sticky with shame and shyness.

Kat flops onto the bed, sliding down right on top of the newly smoothed surface and staring blankly at the ceiling. "That's not what I meant, not really."

She waits, and I know what I should do, what a normal person would do. I try to reach for her, but my face burns, my arms are stiff and heavy at my sides. I look at Katy lying there, and I'm lost, utterly lost.

"I guess it's complicated," she says. "It always has been."

What is she talking about? Irrational anger—a flash fire of something bewildering and stupid—ignites in the pit of my stomach and travels up my spine like the mercury in a thermometer.

"Get off the bed! You're messing it all up." I grab her arms to pull her up, off the bed, but Kat fights back, wrestling to free her wrists from my grip.

The anger of a moment ago twists within me, transforming into panic.

"Get up! I want . . . I want to leave, okay?" I can feel her trying to trap me here.

We're almost really fighting now; I try to drag her up off the bed, and Kat struggles to escape me. We push and pull, equals in strength, grappling like children on the playground.

She lands a kick, a sharp pain in my right shin, and then she sweeps my feet right out from under me. I fall in an awkward snarl on the bed, flailing around like a cat dropped into the bathtub. Damn it, I'm not going to Mexico. She can't make me. I push her, crowding her toward the edge of the bed. Katy rolls and pins me, a knee on my chest.

I'm trapped. I try to stuff this strange panic down. "Let's get out of this place!" I can hardly breathe. "Let's just get the hell away from this creepy family!" My voice has that hysterical lilt to it, and it shames me almost instantly.

"Uh-m." An awkward throat-clearing sound comes from behind us, and I turn to see Pastor Shepherd standing in the doorway. "Pardon me, ladies, I just wanted to make sure you didn't forget this." He holds up the atlas that we were looking at over breakfast. "In your haste to leave." He smiles.

We're frozen in a scandalous tangle of arms and legs,

sprawled across the ruined bed. Neither of us can move, and likewise, Pastor Shepherd seems similarly stuck, holding out the atlas with a sort of half-horrified, half-rueful look on his face. I want to disappear, or worse than that. I want to be *vaporized*, like in some goofy science fiction movie—every bit of who I am blasted irrevocably into subatomic particles.

"Can I pack you girls a lunch?" Angela Shepherd's sweet face peers around the door frame. She takes the atlas from her husband's hand and bustles over to the edge of the bed, where Kat has placed her satchel. "Wouldn't want you to leave us with an empty stomach," she says, oblivious to the tension in the room, which dissolves in her presence like a sugar cube stirred into a steaming cup of tea.

The anger—the shame, the fear—*it* vaporizes instead of me, and I giggle, helplessly, tears streaming down my face. Hysteria squared. Of course it's contagious. Before long, Kat and I are rolling with peals of laughter.

"Lunch. Awesome," says Kat at last, when she can breathe. "And then we're off!"

I look around, but Pastor Shepherd has disappeared, and even though it might be ungrateful to think this way, I'm not sorry to see him gone.

We spend the next few nights at a campground in the Black Hills, where Kat discovers she is a pretty kickass cook on a campfire. I discover that the pine trees smell like vanilla and the squirrels are vicious.

My father sends me two texts in a row, unprecedented communication skills. The first one is sort of cryptic: *Returning to church is a journey.* The second message encourages us to visit Mount Rushmore. He doesn't mention Mom, though I've known about Rushmore since I was a baby. It was part of their song, from that time before I existed, the time when they fell in love.

"You don't want to see it, just to see it? It's like, some kind of American . . . *thing*, isn't it?" Kat looks up from painting her toenails. "I mean, I don't care. Whatever you want."

"Not Rushmore." My parents met there on a church retreat when Dad was in seminary and Mom was in college. The stories they used to tell in tandem—about Mom asking Dad to take a photograph of her with her best friend next to the monument; how he had accidentally opened her camera and exposed the whole roll of film. Too many details—ones that I remember—the way they finished each other's sentences. And later the photograph album of their Mount Rushmore honeymoon trip—pages of snapshots with their bright, youthful smiles so full of the expectation of future joy—all these details crowd out any appeal I may have found in the mountainous sculpture.

I send him a response: *Take a step. I'll save Rushmore for you.*

"All right, cool. Carving a bunch of giant, dead white guys seems such a stupid thing to do to a sacred mountain." She wiggles her toes.

Devil's Tower is pretty much as we expected, minus the aliens. We shuffle around the base in a crowd thick with strollers and toddlers wearing backpacks with leashes attached, and sunburned young lovers handing their cameras over to strangers to capture their bliss with the otherworldly rock formation rising above their heads.

Kat rubs the back of her neck and scratches at a mosquito bite on her ankle with the edge of her other flip-flop. "Let's get out of here."

"That's cool with me." I have a headache.

The air inside the car is thick and hot, and it ripples out across the parking lot in waves. There is still a freshness in the air, though, in the smooth June sunshine that isn't yet oppressive with midsummer humidity. "Next stop?" I pull out the atlas.

Kat shrugs, looking a little peevish. "I don't care. Will you drive, though? I get so bored."

I trade the map for the keys and climb into the driver's seat, a flash of pale, freckled legs peeking out from underneath my skirt. I frown at them and wish, for the millionth time, for some pigment. "God, look at my legs. I look like a ghost."

Kat doesn't look. "I like your legs."

"Yeah, well, you're alone in that opinion."

"Not true. The boys in A.P. Lit. used to go on and on about them every time you wore a skirt."

Yeah, right. The boys in A.P. Lit. were too busy geeking out over their role-playing games or whatever to notice my legs—of that I'm sure. I roll my window down all the way before closing the door. "Oh my god, it's so hot in this car, I swear I'm going to melt." I lift the hair off the back of my neck. "Whatever, Katy. There were no boys ogling my legs. You made that up."

"Why would I make it up? That would be kind of weird."

"You know you're always trying to make me feel better about myself. And it's not like I'd ever know, with a lie like that. It's not like I'm going to call up Danny Nash and Norman Whatshisface and be all, 'Hey, did you used to look at my legs?'"

Kat grabs my arm. "Call," she says. "Call them and ask. I'm serious."

I roll my eyes and point at the map on Kat's lap. "Find me a road. I'm ready to move."

"Fuck you." She fiddles with the music. "You're not listening to me, Anna. You have no clue how many people lusted after you."

I shift into reverse and back out of the parking spot. "What do you mean, 'fuck you'? Which way should I go?"

"I mean fuck you, you don't even realize when someone's crazy about you, Your Royal Aloofness."

"My Royal Aloofness?" I frown. Is that what people think of me?

There's a pause, and I look over to see her fumbling with

her sunglasses. She gestures. "Go right. Down to that green sign, and then hang another right."

"People think I'm stuck up?"

"Does it matter?"

"Do *you* think I am?"

She sighs. "Maybe a little bit, senior year, but it doesn't matter. We all knew you were sad." My phone beeps, and Kat reaches into my backpack to get it. "Your dad," she says, and then she reads the message. "*There are ducklings.* That's all he says."

Ducklings. At the pond, in the park. I laugh. "It's been years since we went down to see the ducks." We used to go to the river all the time and watch the ducklings as they grew up. Sometimes people would feed them bread crumbs or whatever, but my mom always said it was better to just watch, that they had plenty of food in the pond and would come close if we just sat still and silent.

"Hey, do you think he went down there? Down to the pond, looking for ducklings?"

The thought of this makes me so happy I almost miss my turn picturing him sitting quietly on the banks, waiting for the mama ducks to lead their little families past him. "Katy? Are you serious about stupid boys from high school liking me?"

"They all wanted you," she says. And then, after a short silence, "It wasn't just the boys."

I'm not sure how to answer that.

We both roll the windows up halfway as I reach full speed on the highway, and for a while we sit there listening to the sound of the air rushing into the car, feeling the chill on our skin, and then we roll them up a little more so we can talk.

It's hard to know how to begin. I clear my throat. "I'm sorry for freaking out on you this morning." I pause, but Kat doesn't look at me. "Pastor Shepherd . . . he . . ." I shrug. "Something about him makes me nervous." It's not everything I want to say, but it's one thing. I can talk about one thing, anyway.

"I liked him. You were scared he'd make you believe again."

"Oh, *please*, Katy." I scowl. What's that supposed to mean, anyway? This isn't about *me*. "He's too . . . slick, like some kind of door-to-door God salesman."

Kat raises an eyebrow. "Watch out for the lightning, there."

I can't help it. I have to laugh. "Well, I didn't trust him."

"I thought he was nice. And so was Angela. I just got this . . . *feeling*. Like we were meant to meet them. Like we'll meet again."

"See? Now you sound just like him." I don't believe in that cosmic coincidences junk. What good is free will if everything is already fated, if it's all just waiting there for us? What's the point of making good decisions or doing good deeds, if it doesn't change anything, if our fate is preordained? So my mom was *meant* to die, then?

"Whatever, Anna. I just said I have a feeling we haven't seen the last of the Shepherds." Kat sighs. "Sometimes it's like you're just looking for a reason to get pissed off at the world, you know? Maybe you could give some other emotion a chance."

We ride in silence again for a while, driving west right into the setting sun. I squint at the bug-splattered windshield, my forehead drawn together in a frown. What the hell does she know, anyway? Finally I speak. "Text my dad back for me," I say. "Tell him God won't leave me alone."

Kat grins and taps out the message. "Perfect," she says. "Now. You wanna hear me read some Kerouac?"

I smile, forcing myself to relax my brows. Maybe she's right. Maybe I am always looking for a reason to be angry. Maybe I should chill the hell out. Maybe this book will be good for me. "Bring on the dharma!" I say.

Here Is A List of Words
I Cannot Say

Yes,
I am
angry,
but
I have to
fight
back
the fear
of losing you.

6

Straining at the padlock,
the garage doors
At noon
—Jack Kerouac

Here is what I love most about Kat. She knows how to be quiet when it really matters. Also she knows how to say what needs to be said, unlike me. I always have the words waiting in my mouth, poised behind the fence of my teeth, unable to form my lips around the syllables for fear of how the words will twist during the passage.

Here is a secret: I wonder if she's right about Pastor Shepherd—that I'm afraid he'll make me believe again. And if that's not it, what am I afraid of?

I ease the car into the parking lot of the garage. The oil light came on about twenty-five miles ago, and we spent another ten or fifteen minutes driving around the tiny town of Gillette, Wyoming, searching for a mechanic. At four thirty on a Saturday afternoon, this little quick-change oil place looks to be our only option.

The tall guy in coveralls who walks into the tiny waiting room has nice eyes and a black smudge of grease along his left cheekbone. His face also reveals a five o'clock shadow and wistful thoughts of quitting time. "Hello," he says, wiping his hands on a rag so grimy it can't possibly be helping the situation. "You got here just in time. I was on my way out to turn off the sign." He nods toward the neon sign in the window.

I flash a nervous smile, and wait for Kat to turn on the charm, to get this boy wrapped around her finger and ready to spend his evening solving the puzzle of our car trouble, but Kat flops down in one of the plastic chairs and leaves it to me.

"So what's it going to be?" asks the mechanic. "Standard oil change? Air filter?" He smiles, seeing my nervousness. "Oh, it's okay, don't worry. I'll stay to get you set up. If I don't, I dunno where you'd get an oil change 'round here till Monday."

"I think—" I say, and my voice sounds far away and wrapped in layers of gauze. "I think maybe we have some bigger problems?"

His eyes stray for just a tiny fraction of a second toward the front window, toward that sign he must wish he had unplugged ten minutes ago, but he remains professional. "All righty. Well, let's take a look. Pull her into the first bay there, okay?"

I toss the keys to Kat. I hate driving into garages, especially the kind with the big hole in the middle of the floor. Even when I go super slow, I can't imagine how I'll avoid crashing into the door or dropping a portion of my vehicle into the pit. I wander over to the coffee pot and sniff at it once before pouring myself a Styrofoam cup full. My mom and I used to tease my dad about what a coffee snob he was— Mom would do things like microwaving old cups of coffee just to drive him nuts. To me it mostly all tastes the same. Still I find myself imitating his habits—sniffing the brew as though I will turn it down if it has been on the burner all afternoon, when in reality I would probably drink it even if it were mostly solid.

After a while, Kat comes back in looking worried. "So it turns out we were supposed to stop driving the car when the oil light came on," she says.

"I told you!" I had, indeed, advocated for immediate stopping, but Kat had insisted we keep going.

"Well, apparently the oil is kind of necessary. And we don't really have any left. Something about the plug in the oil pan leaking or maybe it's missing?"

"Missing?" I squeeze my arms in front of my chest, holding myself together. "I mean, wouldn't all the oil just pour right out?"

"Well, yes, Anna babe. That's why we don't have any left." Kat flops down on the chair again and picks up an old fishing magazine. She shrugs. "I guess it wasn't all the way gone. The guy says the plug was like, in pieces. So some of the pieces were still all stuck in there, which slowed the oil down some. He says he got all the pieces out."

"Well, now what? Can he just put another plug in, fill it up, and off we go?" I look outside at the bleak gray sky, the scrubby expanse of parking lots and fields that line both sides of the road as far as the eye can see. "I mean, we can't stay here until Monday. Where would we even sleep?"

Kat pulls her hands through her hair, twirling it around her fingers. "It's just . . . he doesn't have the part. The plug, I mean. And it's time for him to go home, you know? I don't really know what we should do, but we can't drive the car, not without any oil in it." For a moment Kat's face seems etched in glass—her expression still and nearing transparency. It scares me to see her so fragile. What will we do?

The bell on the front door jangles, and a thin, timid-looking woman with a fuzzy-headed toddler comes in. She smiles at us and settles the little one next to the faded toy box in the corner.

Moments later, the mechanic comes back into the waiting room, this time scratching his head. He shoots an apologetic look at the woman and then nods a couple times as though reassuring himself that he knows what he's talking about. "I took a look at it—looks like the last person who changed your oil stripped the threads on the plug, then cracked it in half when they were trying to tighten it." He glances at Kat. "You didn't notice it was losing oil? That the stuff was dripping on the ground?"

The little boy catapults himself toward the mechanic's legs. "Daddy! Daddy home now?"

"Whoa, buddy, easy." He scoops the boy up into his arms.

Kat shakes her head. "I guess I never really pay attention to the oil." She scrunches up her hair again.

The mechanic nods. "Well, I'd say you've been losing oil slowly but steadily for a while now. I can order the part from Casper, but honestly, Tuesday's probably the soonest we'll get it. *Maybe* Monday afternoon, but with the way stuff stacks up over the weekends, I don't know. I already tried to rig a few temporary options, so maybe you could limp it down to Casper or something. I could try a few more things . . . " He trails off, looking at the young woman in the chair. She smiles sadly.

Kat raises her eyebrows at me, and I look out the front window again. The wind has really picked up, and dust whips wildly across the parking lot.

"Is—is there a campground or something where we could stay, somewhere close by?" Kat keeps twirling her imaginary pigtails and pursing her lips.

The mechanic and his wife both shake their heads. "There's the Comfy Time Motel," says the woman softly. "I could give you girls a ride there."

We stand awkwardly in the middle of the room, between the couple. I tap my foot, nervous energy coiling and uncoiling in my legs, in my stomach. Kat was supposed to figure out all the car stuff before we left. It was on the list. We don't have the money to drop on a motel room for two or three nights, at least not this early in the trip. I mean, we could do it, but it would set us up for problems later on. We have a pretty tight budget for lodging, although we do have some "fun" money set aside. I suppose we could use that on a motel and forget about having fun.

"No, give me a little while. I can rig up something," he says. "Probably." He looks apologetically at the woman—his wife? Girlfriend? "I mean, it's still pretty early, really."

She smiles, but I can see the weariness in her eyes, how much she really wants him to come home. "Yes, honey, work on it awhile more. It's okay. We can come back for you later."

I can't do this to them, intrude on their weekend like this. It's not right. "We're ruining your night," I say. "It's fine. We can figure something out." We step outside to give them a chance to talk, and the wind nearly knocks us over. It's major dust bowl action going on in the town of Gillette. Acres of topsoil whip through the air, swirling and eddying across the pavement.

Kat shouts, throwing her arms up over her face. "Let's go around the building!"

We run to the lee of the garage, bent nearly double against the wind, which seems to suck the words out of me and fling them into the next county. "This is going to be a crazy night!"

Kat huddles in closer. "I know!" she shouts in my ear. "What should we do? Motel, you think?"

I'm facing the parking lot, so I'm the one to see the squad car drive up. My heart instantly goes into a tap-dancing routine on speed. "Oh my god!" I push Kat back from the corner of the building, toward the alley behind. "It's the cops!"

Even with her natural skill of composure, Kat's face still registers a little flash of fear.

"It's those guys we ran over!" The grim headlines return to my mind, and I can see it all laid out in front of us—jail, court, testimony, even prison. I imagine my dad's face gone all skeletal with worry, that lank gray hair he used to keep so clean and shiny clinging to his disappointed face.

It takes Kat only a second to regain control. "For the last time," she shouts, "we did not run anybody over!"

We scramble back around the corner of the building,

leaning into the wind. Kat pushes me the last fifteen feet toward the door. "Go, you moron!" Her hands are firm on my
shoulders. "Get a hold of yourself. It's just the local police."

I consider this. It would probably be some other kind of
law enforcement, if they were tracking down two hit-and-
run killers who had crossed the state line, wouldn't it? The
thought casts enough doubt in my mind to propel me inside, though I swear my wrists can already feel the weighty
shackles snapping shut.

"The whole north side of town ain't got power," the
cop says as we enter, struggling to close the door against
the bluster outside. His rodentlike face twitches with im-
portance. "This storm rollin' in, gonna be out all rest of the
weekend, I reckon."

Oh, thank God. He's here about the weather, that's all.
My spastic heart slows to a nervous trot.

The cop turns to face us, nods, and twists his face into a
smile. "That your little Toyota in the shop?" he asks.

Kat nods, pressing her lips together.

"Long way from Minnesota, ain't ya?" He says Minnesota like Mini-soda, and I'm struck by the thought of one of
those tiny little cans of soda pop. I don't exactly giggle, but
enough amusement shows on my face that the cop narrows
his eyes. Cops are so suspicious of a good time. I have to dig
my fingernails into my palms to stop smiling.

"You girls stayin' in town, then?" His eyes are shrewd,
and his narrow lips quiver.

Kat slips her arm tightly around my waist and gives him
a saucy smile. "We might stay all week," she says, raising
her voice over a sudden groan of wind that shakes the whole
building.

I watch the nervous little man's face flicker with conflict-
ing emotions as he eyes the two of us, Kat with her grinning
and me biting on the edge of my finger. It's like he wants to
find us guilty of something, but he can't quite decide what.

At least he doesn't seem to react to our license plates. If

the guys from the Sage Creek Campground had been able to remember the plates, or the model of our car, that information would have been disseminated to all law enforcement in the area. Either those guys had been too drunk to notice or remember the information, or Gillette, Wyoming, was far enough away to escape notice, at least for today. I pull my hand away from my mouth and curl it into a fist. What about tomorrow? And the next day? Tuesday is a long ways away. Anything could happen.

"You're not planning on being here too much longer, then, are you, Leroy?" The cop talks to our mechanic, who shrugs. "I'll drive by a coupla times tonight and tomorrow, like usual, make sure everything is in order. If you lose power over on this end, I'll come through a little more often."

"Oh, you know, that's okay," says Leroy. "I mean, things will be fine. I'm just going to see what I can do for these girls and then head home. Have a good night, now, Officer Henley."

The cop nods to the woman. "Evening, Donna. You take care now!" He tips his hat to the little boy and then hurries out to the cruiser he has left running in the lot.

"We'll just get out of your way now, so you can close up," Kat says. "Do you think you could point us toward someplace with power, someplace we could get some dinner?"

I nod, drawing my arms around myself. "Maybe pizza?"

The mechanic's wife looks up, her whole face brightening. "How old are you girls?" she says.

"Eighteen," says Kat. I'm seventeen for three more weeks actually, but it's close enough.

"I'll call my little sister, Casey. She's seventeen, and I bet she and her friends would show you around. She's a lot of fun. Can I give her a call?" Donna has her phone open already.

Kat reaches over and pulls my finger away from my mouth. "That would be awesome," she says. "Road trips are more fun when you've got a local to show you the ropes."

Kat's grin is so easy; I force my mouth into a sort of gri-mace and wonder what it would be like to be so comfortable around people all the time.

Leroy nods to me. "While Katherine is setting up your dinner plans, you need to get anything out of your car? I put it in the back parking lot." Kat hands me the keys, and I head uncertainly toward our car. How long would we be gone? If we stay at a motel, will we be able to grab some things later? I shove several pairs of underwear into my backpack and peer into the backseat, trying to decide if anything needs to be moved to the trunk or taken with us. Is the gun in there somewhere? The weed? In the end, I'm too besieged by the buffeting winds to stick around. I run to the front door, holding my arms in front of my face to keep the grit out of my eyes.

Leroy holds the door open for me, and I step into the waiting room, where Leroy's wife, Donna, is talking on her cell phone. "Oh, I see you right now," she says, waving out the window toward a set of headlights pulling into the lot. "Okay, 'bye." She snaps the phone shut.

A car zips across the lot and parks carelessly askew, and two girls jump out; they race toward the door in tandem, their coifed blonde hair withstanding the worst of the wind. As they spill in the door in a hiss of giggles, my stomach tenses, my voice retreats. These girls are plastic perfect—from their bubble-gum lips to their shiny heels.

"Sissy!" squeals the slightly taller Barbie, the one who was driving. She runs over and embraces her sister, kissing both her cheeks in a great show. She turns to the little boy, who grins. "And how's my favorite little man?" He runs to her to be tickled, while the other girl examines her cuticles near the door, tapping her impossibly pointed patent-leather toes.

This is my worst nightmare. I hate girls like this, so flawless they must be unreal. I feel an arm slide around my waist and lean into Kat with a sigh of relief. She senses my vulnerability, helps hold me together in the face of this uncertain evening.

The sister turns toward us at last, smiling with her straight white teeth, the kind that glint too brightly to be natural. "You're the refugees, huh? I'm Casey," she says. She nods to her friend. "That's Sammi, my best friend." Her eyes slide over me from head to toe. "You're hungry, huh?" I tug at the bottom of my shirt. My hand creeps up to touch the edge of the pink bandanna I've tied around my dirty hair. I feel pinned under the scrutiny of her gaze.

Kat grins, completely at ease. "We're starving," she says. "And what do people do around here for fun?"

Casey laughs, her voice that of a celebrity sex kitten being interviewed on late-night television. She and her plastic friend exchange a glance, a secret smile. "We can show you a thing or two."

7

The purple wee flower
should be reflected
In that low water
—Jack Kerouac

*In some ways our journey begins in earnest on this night, the
night of two lotus blossoms shimmering on the surface of the
pond. The things that come before are important, of course.
They are the roots in the mud, the two stalks that labor up to
the light—delivering the blossoms to the dawn. The stems twine
together; the roots curl and tangle in the depths. The twin blossoms turn as one, opening in tandem, following the sun each day
to his fiery bed in the West.*

> *I watched your mouth—the smile
> deepening the corners of
> your lust for adventure.*

This is the night I felt too much and lived to tell about it.

"You're driving, Sammi," Casey says, in a tone that
shows she is used to giving the orders.

Sammi snaps her gum, takes the keys, and climbs into
the driver's seat while Casey opens the passenger door and
tips the front seat forward for us to climb in. Then she winks
at me while Kat clambers over. "Your girl is hot," she says,
under her breath.

I scramble to respond, but I'm too slow. My face heats up—I try to hide it by climbing in quickly after Katy, wishing fervently that I could disappear, or at least come up with something casual and witty to say.

Is that what people think, then? A startling tingle travels through me at the thought. I lower my eyes, suddenly shy. Your girl is hot. *Your girl.* Do I have a girl? And okay, I'll admit it isn't like it's the first time I've entertained the possibility, but hearing someone else say it—I sneak another glance at Kat, who leans toward the front seat, laughing at something that Casey or Sammi has said. I see her tiny overbite, the small mole on her cheek, and I wonder. My girl? Am I . . . am I *into girls?*

My head spins. I remember the way she kissed me in the Shepherds' guest bed. As a friend? She hasn't ever kissed me like that before.

A smell. Sammi turns and laughs, smoke curling out of her mouth as she does. The smell, sweet and cloying, wrapping around me like the tendrils of a vine; I close my eyes for a moment. Clove cigarette. I fight against the memory.

My mother found it in my dresser drawer, tucked into a little wooden box that used to have tea bags in it.

"Why were you digging through my stuff?" My throat still hurts when I remember how I shouted, when I remember the shouting that came later that same night, through the smoke. Shouting for her.

That stupid, stupid night. I remember it in sound bites and images—my father's voice as he stepped in to temper the heat of my mother, the flint in her eyes. Dad said they didn't have any more kids because they liked the balance of our group of three, but I wonder how close we came sometimes to tearing him right down the middle. I remember the ache in my left heel from when I stomped upstairs to my room. The smell of the clove cigarette, clutched between my angry fingers. I smoked it to spite her, right there in my bed. I remember stabbing it out in the fichus plant, feeling dizzy. I remember putting it out. I'm sure of it. I'm positive. But that doesn't erase the sense of guilt, as though it really were my cigarette—my act of stupid defiance—that set the whole night on fire.

Besides, I can find guilt anywhere. If she hadn't been upset with me, maybe she wouldn't have taken her pills. If she hadn't taken them, maybe the smoke alarm would have been enough. *If . . . maybe.* If I believed enough in God, maybe he would have saved my mother.

I snap open my eyes and choke on the smoke that hangs heavily in the car. I roll down my window with a shaking hand. I hear nothing but the roar of blood in my ears, feel nothing but my heart.

Kat is looking at me. So is Casey, twisting around on her knees to peer over the back of the passenger seat. Kat looks concerned, Casey curious.

"Are you, like, going to throw up in my car?" The curiosity grows closer to disgust.

I force my eyes up to meet Casey's. I shake my head, searching for the voice I left buried somewhere. "N-no," I manage finally. "I'm okay." My face is hot, my breath sucking in and out of my lungs noisily. I turn to Kat, fumbling for an explanation. "I—I couldn't breathe all of a sudden. It was like, my heart . . . it won't stop racing." I can still feel it galloping in my chest, and I reach over—bridging the distance between us—I reach over for her hand and hold it tightly to my chest. "Feel."

Kat nods, her eyes serious. She doesn't seem at all fazed by the fact that her palm is pressed against my chest. "It's really racing, Anna babe. I think you should lie down." She scoots over a little and helps me recline, my head in her lap. I feel her fingers pressing into the pulse point in my neck. Her touch sends strange shivers through me. "It's slowing down, babe. Just breathe."

Casey is still peering over the seat at us. "You're having

a panic attack," she says. "I get those all the time. Or at least, I used to. I don't know why, but they stopped awhile ago." She nods. "Lying down helps."

How completely humiliating. I close my eyes. Kat's fingers are soft against my eyelids, slowly moving in tiny circles, calming me even as they send waves of tingly confusion over me. I take a deep breath and try to picture my life with a girlfriend, with Katy. Suddenly my chest spasms, and I snap open my eyes, frightened again.

Kat giggles. "Hiccups, babe. You have the hiccups."

Oh, wow. I start to giggle then, and so do the others, all of us laughing together. I roll halfway over and struggle to sit up, random hiccups escaping as high-pitched exclamation points interspersed with laughter. Stupid hiccups.

Casey spins around and faces forward again, turning up the music. Some pop diva whose name escapes me sings brightly about lust and sex, and for a while we all just sit and listen, a ripple of giggles running back and forth among us, punctuated by an occasional *hic*.

When Casey turns around again, she holds out a joint and a lighter. "Either of you care to light this?" Kat reaches for it without hesitation, and I watch her set the tip on fire.

"Where are we going?" We're driving along a rather dark highway. "In fact, where *are* we?" I take the joint, pressing it into my index finger like Katy shows me, but then I hold it, looking at her helplessly.

"Suck it straight into your lungs," she says softly. I look into her dark eyes—the *interesting* eyes that challenged twelve-year-old me to take a dare. I think of her laughing with Sammi and Casey, the way they all seem to be having fun. I think of my daring so long ago, the way I surprised us both by kissing her. I'm tired of being the one who can't have fun. I lift the joint to my lips.

The smoke fills my chest and then my head like a cloud, and I cough, gasp, choke. "Oh," I say, when I get my breath back. I feel such a spiraling mess inside me.

"Oh," I say again, barely a whisper. "I think I just did drugs."

Kat laughs. "Anna, you're adorable."

I'm adorable? What does that mean? I cough. Casey takes the joint from me and holds it up to Sammi's mouth. I'm worried about that, about her driving while stoned. I should say something, shouldn't I? I'm supposed to, like, get out of the car right now and call my dad or something. But I don't want to get out of the car. I don't want to leave these plastic-perfect girls and their pop songs and this spiral, this tingly suggestion—this promise of excitement. I'm torn between fear and adventure—uncertain.

I try to pay attention to what Casey is saying.

"You didn't think we were going to show you around *that* little dung heap of a town, did you?"

The joint makes its way back to me again. On the second round, my lungs feel less constricted as I inhale the heady smoke. I don't hear any sirens, no officers of the law bent on throwing me in jail. No Hand of God interferes. My stomach growls.

I pass the joint up to Casey and lean back against the seat, watching the flicker of headlights as a car passes. "It got dark," I say, my tongue loosened to the point of stating the obvious. I look to Kat, whose profile is shadowed against the fading glow from the window behind her. "I'm hungry."

Sammi laughs, a little hint of cruelty in the ring of it. "Anna's got the munchies."

Even though I can't really remember taking it, I seem to be holding the joint between my fingers once again. I suck in the smoke, feeling confident—an old pro at this. The roach is tiny, and little hot sparks scorch my lips, but I don't even flinch.

All at once I'm giddy. Kat and I exchange a smile, and I see her relief—she's glad I'm okay with this.

And I *am* okay with this—with this adventure. With more than that? I steal another glance at Katy and find that I'm glad to surprise her. I cough.

"You're so messed up," says Casey, and I reach over the seat to give her the roach, but I'm clumsy, and I drop it somewhere.

"You idiot!" Casey scrambles in the dark.

All my confidence vanishes. I feel tears spring to my eyes.

"These seats are *leather!*"

Sammi turns on the dome light, flooding the car with a surreal illumination. *"Shut that fucking light off!"*

Sammi snaps the light off, and Casey triumphantly holds up the roach, which is still lit.

"I—I'm sorry." I don't know what to say. "Did it burn the seat?"

Casey grins over the seat back. "Oh, I don't know," she says, sucking hard on the roach. "Whatever. I don't care." She laughs. "Besides, it's *so obvious* you're a complete amateur. I don't know why I even gave it to you when it was that small."

I watch as she holds the roach to Sammi's lips, trying not to think words like *tragic* and *head-on collision*. I hate this unfortunate habit I have of imagining grim newspaper headlines about my own life.

I squeeze my eyes shut. *This is the kind of situation where I used to pray.* Instead, I take a deep breath and lace my fingers into Katy's, trusting the darkness to cover the hot blush that accompanies my daring.

Casper isn't huge, but it has that smugness of being the biggest thing for miles around, and the lights of it are enough to blow my mind as we drive in. I've been sitting there in the dark car, quietly stoned out of my mind, and when I see the glow of the lights, and the distant shadows of the Casper Mountains looming in the background, I gasp. All of it seems to shimmer, to expand and contract.

I pull away. "Katy," I say. "You know that part you were reading in *The Dharma Bums*, about that lady, Rosie, the one who was trying to kill herself?"

Kat nods, serious.

"And he told her to relax, that she *was* God?"

"I remember."

We are pulling into downtown. "And then when she dies, when she jumps off that roof, and the cop grabs her robe, but she falls naked like a newborn down to the ground, and then Kerouac realizes that Heaven is everywhere all the time, and all religions are one, and we are all a part of God?"

Kat squeezes my hand to let me know she hears.

"That was cool, wasn't it?"

"You're stoned, Anna," Kat says softly, and I'm about to protest, but her mouth collides with mine, and then she's kissing me. For a crazy instant I feel like our mouths are actually two parts of the same person—two perfect halves of some divine whole, a fruit full and ripe, waiting to be consumed—and then I laugh, a ridiculous giggle. She's right. I'm so stoned.

I'm also starving. "Someone please tell me there's a pizza shop in this town that's open late and isn't a hangout for bored cops."

The others immediately agree, and Casey directs us to a tiny hole-in-the-wall with a bunch of teenage boys in the kitchen and a handful of narrow booths in the front. The place is deserted, and the lighting is dim. Kat and Sammi order pizzas while Casey and I drop some quarters into the dusty pinball machine. I'm starting to feel more normal. I have what feels like a perfectly dignified conversation with the counter girl when I go up to buy a soda out of the cooler, and I get a decent score at pinball as well.

"I want more quarters," Casey says. She drags me by my elbow back up to the counter, and I can't be entirely sure, but this time it seems like the girl stares at us.

"Quarters, please." I giggle a little as I hand over the money.

The girl just raises her eyebrows and hands me a stack

of eight quarters. "You're having an interesting night, huh?"
she says.

Casey leans into me, wrapping her arm around my
neck. "Anna's *my* girlfriend now," she says to the counter
girl. "We're going to run away to Mozambique." She leans
over and licks my earlobe.

I pull away, my hand flying up to my ear. "What are you
doing? Gross!"

Casey laughs. "Do you even know what that is?"

"What, Mozambique?"

"Eargasm!" Casey giggles.

The girl at the counter laughs.

I cover my ear and laugh, too, feeling lighter than I have
in a long, long time.

"So what should we do now?" I pick at the edge of my
last slice of pizza. I'm too full to eat it, but it tastes so good I
almost can't stop myself from trying. It has to be past midnight, and even after our second round of energy drinks,
I'm wilting. I wonder about sleep, about what comes next.
My chest tightens.

"Yeah, we should *do* something," Kat says, her voice
dreamy. Her head is on my shoulder.

"Like what?" My brain is empty, my stomach so full it
feels like I've swallowed a washtub full of wet denim.

She sits up straight and opens her eyes. "I know!" she
says. "Let's get matching tattoos!"

Casey and Sammi exchange a look, grins spreading
slowly across their faces. "We could go see Shaggy," Casey
says, her smile growing even wider, a little sigh escaping
her lips.

Oh, god, a tattoo. Of course Katy *would* come up with
something like this. Something to test me, to find my limits.
Three sets of eyes turn on me, waiting for my reaction—
there is no question among them who is the lamest, the most
likely to chicken out of this plan. Well, I can play this game.

"Sounds awesome." My tone gives away none of my uncertainty. "What kind should we get?"

"Is he any good?" says Kat.

Casey nods dreamily. "Shaggy went to high school with us. He's the real thing."

"An artist, like for real," adds Sammi.

"An anarchist," says Casey.

"An anarchist?" Kat twists, twists her pigtails. "So what?"

Casey leans against the back of her booth, her eyes half-lidded. "Oh my god, but he's good," she says. "At more than tattoos."

Damn this stupid blush. "I have to use the restroom," I say, nudging Kat. "You?"

Kat smiles. "Be right back," she says, and the two of us head around the corner to the bathroom.

We stand close in front of the dingy mirror, two girls, two little dharma bums. Best friends? I look into Katy's deep blue eyes and wonder what she sees.

"Are we really going to get tattoos?" My eyes are locked on the eyes in the mirror, and it reminds me of that strange feeling I get when the phone rings but nobody is there except a sort of echo of my own voice saying "Hello?" again and again. I can barely bring myself to hang up, to leave that echo of myself out there in the void.

In the mirror, Kat nods. "A lotus, turning, following the sun. Wandering west, like us."

I don't know what meaning Kat has attached to these words, but I drink them in, savoring the sound in my ears. "You kissed me." I tear my eyes away from the mirror to face her. We are close, so close standing here. My lungs might be carved out of granite, cast from bronze, the way they refuse to expand, to fill with air.

"You kissed me back," says Kat softly.

I nod. There's nothing more to say.

8

Fiddlydee!—
Another day,
Another something-or-other!
—Jack Kerouac

My first crush was this boy in fifth grade named Earl.

The popular kids in my class, who had trendy names, of course—Austin, Parker, Caden, Ashley, Madison, and Cole—called him a sissy because he played the piano and had long, dark eyelashes that could make my heart stop with one flutter in my direction. To me, he was every bit as noble as his name, and I thrilled at any small, fifth-grade chance to show my affection for him. I strategized carefully when we lined up so that I would be opposite him. I put an extra stick of cinnamon gum in his valentine. At recess I made dandelion voodoo dolls of his tormentors and pinched their heads off each time they called him "Earl the Girl."

He was oblivious, and of course that was part of his charm. His complete lack of interest in girls was as cute as those smoky gray eyes or his rumpled curls or his long and dainty fingers. I filled my time around the edges of the busywork, the time when I was finished but the rest of the class still plodded along, with sweet daydreams of Earl.

Until the day of the Milk Joke. This was the day I looked over during snack time and watched Earl take a big swig out of his carton of milk just as Madison Miller leaned in and said something funny. To begin with, Earl My One True Love was not supposed to laugh at jokes told by pretty little blonde girls with trendy names. This was bad enough, a grievous betrayal. But possibly even worse, Earl simply wasn't perfect anymore once I saw milk shoot out his nose.

Ever since the day of the Milk Joke, I've tried to remember this about "true love": how mutable it is. How it can disappear in an instant, especially if that instant involves mucus or betrayal. Most decidedly if it involves both.

And yet here I am in this tattoo shop, and I've agreed to leave here with a permanent reminder of Katy etched into my skin. Luckily, she hates milk.

Shaggy's arms are a sketch pad, showing the evolution of his art. He leans over the drafting table drawing, sandy blond hair tangling around his ears. A bright desk lamp illuminates his painted arms—a jumble of images and techniques fading into and out of one another like a crowd of strangers who are forced by circumstance to work together.

He nods at us as we come in, smiles a little around the hand-rolled cigarette that hangs from his lips, unlit. "I'm workin' in the back right now, ladies, but I should be ready for ya in about ten minutes. Take a look around."

With that, he disappears, sketch in hand, pencil stuck behind his right ear. The walls are hung with glass cases filled with page after page of tattoo renderings, some in black and white, some full color. Skulls. Roses. Tropical fish. Hearts of all sizes and accompaniments. Frogs, tigers, hieroglyphics, and tribal patterns merge into an eclectic display. Katy and I browse while Casey and Sammi giggle over a book full of butterflies and care bears.

"Do you see any?" I halfway hope we won't be able to find the right picture. It would give me an easy out, a way to back away from this precipice. But the rest of me hopes for the perfect image, the one that will strike me speechless and make me certain this is the right thing to do.

"I don't really like these lotus blossoms," says Kat, pointing to a wall display. "But I like his original designs."

"*You* could draw one, Katy Kat. I love your drawings."

She nods. "Oh, I know I could draw one, and it would be awesome." She laughs. "But see . . . it's like this. Shaggy will draw us a lotus, and I'll love it. I'll love it forever. I could draw us a lotus, and I'd love it. But then . . . I mean, I'm trying all the time to get better as an artist, you know? To evolve. And having my own art permanently etched into my skin? I feel like . . ." She trails off.

"You'd be making comparisons." I understand, even without being an artist. It's the reason I don't show anyone what I write. "You'd be embarrassed of its flaws."

"Well, it's more complex than that, but yeah."

The door to the back room opens, and Shaggy comes up front, stripping off a set of gloves. "All right, ladies, I'm all yours. Oh, hey, Casey, what's up, girl? Haven't seen you in a while!" He goes to her and wraps her in his arms for a tight hug, then looks her up and down. "Lookin' good, lookin' good," he mutters, smiling.

Casey laughs her perfect laugh. She bounces a bit. "Came in for tats! All of us!"

Shaggy nods in my direction. "New friends?"

Casey rolls her eyes. "Refugees from Minnesota."

"No kidding?"

Kat steps forward. "Katherine Amundsen," she says. Shaggy shakes her hand, flicking his fingers off of hers and bumping her fist. Kat follows his lead perfectly. I hope he keeps his weird handshake things to himself so I won't humiliate myself. He does, merely smiling at me. His eyes are strangely compelling, and he holds my gaze for a little longer than seems usual.

"So what's it going to be, then? Are you all getting the same thing?"

"We're thinking of getting a butterfly, or maybe some of these little daisies on the back of our neck?" Sammi points to a page in the book she is looking at.

"Sammi Richards? Seriously?" He laughs. "Wow, you have changed!"

I see the flash of shame that flickers across Sammi's proud features. "Yeah, well, that was a long time ago," she says.

Casey is oblivious. "I know! Isn't she hot? Gastric bypass, baby!"

Sammi's eyes narrow and flick over in my direction. "Anyway, about the tattoos?"

Shaggy nods. "Sure. So, butterflies and daisies all around, then?"

Kat clears her throat. "Can you show us any lotus blossoms that are a little more . . . delicate?" She gestures up at the gaudy magenta and blue designs, all full of bright flames and glowing jewels. "Something smaller, lighter? I'm thinking sort of wispy and a little stylistic."

Shaggy's face is thoughtful. "Sure, yeah . . . hold on." He slides into a rolling chair and rolls over to his computer. Within moments, he beckons us over to see some images on the screen. "Maybe find a particular angle you like in one of these photos, and then I'll do a drawing based on that."

He moves out of the way, and we share the chair to look over the images, scrolling through the pages in silence. My chest is so tight I can barely draw in a full breath. "Are you sure about this?"

Kat smiles and doesn't even move to twist pigtails into her dark hair. "I think it's a great symbol." She pauses and then reaches for my hand. "It will be our vow to each other. Forever friends."

My phone beeps, and I pull it out to discover a text from my dad. It's late, but that doesn't surprise me since he's always been a night owl. *You won't be alone anymore,* he says. For a second I'm confused, but then I see that he's responding to my text about God refusing to leave me alone. Still, it's kind of funny the way it arrives right now. I hold the phone up for Kat to see. "Dad says go for it." I glance back over my shoulder at Shaggy, hoping he won't ask for my ID, since I'm not *quite* eighteen. And I doubt this cryptic text message would count as parental consent.

"Have you two settled on a butterfly, then?" asks Shaggy, moving to the other side of the desk to where Casey and Sammi are poring over the book. They point and discuss the relative merits of several pictures while Katy and I peruse the lotus flowers.

Kat clicks on to a new page, and the image that pops up on the screen makes both of us catch our breath. We look at each other.

"It's perfect." I can't find any other words. "Absolutely perfect."

Casey is right. Shaggy can do much more than trace a pattern onto skin. He transforms the photo of the lotus blossom into something almost ethereal—delicate, yet containing the promise of strength within its mysterious depths. He finishes the drawing with a subtle rendering of the om symbol from Tibetan Buddhism, a nice touch. The curves of its strokes melt into the petals of the lotus as though he just discovered them there, outlined in morning dew. It isn't the least bit tacky; it's the merest suggestion of a tattoo.

"That's amazing." My words are muffled, both hands pressed up against my mouth. All my doubts fall away, and I turn to Kat with a grin.

"I'm ready," I say. "Let's do this."

Shaggy starts with me. I recline, tilted to one side, while he outlines the design in the soft flesh above my left hip bone. Kat is getting the mirror image, on her right side.

At first the needle hurts, but after a while the sensation deepens into something else entirely, something almost living, and I imagine that the lotus is actually rising up from my insides—tiny points of my bones and sinews rising to form an intricate mosaic on the surface of my skin. This thought rushes over me like a wave, and Kat presses her hand to the side of my face. I'm dizzy.

"Easy, babe. You're looking a little pale," she says. "Can I get you a Coke?"

Shaggy chuckles. "I get so many people in here all worried about whether or not they'll be able to deal with the pain. Pain is one thing. What people can't take is feeling so much, so much of anything." He pauses, blotting at my skin with the edge of the paper sheet he has draped over his skinny jeans. He nods. "You're doing great, though. This outline is the hardest part." He blots my hip again and then the roaring drone of the needle is back, rattling my core, but now it's as though he has softened the blow, pulled out the tiger's teeth.

So what I'm afraid of isn't pain. It's feeling. My chest expands, breath flooding through me. I can do this. Kat is here beside me, holding my hand.

The sound, the feeling, sinks into my body. I close my eyes. This is forever.

It feels as though several millennia have passed since the garage in Gillette. My left side is sore, and my brain is tired and droopy. Shaggy finishes Kat's tattoo, and even in its red freshness it is beautiful. There's only a hint of color, a blush of soft pearl on the lotus petals, a touch of pink highlights. Kat's light olive skin gives the image a duskier feel than my own pale cream, lightly dappled with freckles, but the blossoms are still mirror twins, and my face burns at the thought of our hips touching, skin to skin. Has she thought of it, too?

Shaggy snaps the needles into the sharps bin and peels off his gloves carefully. "All done, you two. Here, stand side by side so I can see them together. Easy does it, Katy." He holds her arm. I'm surprised at the brief surge of jealousy that flares in my chest when he uses her nickname.

Kat stands, a little shaky at first but smiling, and I go around to her right side so our tattoos are close, our arms around each other's waists. I stare into the mirror, trying to make this new image fit into my vision of myself.

"Can I take a photo for my wall?" Shaggy asks, pointing over to the bulletin board full of smiling patrons displaying his artwork.

I bite the inside of my lip, feeling a little shy, but then I nod. It's not as if anybody knows me here, anyway.

Shaggy snaps the photo, and I look at it in the display on the back of his camera with a kind of wonder. "There we are." There I am. With a tattoo. And . . . a girlfriend?

"There you are," he repeats. "And here are your after-care instructions. You can cover it up lightly, like this, to keep your clothes from touching it. They look nice, ladies. Really nice. That was fun." He smiles.

We all troop out to the front room, but it's empty; Casey and Sammi are nowhere to be seen. "Maybe they got bored?" says Kat. We walk to the front door and peer up and down the street, which is dark except for the occasional neon splash. The sky has a faint brush of violet across the black, and I wonder once again what time it is.

"I guess they'll be back soon," says Kat. Her voice is bright, but I can sense the uncertainty beneath the confident words. Where are they? Why didn't they say something if they were going to leave?

We go into the back room, and Shaggy packs a bong. I accept it when Kat hands it over, but it feels less like an exciting adventure and more like an amplifier for the anxiety building up in my belly. We smoke mostly in silence. I pass on the last couple of rounds, but it keeps going back and forth until both Katy and Shaggy are practically catatonic. I look from one to the other, and I hate it. I feel trapped.

"What do we do if they don't come back?"

"They'll come back," says Kat. "Why would they just leave?"

"Because that's who they are," Shaggy says, his voice dark. "They're just the kind who would find it funny to abandon you two here." He shrugs. "I'm not sayin' that's what happened, you know. I'm just sayin' that girl Casey is classic mean. Way back even as far as middle school, she ruled this little crew of mean girls with a combination of charm and brute force. Sammi was her sidekick, the desperate fat girl. The one who took the brunt of Casey's abuse and kept coming back for more, just for the privilege of being included."

Kat nods. "Yeah, I can see that," she says. "But Casey definitely likes you."

"Bad boy complex," he says, waving his hand dismissively. "I was two years ahead of her in school, had a motorcycle, you know. She was always hanging around, looking for danger and something to piss off her parents. Luckily, I was good friends with her brother-in-law, and I knew better than to mess with her."

"You know Leroy." The mention of our mechanic fills me with relief somehow. Leroy feels like an old friend, and if Shaggy knows him, well, there's hope of us getting back to our car, even if Casey and Sammi did abandon us.

"Yeah, Leroy and I grew up together. His wife, Casey's older sister, now she's a classy girl. Donna got all the goodness, all the sweetness in that family."

"But you don't really think Casey would just leave us here, do you?" I can't quite believe in this kind of mean. Like, in the abstract, sure. I know there are people who are that mean. But to me? To Katy? "They probably just went out to get some coffee or something." My confidence runs out. "Don't you think?"

Kat twists her hair. "How far away are we? From Gillette, I mean."

Shaggy shrugs. "About a hundred an' eighty miles, I guess. Takes two and a half or three hours to get up there."

"Maybe we could rent a car," says Kat.

"And anyway, I was just running my mouth, you know. Things change. People change. I mean, look at Sammi."

I realize I'm chewing on the side of my index finger,

and I pull it out. My side hurts, a dull ache like a sunburn. The kind of change that Shaggy's talking about—the kind where nasty high school girls mature into reasonably kind and accepting people—that kind of change isn't about losing a hundred pounds and getting a nose job.

"Maybe we should see if we can find their car," Kat says. "You remember what kind it was, Anna?"

I search through my brain for details, but it feels kind of like an office building after hours, with lights clicking off on all the floors, one by one. I muddle around in the dark for a bit and come up with, "It was light blue. And it had two doors."

Kat laughs. "Well, that ought to help. Let's settle up with Shaggy and then go out and see what we can find. I'm up for a walk, anyway; maybe a little fresh air would wake me up."

"Okay, lemme grab my wallet."

I grab my backpack from the floor behind Shaggy's desk and unzip the main pocket. Where's my wallet? I try to recall the last time I had it—the pizza place, I'm pretty sure. Yes, I paid for the pizzas, for all four of us. I breathe deeply, forcing myself to stay calm as my fingers reach around the bottom of the backpack, making sure before I check the smaller pocket. Nothing. I pinch the zipper pull for the small pocket, the whole time racking my brain for an image of myself paying the bill. I have almost zero hope of the wallet being in this pocket, but I check anyway.

Empty. My stomach plummets. My hands shake. "Hey, Kat?" My voice quivers pathetically.

Kat stands by the door, peering out for a sign of Casey and Sammi. "Yeah?" She doesn't turn to look.

I can't bring myself to say it. I mentally run through all of the wallet's contents: about two hundred dollars cash, an ATM card for the account where Kat and I have all our money for this trip, my driver's license, a credit card for my father's account that I've been instructed to use only in case of dire emergency. Some photos. A gift card for the coffee place at home.

Kat senses the emergency and comes to me, concern on her face. "Anna babe, what is it?"

"My . . . wallet. It's missing." I sit down on Shaggy's wheeled chair, closing my eyes. I have photocopies of both sides of all the contents of my wallet in the car, in the glove compartment. All the numbers to call in case things get lost or stolen. All two hundred miles away.

"No way."

Shaggy comes out of the back room. "Still no sign of them, huh?" he says. He sees the way we're staring at each other. "Whoa . . . what's going on?"

"They stole Anna's wallet!" Kat looks ready to kill.

"Well, maybe not." I can't jump to that conclusion, not yet. "Maybe I left it at the pizza place. Can we call them and ask?"

Shaggy shakes his head. "It's four in the morning, sweetheart. They won't be open until noon tomorrow. Wait. Tomorrow is Sunday. I don't think they open until two."

"No," Katy says. "I'm *sure* you put it in your backpack after we paid for the pizzas. I'm sure you did."

"I—I can't remember." I hate my pathetic, anguished voice.

"You didn't leave it anywhere," says Kat. "You put it back in your bag, I know you did. You're always completely organized, Anna. They took it. They must have."

I feel the tears fighting to the surface. How the hell are we going to get back? And then I remember Shaggy. "We'll figure out a way to pay you, I promise." The tears win, and once the dam is breached, the flow is heavy and fierce. I search my pockets for a tissue, sniffling. I am such a mess.

"Hey, hey, here you go." Shaggy holds out a handful of tissues and pats my arm awkwardly. "Don't worry about it. I know you'll pay me. It's okay."

Kat is pacing, her eyes full of fury. "I'll kill them," she

mutters. She turns back to me. "I cannot believe this, Anna babe."

A sort of resignation settles over me in the face of Kat's indignation. "Do you have my phone?" Maybe this is it: our car broken down, our money gone. Maybe we'll have to wave a white flag and wait for Kat's parents to come and save us.

No. That last is too much. Kat tosses my cell to me, and I slide out the keyboard and begin typing. "*Bad things are not a punishment,*" I write. "*Bad things are just bad things.*" Things we can't control.

"What did you tell him?"

"Nothing." I don't feel like sharing. I turn back to Shaggy. "You're being so nice to us." I can't even believe how embarrassed I am. Looking at him is painful. "Can I ask you one more quick favor before we get out of your hair?"

Shaggy grins and hands me something. I look down at my hand to find a twenty-dollar bill. "What's this? No, no, I can't *take* your money. I need to *give* you money." I can't believe this. "I was wondering if I could use your computer for a second." Maybe I can look up my bank account; maybe there's a way to contact customer service. That's not my main reason for wanting the computer, though. My main reason is both more and less important than that.

He pushes the twenty back into my hand and offers me the chair in front of the computer. "Seriously, Anna, I know you two are going to pay me back. I just wish I could help out more. I mean, if I knew someone who was driving up to Gillette, I'd totally figure out a way to get you up there. But this"—he nods at the money—"this is the least I could do. Maybe get some breakfast or something."

I force myself to smile. "Thanks, Shaggy. You're awesome." I log in to my bank statement and discover that my account balance is untouched, so far. There is a twenty-four hour customer service number on the Web site, and I jot it down. At least I still have my passport, but only because my mother always told me to keep it separate from my wallet.

"Any luck?" asks Kat, standing by my shoulder.

"Well, they haven't used the debit card."

"What are you doing now?"

"I'm curious." I type a couple of words into the search engine.

Kat laughs, the sound loud in my ear. "Anna babe, how many times do I have to tell you? *We did not kill anybody in South Dakota!*"

I look quickly at Shaggy, but if he hears our *Thelma and Louise* drama, he doesn't let on. "All right." I find nothing in my search, not a single mention. "I believe you, okay? I just . . . had to check."

"I'm sick of waiting for them to come back." Kat tugs at the strap on her satchel, pressing her hand against the bag. "You want to take a walk, see if we can figure out what to do next?"

Shaggy perches on the edge of his drafting stool, sketching. He's giving us room to figure out what we need to do. Looking at him this way, knowing how kind he has been, it's like I'm seeing him for the first time. Instead of his stringy hair and ragged skinny jeans, his faded black metal band T-shirt and his scruffy face, I notice the fine bones in his hands—the effortless way he sweeps his pencil across the page. He looks up at me, and I am humbled by the kindness in his hazel eyes.

He mouths his tongue stud thoughtfully. "Um, you girls could crash at my place," he says. "I mean, it's only a room at my brother's place, but I've got a futon."

Kat and I exchange a glance. She looks as though she thinks it's a good idea. She's tired. I look back at Shaggy, with his delicate hands and his kind mouth, and . . . I think about what this might mean—sharing a futon with Shaggy. What if I ended up sleeping with him? This question comes to me out of nowhere, like a fortune pulled from the remains of a cookie, and the thought makes me crumble a little inside. Is that what I want?

It would be one way to do it, to get over my stupid virginity. It wouldn't be the worst of ways, either. And then it would be over. I shrug. "I guess . . ." I say, my eyes on his. "I mean, are you sure?" I remember how Kat said that maybe we'd get laid on this trip. Was this the kind of thing she meant?

He doesn't look away, and I can see he's had the same thought. "It's up to you," he says.

I put my hand on my side, where the new tattoo feels tender, hot to the touch. *Forever.* "No, I . . . I think we'd better go." My voice shakes. My legs tremble as though I've been running, and I wish I could run away right now, the faster the better.

Kat looks from me to Shaggy and back again, her eyebrows raised. "Okay?"

"Okay," says Shaggy.

"Can I get your address and stuff, so I can send you the money?" I take out my notebook and scribble down his information, keeping my eyes on the page—and away from his hands.

"So what was that all about, anyway?" Kat leans back against the granite bench. "We could be sleeping on a futon right now instead of curling up in a dark graveyard."

Dark graveyard is somewhat of an exaggeration, really. It's bright enough to read in this cemetery, thanks to the streetlights, and it isn't as though we're snuggling up against some mossy headstones from the sixteenth century. On the edge of a wide path, we found a bench that is big enough for both of us to recline on, although the granite is proving to be cold and uncomfortable.

"You want to read a little more of the dharma?" I'm not quite ready to discuss what happened at the tattoo shop. I don't know if I can ever discuss it.

"Sure," says Kat, and she takes the book out of her bag and hands it to me. "I left off right where he was sleeping by that little river bottom in California."

I find the spot and read out loud, stretched out on the bench with Kat's feet on my lap, my own feet tucked in behind her. We commiserate with the troubles that go along with being homeless, the truth of it biting a little deeper than either of us like.

"'Either side of the border, either way you slice the boloney, a homeless man was in hot water. Where would I find a quiet grove to meditate in, to live in forever?'" I shift on the cold stone bench.

"Ha! So true," says Kat, laughing humorlessly. "Here we are cowering in a cemetery, two sad little dharma bums, just like Jack."

I shrug, but I keep my response to myself. I'm not sure we really qualify as dharma bums. I mean, maybe right now, at this exact second, we're closer, but, you know? Even now, we're one phone call away from someone jumping on an airplane, scooping us up, and carrying us back home like helpless children.

I pick up the book and continue reading; for a while, we're quiet, focused on the story. I move around, trying to get feeling back in my legs. "This bench was a stupid idea." I can say so because it was my idea. "Here we are, surrounded by soft grass, and we go for the most uncomfortable place to sit down, just because this fits our idea of something to sit on."

Kat laughs. "Oh, Anna, you're starting to sound like Kerouac. Pretty soon you'll be saying that the bench doesn't exist, and comfort doesn't exist, it's all emptiness." She stands up, offering me a hand. "So, what's next? If we want to be true dharma bums, I think we should hitchhike."

I stretch, yawning. I'm so tired. "I dunno, Katy. I think hitching rides now is different than it was when Kerouac was roaming around the country. I mean, maybe there were fewer psychopaths back then. Or people were just generally nicer? I'm not sure."

"People *are* nice," says Kat. "I mean, look at Shaggy. Look at Pastor Shepherd."

"Look at Casey and Sammi. Look at those freaks at Sage Creek." We walk aimlessly along the path, stomping our feet against the pins and needles.

"Leroy and his wife. They stayed late on a Saturday night just to get us all settled. It's not their fault that Little Sister is a klepto."

"There are good people and shitty people." I suppose it's a pretty even balance between the two, really. But so what? "That means we're just as likely to get picked up by a serial killer or a rapist or . . . a cannibal as we are to get picked up by a nice person."

"Actually, I think the odds are skewed more toward the rapists and maybe the serial killers," says Kat. "Nice people are scared of picking up hitchhikers. I'm not all that nervous about cannibals."

"All I know is that I can't walk to Gillette, or even hitchhike to Gillette, feeling the way I do right now. I need to sleep, and soon." I wish we could find a nice spot in the woods where we could sit down next to a twin pine like the guy in the book. I'd learn to meditate. After I sleep for like twelve hours, I mean. I yawn again.

"So where to now?" says Kat, leading the way out of the cemetery. "It's starting to get light." It's true; the sky is fading to a grayish purple like a black shirt washed too many times.

"Oh, I don't know, Katy. Maybe if I could have a cup of coffee and wash my face, I'd feel a little more human."

We walk in silence, past blocks and blocks of closed-up shops and dark houses. Everything looks desolate—the doors barred. My feet are tired and pinched in these stupid flimsy canvas shoes I was wearing in the car, back when our only concern had been a stripped oil pan plug, and finally I stop and sit down on the edge of the curb. I slip the shoes off, and even though the early morning air is cool, I swear I see steam rise off my toes.

"I don't know where to go." My voice borders on a whimper,

89

if the truth be told. "I'm sorry, Kat. I should have said yes to Shaggy."

Kat puts an arm around me in that easy way she has, resting her head softly on my shoulder. "I dunno," she says. "What would you have been saying yes to?" She turns her face until I can feel her breath on my ear. My own breath catches; I lean down to fiddle with my shoes, a nervous laugh spilling out.

She knows. It shouldn't be a surprise, really; Kat always knows my secrets, sometimes before I do, drawing my thoughts out like witching a well.

"I could have done it," I whisper. "At least we'd have had a place to sleep." Kat doesn't answer, doesn't move at all, just waits. There is nothing but the sound of us breathing in tandem.

I break away at last. "I couldn't do it, though," I say. "I mean . . . I don't want to be with *him*." I know the words I should say next; I can feel them rattling in my mouth like steam building up, knocking about in an old radiator, but it's no use. I can't even whisper them. Instead, I sit here, looking at her helplessly.

"I know," says Kat softly. "Let's get moving."

I stand up, looking back the way we came. "Actually . . ." The idea forms slowly. "Let's go this way."

"No freaking way, Anna. I am not breaking into a *church*."

"Not *breaking* in, Kat. More like . . . sneaking in."

Kat raises an eyebrow. "Yeah, I'm sure God is making those fine distinctions in his notes."

I roll my eyes. "We're just getting to church early, that's all. There has to be some little room somewhere that we can duck into and sleep, and lots of times there's food served in between services, you know? At the very least there will be coffee."

Still, I feel like a creeper watching an older man get out

of his van, whistling in the soft glow of early morning. He retrieves what looks like several cake pans from the front seat of his car and disappears into the church.

I lead the way, acting like I have every right to be there. This is no big deal. Once inside, Kat pulls me down a set of dark stairs, and we tiptoe along a tiled hall lit only by a red Exit sign at the very end.

I try one of the doors leading off the hall. The room is dim, and I'm barely able to make out the shapes of low tables and tiny chairs in the growing light shining through the small windows near the ceiling. The walls are painted with animals, two of every kind. "Definitely a classroom," I say.

Quietly, we examine each of the rooms leading off the main hall but find only identical classrooms, which will soon be filling up with little children watching Bible stories play out on flannel boards while drinking grape juice from tiny paper cups.

"Upstairs, then." We slip up the stairs. At the top of the first flight, near the door to the sanctuary, is a coatrack, an elevator, and another flight of stairs, leading to either a balcony or maybe another wing. I hesitate, then take the stairs up.

Kat nods. We're not quite to the top of the stairs when suddenly the side door swings open and pale morning sun floods the entryway. We freeze.

I hear a rustling of coats and hangers and a woman's voice. "Here, Richard. I'll take the cake downstairs if you want to go up and fetch the bulletins. Michael folded them all yesterday evening, but you'll have to show the ushers what to do."

Heavy footsteps approach the bottom of the staircase, and Kat's eyes grow wide. If we move now, the man will see us for sure, but if we don't, he'll run right into us! "Act pathetic," I whisper. It's a church; churches are supposed to welcome the needy, the afflicted. Still, we've been sneaking around like thieves. Maybe I should have asked someone for help in the first place. My heartbeat is so loud, I'm sure he's already heard us.

"Richard? Wait, Richard, I completely forgot about the offering envelope. It's sitting in the car. Be sure to get that first, so we don't forget."

I let out my pent-up breath as Richard turns away from the bottom of the stairs and sighs. "Yes, dear," he mumbles as he steps back out the door. We race to the top of the stairs and run blindly through the first door we see.

"What the hell is this room for?"

"Anna! We're in a church!"

"So?"

"It's . . . *rude* to swear in church." Kat flips on the light switch.

"It's just a building." My own home had once been attached to a church, and it certainly hadn't been sacred ground to me. "But seriously, did they make this room just for us, or what?"

The room is small—one long narrow expanse, like a hallway with big aspirations. The walls are covered with faded yellow wallpaper, and there are framed prints of vaguely pretty scenes. At the end of the room is a small window, trimmed with gauzy white curtains. But the most interesting features are the lock on the door and the two plush couches lining the walls.

Kat grins. "Thanks be to God." She kicks her shoes off and collapses on a couch. "Hallelujah! Turn off the light and lock the door!" I think she's sleeping by the time I turn the lock. I smile at the sound of her measured breathing, but I can't sleep, not yet. Being here, in this church . . . I am haunted by memories of my mother.

Words I'd Scrawl Across These Yellow Walls
if Only I Dared

- *I miss you.*
- *I miss you.*
- *I miss you.*
- *Who am I now?*

9

Mist before the peak
—the dream
Goes on
—Jack Kerouac

A man sits cross-legged beneath a tree. He is weaving a small
mat out of long grasses, which he pulls strand by strand from an
old plastic bucket of water that sits beside him.
"Jack?" I say. He doesn't look up, his eyes fixed on the work
in his hands.
A desperate need crushes me. "Please." I kneel beside him,
plunging my hands into the bucket. The water is shockingly cold;
it freezes around my hands, and I can feel the edge of the ice
biting into my wrists as I struggle to pull out a handful of reeds.
Blood from my wrists pools on the ice, sizzling where it
touches.
"Open up," says the man, pointing to my fists, which still
clutch the reeds. He moves his hands like a magician releasing
a dove. And then I am alone. The bucket is gone, and my hands
rest in my lap, clutching a scrap of green cloth. A green silk scarf.
Mom?
I open my hands like he did; the fabric lifts in a sudden
breeze and floats up, a spiral above me, and I watch it rise,
shielding my eyes from the glare of the sun, until it disappears—
a tiny dot—and my neck aches and my eyes hurt and the ground
is soft on my cheek when I collapse.

The first sound that trickles into my consciousness is a sort of droning voice, a man's voice, chanting something. I lift my head and wince, my neck muscles pinching. What is with that voice?

I try to get a handle on the juxtaposition of images in my head—forest glade to bloody ice to yellow wallpaper. Across the room Kat is curled up on a pastel-striped couch, her dark hair hanging over her face.

The voice drones on, and then it stops, followed by the sound of a whole group of voices repeating the chant, or answering the chant. It sounds . . . familiar. A lullaby I've almost forgotten. I rub my eyes, and I'm startled to find my cheeks wet with tears. I wipe at them with the edge of my sleeve and roll my head from side to side, rubbing the back of my neck with one hand.

In this way I spy the source of the voices: a small set of speakers mounted near the ceiling. Ah, yes, the church service. I wonder if this is the first service or the second, and I attempt to judge by the amount of light coming in the window and by whether it feels like I have slept for one hour or three all squished up on this short couch. Probably three. I reach for my notebook to capture my dream so I will not forget it.

I walk a little circuit of the room, which contains only the two couches and the window, plus the speakers. My legs are sore, and shaky, as though I've just finished a marathon. I sit on the rug and stretch, leaning back against the couch where Katy still sleeps.

She's so peaceful, so untroubled. The strong angle of her narrow nose, the thick line of lashes against her cheeks. The plum of her lips. She looks younger when she's sleeping, like a child fiercely guarding her secrets.

I ponder the dream again, holding my arms in front of me, examining my wrists for marks, but all I see is pale freckled skin. I can still feel the bite of that ice, though, can still see my blood spreading in a dark stain.

The cloth, the green scrap of fabric. In my memory, it flits just out of my reach; I can touch its shadow but not the thing itself. "That's all anything is," I say, my voice hoarse and raspy. "Empty shadows, like Kerouac says."

Katy stirs, twists on the couch a little, and opens her eyes. She sees me and smiles. "Hey," she says, her voice just as ragged as mine.

"Hey."

"You all right?"

I smile. "I'm okay. You?"

"You're crying."

"No. I was, I guess, but I'm okay now. I had this crazy dream . . ." I'm gathering my thoughts to explain the dream, to speak it out loud and disperse some of its power, when I'm interrupted by the sound of someone twisting the handle of the door.

Jiggle.

Twist.

My heart triples its pace, and Kat sits up stealthily. There's not much we can do, trapped as we are in this room, except try to be quiet and hope this person will not persist.

A light rap on the door. A woman's voice. "Hello? Is someone in there?"

I don't dare breathe, don't move a muscle.

I hear the sound of an infant fussing, and again the woman raps on the door, calling out a little louder this time. "Hello? Can you unlock the door?" She jiggles the handle a couple more times, and then I hear soft rapid footsteps heading away.

"Let's get the hell out of here!"

"Anna!"

"I told you! It's just a building."

We burst out of the room. "Please God," I mutter under my breath as I try the knob of the first door I see. Locked.

The knob on the next door turns, and I open it a tiny crack, peering in. An empty office. It will do for the moment.

"Excuse me!" A man's voice calls out from behind us. "That's the pastor's study!"

"Goddamn it," says Kat.

"Now there's a word you don't say." I smile, but it's the resigned smile of the condemned.

We face our accuser. Katy turns on the charm.

"Oh, sorry?" she says, smiling sweetly. "We were just looking for the restroom, that's all." She waves her hand toward the door of the room we slept in, which I notice bears a yellow stenciled sign, Nursing Mother's Lounge. "We thought that was it, but we were wrong, I guess."

I wonder if we look like homeless people who have slept a maximum of three hours on a couch. I run my hand nervously over my hair, adjusting my scarf.

"Are you with Pastor Shepherd's group?" the man asks, veiled suspicion in his eyes. "I didn't remember anyone so young."

Kat and I exchange a look. "Pastor Shepherd? We're meeting him here," says Kat.

Could it be the same Pastor Shepherd? What are the odds? And if it is him, are those odds in our favor?

The man still looks uncertain. "Well, you'd better come back downstairs," he says. "The service for blessing the mission is just about over." He turns to the woman standing behind him, the one holding and rocking a fussing infant. "Looks like it's open now, Jeanne. Sorry for the inconvenience." He nods politely to the woman as she slips into the nursing lounge, shooting a scathing look at us before she does.

What will happen when it becomes apparent that we are not, actually, members of Pastor Shepherd's mission trip? We should have told the truth. "Um, the restroom?" I'm looking for a chance to stall, to escape.

The man presses his lips together, still looking at us somewhat dubiously. "Oh, right," he says. "Well, I'll show you the one right outside the sanctuary. I'm not sure how you missed it, actually."

We follow him obediently down the stairs and enter the restroom, which is, like he said, plainly visible from the main door of the sanctuary. Once inside, I set my backpack down on the floor and go immediately to the sink, running my hands under the cool water and splashing it onto my face. It feels good; it clears my head.

"What should we do?"

"Do you think it's *our* Pastor Shepherd?" Kat says.

"Katy, you can't seriously think we're going to walk in there and pretend to be a part of this mission trip."

"Well, but I *told* you. I had a feeling we would see him again, that we met him for a reason." She runs a brush through her hair, watching her reflection. "I think we should figure out a way to talk to him."

"I'm not going to Mexico." I have such a terrible feeling about all of this. Goose bumps rise up across my neck.

Kat's brushing stops for a moment, and she glances away from the mirror to look at me. "Anna. I didn't say we were going to Mexico."

"But you thought it."

"I did not."

"Well, you were about to think it, then. And I'm not going. *You* can go, if you really want to. I'll hitchhike back to Gillette all by myself, I don't care. I'm not going to Mexico." I can feel myself digging in, setting my jaw.

Kat shoots me a look. "Anna, relax, hey? Nobody has said anything about going to Mexico." She throws the brush back into her bag and moves to put her arm around me, but I pull away.

"Don't tell me to relax," I snap. "This whole thing is all your fault. I never even wanted to come on this stupid road trip." I always get irrational when I go without sleep. "Plus, you never listen to me." I wince inwardly at my petulant tone, but I'm powerless to stop. "If you would have pulled over when the oil light came on like I told you, we could have fixed the car problem before getting stranded in the first place, and I'd still have my wallet and we wouldn't have gotten busted sleeping in a church breast-feeding room." The cold tile digs into my knees as I kneel down and furiously pull things out of my backpack.

Kat laughs, but her eyes are sharp. "Oh, this is all *my fault*, is it? What the hell, Anna? You've been calling the shots all along, and I haven't complained once. What is your problem?"

"I'm not the one with the problem." I continue emptying my backpack onto the bathroom floor.

"Like it would be so awful to go on a bus trip to Mexico for a couple of weeks. Do some hard labor. Church and old people, Anna. That's two things on our list."

"No. Stop trying to change my mind." I hate it when she does this. She knows I can't refuse her. But I don't want to do this. Do. Not. Want.

"You're every bit as afraid of living as your father is, Anna."

I glare at her. Staying angry is the only way to keep from crying, and I am *not* going to cry. "No." My quiet voice walks the edge of desperate. My hands tremble. My head aches.

Kat shakes her head. "Whatever. You know what, Anna? I'm sorry for not stopping when the oil light came on. What else do you want me to say?"

My anger wilts. "I've had enough church people to last me my entire life, I swear." I've been surrounded by church since birth—church people feeding me, caring for me, praying for me, but above all making every moment of my life their business.

Kat picks up the *The Dharma Bums* from the pile on the floor. "Well, let's see what Jack says." She flips the pages, and I stab my finger into the book, praying for something that makes sense, something she can't twist to mean what she wants it to mean.

Kat reads. " 'It don't make a damn frigging difference whether you're in The Place or hiking up Matterhorn, it's all

the same old void, boy.'" She nods excitedly. "See? What difference does it make, Anna? A free trip to Mexico and back?
No paying for camping every night? Looking for God?"

"I told you this was going to happen. I *knew* you'd start
in with this Mexico idea." I grab *The Dharma Bums* out of
Kat's hands and open it up angrily. "'I climbed up the ar-
royo, so finally when I turned and looked back I could see
all of Mexico, all of Chihuahua, the entire sand-glittering
desert of it, under a late sinking moon that was huge and
bright just over the Chihuahua mountains.'"

Fuck this. I snap the book shut. "I don't like it," I say.

Kat gathers my things and shoves them into my backpack. "Why are you taking all this stuff out, anyway?"

"I thought maybe if I looked again, I'd find my wallet." My phone beeps, a text from my dad. *Erica Randall
brought over her new kittens yesterday afternoon,* he says. Erica Randall? That was the woman with the SIDS baby the
year my dad started up the church. So sad. She has a son,
a couple years younger than me, I think, and a bunch of
girls younger than him. "My dad texted me about kittens,"
I say. Who could be afraid of life when faced with newborn
kittens?

"That guy is going to wonder what we're doing in here,"
says Kat. "Let's go out there and say hello to our old friend."

He stumbles midsentence as he recognizes us. Actually, it's
less of a stumble than an all-out speechless pause, during
which every head in the congregation turns to stare.

"As . . . as I was saying," he continues, "God has called
us on this mission because He knows that lying dormant
within each of us is a strength untapped, a strength of spirit
and love that is waiting for circumstances to present themselves that will challenge that strength to rise up." His voice
again. Is it like my father's?

Kat elbows me, frozen in the stares of the room full
of people, and we move toward a seat near the back of the

group, about halfway up the aisle. "Sit down," she hisses, and we do.

"I have to stop for a moment and tell you all something, something extremely important to me." Pastor Shepherd advances as he speaks, his eyes never leaving us. The people all twist in their seats and follow him as he moves.

"These two young girls that you all watched enter the room, these are two friends of Jesus whose paths crossed my own two nights ago as I was sitting at Celeste's Diner, preparing my sermon, as many of you know I am wont to do."

There are murmurs of assent in the crowd; heads nod.

"Well, I'm not going to lie to you, I was having a difficult time that night, trying to prepare words for you—for you wonderful believers who are following the call to Mexico with me, going into what hardships I cannot imagine. My words fell flat on the page. I couldn't seem to find the passion."

The people shake their heads sadly. I feel my face burn, and sweat forms between my breasts, though I'm inexplicably shivering. I want to disappear. If there is a God, he certainly hates me.

"But then I looked across the back of the booth behind me, and here were two lovely young ladies, their heads bent over an atlas, their hearts so pure and loving I could just feel the divine light streaming from them." Okay, no. My father never spoke with such . . . melodrama.

I jab my elbow hard into Katy's side. Pure and loving hearts, yeah. We were only arguing about whether or not we had killed several people and abandoned their bodies in the middle of the wilderness. I cover my mouth with one hand and bow my head, hoping I look pious instead of rude.

"These two young women are on a remarkable journey, my friends, a pilgrimage across America, looking for proof of the existence of God's Unconditional Love." Pastor Shepherd takes a deep breath and holds the room in the center of his own dramatic pause before he continues, his voice (which is *nothing* like my dad's golden voice) rising up a notch with a hypnotic zeal.

"As I spoke with them, it was as though my thoughts became free, and I was able to write the words I have already spoken to you today."

He raises his arms theatrically. "When we parted ways, my hope for these exceptional young ladies was that they would find the answers that they were seeking, that God would make His blessed presence known to them. I am certain now that they have been placed in my path according to divine design, and I would like nothing more than for them to join us on our mission. In Mexico, I *know* they will find the proof that they seek, and I am sure that their presence will teach all of us a very important lesson on faith." His hands tremble with fervor. "Anna and Katherine, will you join us in our crusade of spreading God's Holy Word?"

All eyes are on us. I glance at Kat, only to find that she, too, looks a little stricken. Something has to be done.

I clear my throat; the sound echoes through the church. I search for my voice. I can't be this person, this tentative person who goes along with everyone even when I know it's not what I want. My mouth is dry. All those beaming eyes. No. I stand up.

"Pastor Shepherd, we appreciate your invitation, and I'm sure we would find a great deal of inspiration if we joined you on your trip to Mexico."

I've always wanted to go on a mission trip; in fact, my father was organizing a trip to several countries in Africa before the fire cut everything short and sort of put our whole existence into survival mode. But my father's ministry was gentle and humble, without the spectacle, without the slick smiling rhetoric.

"But we can't go with you. Kat . . . Katherine and I are stranded here in Casper, two hundred miles from our car, which broke down in Gillette. We had some things stolen from us, and we only came here for a place to sleep for a few hours." My voice shakes, but I hold steady. Kat stands beside me and takes my hand.

Pastor Shepherd places his hand on his heart, looking at me with such a sincerely loving expression on his face that it makes me squirm. "Oh, my dear child," he says, his warm voice hushed, "is there any way we can help you?"

Heads nod around the room. I'm embarrassed. My face feels hot, like it's stretched too tightly, like if I try to stop this polite smiling I'll find that my mouth won't go back to normal.

"Well, the least we can do is feed them," says a small white-haired lady in the front row, her voice rather indignant. "Let's go down and have our fellowship meal."

Voices of assent rise in all corners, and Pastor Shepherd smiles warmly. "We would be honored if you would join us for our meal."

Downstairs, they have rolled away dividers and converted the classrooms into one large hall with round tables and chairs. There's a kitchen at the back with a window showing through to the main room, and smiling elderly ladies stand there, ready to put the finishing touches on an impressive spread of pasta salads, homemade breads, roll-up finger sandwiches, and plates full of goodies.

A wave of loneliness for my mother hits me again when I see the food. These kinds of feasts, hosted by the matrons of the church, were always my mother's favorite kind of church event. She moved so easily among the people, a pot of coffee in each hand, smiling graciously and inquiring about everyone. I usually found a chair in a corner to hide, curled up with my cup of watery Kool-Aid and a book or my notebooks. My mother would eventually give up on trying to get me to play with the other kids, and she would softly tousle my hair and place a gentle kiss on the top of my head before she was off again, beginning and ending conversations effortlessly while I peeked over the top of my book, watching in admiration.

Pastor Shepherd insists that we sit at his table; he ushers us through the line and settles us in our chairs before he goes off to get his own food. I stare hungrily at my heaping plate. Kat sits beside me, also looking ravenous. "Is everyone eating, or do we wait for a prayer or something?" whispers Kat.

I shrug. "I don't care. I'm starving." I take a bite, then another. After that, there is no stopping. We almost finish our entire plates before Pastor Shepherd gets back with his loaded plate.

"Ah, you were hungry," he says. "Please, go for seconds."

After a while Angela and another woman join us, and I sit in a stuffed daze through introductions and more polite conversation. My belly full, the danger of being discovered already a thing of the past, I feel a strange, achy fatigue steal over me. My head gets heavier and heavier as the conversation revolves around the room in a pleasant low rumble.

It's only a tiny dream, just a snippet of sleep, but in those few moments I'm falling down, down, spiraling like one of the maple seed pod helicopters Mom and I used to drop from the top of the corkscrew slide when I was a little girl.

"Oh," I say out loud. The single syllable expresses all my thoughts at once. I spiral, around and around, and then all at once I realize that I'm actually standing still, and it's something else—something small and green—her scarf spiraling around above me, rising up higher and higher. Or is it falling toward me?

"I've seen this before," I whisper, and then I wake up.

Either nobody noticed, or they are pretending they didn't. Maybe it was a split second—an extra-long blink. Whatever the case, when I open my eyes, I find Kat nodding and smiling as a woman with ruby lips and an unnaturally white face with black whiskers poking through the makeup on her upper lip talks enthusiastically about her poodle, Windsor. I still feel like I'm spinning. Falling.

Pastor Shepherd holds the hands of another woman—a woman who really does not look well enough to help dig a foundation for a new church in Mexico. None of these people should be working shovels. Like the ancient nodding gentleman propped up next to the piano in the corner. He can't possibly be going on the trip. Can he? I worry, guilt nibbling away at my resolve. Maybe God really does need us to go on this trip, if only for the strength of our backs. I waver.

No. No way. I left Minnesota to escape the church people. Even when they're helping, I can feel the judgments, the unwanted prayers. A church is the last place for me to find God. I know this even if God doesn't. Besides, our car is to the north; I long for my clipboard, my lists, my neatly organized tubs full of all our things. Nothing good has happened since we left our stuff behind.

"Oh, that's just wonderful, Maureen," says Kat to my left. "You must be so proud." The lady has moved on from her poodle and is now showing Katy photos of her grandchildren, or maybe great-grandchildren. The hubbub of conversation in the room, earlier a source of comfort that had lulled me to sleep, now takes on a more chaotic aspect, and I'm dizzy, claustrophobic. I feel like I am drowning in the mundane. I stagger out of my chair, gasping a little, and try not to run as I head for the restroom.

I make it in time, but only barely. My body rejects the delicious luncheon at the precise moment that I enter the stall. I don't even have time to gather my hair behind me, and for a moment I worry about getting clean. Then I can't think at all and only shudder uncontrollably, the cold tile sending chills across my whole body. I shake and shake, my stomach heaving, until finally the spasms cease. I draw a hesitant breath, reaching up blindly for some tissue to blot my mouth. At last I sit back, leaning against the stall divider with my arms clasped around myself, weak and trembling. Tears well up in my eyes, and I'm almost flattened by an onslaught of intense longing. *I want my mother.*

I'm too shaky right now to make it back out to the fellowship hall. I'll wait here until I either get better or someone comes in and finds me. In the meantime, there's no reason to stay awake. My eyes drift closed as though I'm drugged, and I feel my body slouch down farther and farther until I slump all the way to the floor. The white tile—with its dirty grout lines spreading out in a million little hexagonal divisions—presses its pattern into the side of my burning face, and I float away.

I wake to shrieking, a horrible sound of the wild turkey variety, and I wince, drawing a hand over my ear. The room spins lazily around me.

"Pastor Shepherd!" shouts the woman, and I watch the skin underneath her chin jiggle with urgency, which only intensifies her resemblance to a turkey. My skin is sewn up with seams that are stretching and puckering and about to burst, and a part of me knows I must have a fever, but the rest of me has a hard time piecing together reality. I shiver on the tile.

A sound. A hundred thousand feet trampling, and I wait, expectant, for a stampede of cloven-hoofed creatures to thunder into the bathroom stall. That would teach me to swear in church. I try to prepare, to be ready for battle, but the first face I see aside from the turkey-lady fills me with joy.

"Katy Kat, you came for me!" She's beautiful. "I thought you were the devil." That's not true. I try to explain, to differentiate, but the words are like sponges soaking up meanings I can't sort out, so I settle for crying instead. "I want my mom."

Kat kneels over me, carefully lifting up my head and cradling it in her lap. "Anna babe, you're burning up." She pushes several strands of hair back from my face, tucking them into my pink kerchief. I close my eyes. I'm so tired.

"She looks pretty pale," says another voice. I do battle

with my eyelids. Victory brings a vision of Pastor Shepherd's face next to Kat's. The thought of us all squeezed into the bathroom stall makes me giggle, and I shake with laughter, which turns to a fit of violent trembling. Kat's arms hold me close; her dark blue eyes keep me steady.

"Do you think she needs a doctor?" says Kat.

I lurch off of Kat's lap. "I need to throw up."

Katy pulls back my hair. The next few moments are nothing, an emptiness extending out of my soul and spewing indecorously into the larger void of reality.

"I'm empty and awake," I say out loud, when I can talk. The world shimmers and nods, and Kat holds me tight.

10

Whatever it is, I quit
—now I'll let my
breath out—
—Jack Kerouac

I used to joke about how my father could go on about things, how his sermons could stretch sometimes so long that toward the end I could scarcely remember a time when he wasn't speaking—as though his voice were the voice of Creation Itself. Now he sends me these tiny text messages, as succinct as little Kerouac haiku.

> *eight months of silence, broken*
> *only by sighs, now he messages me:*
> *"I remember your laughter."*

> *I reply, punching characters one by one,*
> *hit send before I can't—*
> *"I remember when you were my hero."*

Kat leans over and whispers in my ear as the bus pulls away from the church. "I can't believe we're going to Mexico on this piece of shit."

"I can't believe we're going to Mexico at all."

I was sick for two full days, sleeping alongside the missionary ladies on low cots in a Sunday School classroom, convincing Katy with some difficulty that I didn't need to go to the hospital. The whole time I was gripped with a terrible fear.

I cling to Katy's arm. "I thought you were going to leave me, that you had already gone on to Mexico and left me all alone in that church. I felt like everyone would abandon me if I wasn't careful, only I couldn't figure out what the key was, what being careful really meant."

"I hate it when I have a fever and I get those weird ideas stuck in my head," says Kat. "Everything's always so complicated."

"I am empty and awake," I say. It's my new mantra.

"I can't believe this. How crazy is it that we had to push-start our bus?" Kat laughs, clutching her velvet satchel tightly on her lap.

I smile. It was actually kind of funny . . . especially the sight of all these practically elderly people lined up on a quiet little street, pushing an ancient bus until it got up enough speed to pop the clutch. Something is seriously wrong with the bus; it won't start once it stops, but the driver assures us that from now on, he'll leave the bus running at all times. "We are going into a foreign country in a bus that won't start," I say. "We're a bunch of idiots."

I lean against the window, watching the scenery ripple past. There is a mesmerizing pattern to the mountains and valleys, bright new leaves fresh and bright in the distance. I never intended to be here, on this bus. I must have been still feverish to agree to this; the whole idea has a residue clinging to it—to its every surface—a thin layer of grease on the inside of a drinking glass. Even though it looks perfectly clean, I can feel that there's something not quite right about it. I can taste it—the something wrong—but I can see how badly Katy wants this, and I can't quite shake that delirium fear, the abyss of loss when I thought she had slipped away.

My eyelids grow heavy, and I slouch back against the tall seat, letting myself drift. Sleep slips over me quickly, my head rolling gently over and landing on Katy's shoulder. I guess we both sleep a little.

When I wake, the first thing I notice is our stillness.

"Where are we?" I rub my eyes. The sun out my window suggests late afternoon.

Kat doesn't look up from her sketchbook. "I don't know. Southern Wyoming, I guess. I haven't been paying attention."

"Where did everybody go?"

"Dinner." Kat turns the book upside down and squints at the page. "Damn it," she mutters, reaching for the eraser she has wedged between the seats in front of her.

I massage my neck with one hand. "Why didn't you wake me?"

Kat shakes her head. "Nobody would let me wake you. Not after you were so sick and all." She laughs. "I think they're tired of praying for you."

"Well, I'm hungry." I fold my arms across my chest, narrowing my eyes at the sprawl of fast-food chains and gas stations out the window. This stupid interstate exit looks like every other exit in the country; if it weren't for the mountains huddled on the horizon, we might be in Minnesota.

"Angela brought us food," says Kat, handing over a paper lunch bag. I pull out an orange, and Katy hands me a square of paper towel.

"Are we really doing this?" I work my thumbnail under the skin of the orange, juice stinging a little in a ragged hangnail.

"Really," says Kat.

"I don't get it. What's the big deal here, Katy? Why do you want this so bad?" I suck juice from a segment of the orange.

She doesn't answer right away, but she stops drawing and studies me for a long moment. Finally she smiles and reaches over to wipe my chin with the edge of her sleeve. "You're so gross," she says. "Remember when your mom had to drive me to the hospital from that one weird Bible camp in the woods?"

I remember. "You found out you were allergic to bee stings."

"I was terrified."

I nod. "So was my mom." I remember her talking it over with my dad after the fact—she said she hadn't ever driven so fast before in her life.

But Kat shakes her head. "No, that's just it, Anna. Your mom was so calm. She talked the whole time in this really soft voice. She said, 'Give your fear to God.' It was so normal for her. Like God was someone real for her, sitting there with his hands held out, waiting to take our burdens." Katy looks back at her drawing, frowns, and rips the page out of her sketchbook. She folds it in half, once, and then again and again into smaller and smaller pieces. "The stuff in my head never comes out quite right," she says. "Not on paper, and not in words."

It's weird to think of Katy having burdens to bear, quite honestly. I've always envied the fact that Kat's parents are atheists, that they can discuss any and all topics without once referencing Scripture. I open my mouth to say something supportive, but then I notice how quiet it is, how still. There are no vibrations coming up from the floorboards, through the seats.

"I thought they were going to leave the bus running."

A shadow flickers across Kat's face, a trace of uncertainty. "It died," she says softly. "We had to coast in here, which is why everyone decided we might as well stop for dinner."

I stare out the window, absently licking the sticky orange juice from my fingers. "So. Another push-start, then?"

Kat squirms. "Well, it's just . . . we can't exactly do that here, where it's such a busy street."

"Why not?"

"Something about the brakes." Kat taps the end of her pencil against her bottom lip and turns to a new page. I watch her hands as she sketches in long, confident lines.

"The brakes?" Oh, come on, don't tell me there's something wrong with the brakes, too. I wrap my orange peels in the paper towel and study Kat's drawing. "That's cool," I say.

"What's with all the keys you've been drawing?"

"There's nothing wrong with the brakes, not really," Kat says, closing her sketchbook. "But Michael's worried about being able to stop the bus with the air brakes or something, and Pastor Shepherd is frustrated with the broken-down bus, and they argued a little. It was unpleasant. You're lucky you slept through it."

"Here they come." I nod out the window, where a fleet of gray heads and pastel polyester advances across the parking lot. "Let's go talk to them. I want to know what their plan is." I fold down the top of the lunch bag and gather up my backpack.

We shuffle down the narrow aisle, running our hands along the faded blue seat backs. "What a piece of crap." I can't help being contrary. The whole thing is so absurd it's like a bad joke.

Kat's answering look is pained. "These are wonderful people," she says, her tone terse. "Can you just relax?" Kat stands in the center of the bus aisle. "We promised these lovely people we'd help them on their mission, and it's just possible we could learn something from them. This is the closest we've been yet to being true dharma bums. Look, these tattoos?" She pulls her shirt up, still-tender-looking lotus petals visible above the waist of her skirt. "They mark us, Anna. They tie us together. Please, for once, can you just . . ." She pulls the pencil from behind her ear and bites on the eraser.

"Just what?"

She shakes her head, her dark eyes apologetic. "Just . . . try being open to a new idea, even if it's not yours?"

"All right, fine." I lift my arm, indicating the bus. "But this—this church trip thing isn't going to prove anything to me. It's like the last thing on earth I need right now."

She doesn't say anything, but her eyes tell me everything. It may not be what I need, but this trip is important for her. I guess I can't fathom what it would be like if the idea of belonging to a church—the idea of belonging to a god—was somehow extraordinary and new.

For the second time, I hear the sound of Pastor Shepherd clearing his throat in nervous awkwardness. "Uh-m."

I turn, see him framed in the bus door. "Pastor Shepherd, I—"

"You're awake, Anna," he says, his voice light and pleasant. "Feeling okay?"

I nod and step off the bus, Katy behind me. "So what's our plan? Are we going to call a mechanic? Does the church have some kind of triple A policy or something?"

He chuckles. "We have the best policy of all," he says, with a smile. "All right, everyone, gather around!" I watch the horde of elderly missionaries form a semicircle in front of the bus. Heat waves shimmer off the blacktop parking lot, as cars and buses and semitrucks maneuver around them.

"Come on, Anna, join us!" Kat drags me toward the group.

"Everyone, please lay your healing hands upon this bus and bow your heads as we pray, Dear Heavenly Father . . ." Pastor Shepherd's voice settles into a rocking cadence of bless us and be with us and fix this bus if you love us, God. Alleluia, amen. All around him, pale hands, flecked with brown spots, lift in supplication, touching the bus. No way. This—this is not what I believe.

"Come and pray with everyone," Kat hisses in my ear. "You're being disrespectful."

I shrug. "Come off it, Katy. You know you don't believe in this. We don't need to pray for God to fix our bus. That's why God made mechanics. It is irresponsible of Pastor Shepherd to carry on like this." I raise my voice above a whisper. "I think we should leave and go back to Gillette. Now."

Kat shakes her head so emphatically that her dark hair swings out in a spiky circle. "No," she says, her tone firm. "We gave them our promise. Why would we turn back now?" She looks to the ring of prayer. "And you're wrong, Anna. I do believe there is power in prayer. There has to be."

I roll my eyes and listen to the fruitless sound of the ignition with its ragged chorus—alternating between a hoarse, protracted sputter and silence, except for the drone of Pastor Shepherd's appeal to the divine.

"This is ridiculous," I mutter, and I turn on my heel. Who knows? Maybe I'll just start walking down the highway, as much a dharma bum as Kerouac, even.

Just then the sputter of the bus coughs, catches, trembles. Michael revs the engine, and the semicircle erupts into a chorus of cheers and praises. One woman begins singing—an exuberant modern hymn—and the whole group joins in. Kat runs up to me and throws her arms around me tightly. "See? I told you prayer was a force to be reckoned with," she says.

I laugh. "Katy, seriously, you don't think that God just took a moment out of His incredibly busy schedule to reach down one holy finger and start the engine of our bus, do you? I mean, really."

Kat looks at me for a moment, then shakes her head the smallest fraction. "You know I don't really understand belief," she says. I have to lean in to hear her. "But that doesn't mean I don't think God is possible. And if he *is* possible, well, then, what's there to stop him from starting a bus if a group of people asks him nicely enough?"

"A waste of resources," I say, but I climb back onto the bus along with all the rest of them, fold myself into the seat, and tuck my backpack underneath my feet. "If there is a God, he would have learned to delegate."

There is still snow in the mountaintops, and at first I grip the edge of my seat nervously as the bus twists and turns along the winding roads. This is nothing like Minnesota, not anymore. Michael keeps his promise and lets the bus run the entire time we stop for bathroom breaks and meals. Thankfully, the missionaries are not much into singing; they mostly read their Bibles quietly or talk in soft, earnest voices about their mission. It's almost enjoyable to be moving again, with Katy sketching beside me.

"Where are we staying?" I lean back in my seat and dab some ointment on my tattoo, which is starting to itch. The light is going all red and slanting, and in this mountain region, the sun sinks quickly behind the horizon once it starts its descent.

"We're aiming for some religious compound in northern Utah, I think. Outside Salt Lake City."

I laugh. "What? Seriously? A *religious compound in Utah?* So is it run by a bunch of fundamentalist Mormons with stockpiles of weapons and loads of creepy wives?"

Kat rolls her eyes. "Yeah, I'm sure the polygamists are in league with this lot." She waves her hand to indicate the sea of blue hair and flashing crochet needles.

She has a point. Katy takes my hand and holds it lightly on her lap, and I hope that means she forgives me, for being resistant, for being rigid. It feels comfortable, with the sun slanting ever lower through my window, and before too long, I'm drifting, my eyes falling closed in tiny increments, my head softly lolling and my mind wandering as we drive through the lights of Salt Lake City and turn off onto a small, dusty road.

The bus approaches an uncontrolled railroad crossing, and Michael slows carefully; even with my eyes mostly closed, I notice the bus shudder as he downshifts. The engine sputters. Then stops.

"Oh, shit," says Kat under her breath.

Silence.

"Well, this is lovely." I sit up and look out the window. It's pretty dark out there, but I can just make out the railroad tracks curving out of sight. Wait.

"Jesus, Katy! We're stalled right on a railroad track!" I jump up, grab my pack, and squeeze past Kat into the aisle. "Pastor Shepherd, we're on the tracks! We have to get off the bus!"

All around me, reading lights are snapping on and off, round white heads twisting toward me and then back toward the windows.

"She's right, Pastor!"

"Oh, dear! Look at the tracks!"

"Why, there's a blind corner!"

"We'll be crushed!"

"We need to get off the bus in an orderly manner." My voice is loud and surprisingly authoritative. "Orderly, but quickly." I start down the aisle. The smell of oranges rolls over me; dozens of pairs of frightened eyes watch me make my way to the front of the bus, and my passing spurs them into motion, into gathering their things and standing up to leave.

Michael the bus driver prays, spitting out pleas from between clenched teeth as he turns the key again and again. For a minute or so the bus is quiet except for the grinding of the starter and the shuffle of people gathering their bags. Then Pastor Shepherd's voice stretches to fill the space.

"The Lord is with us," he intones. "Let us surrender to his will and trust in Him to deliver us from our adversity. Join hands, everyone." He takes hands with two missionaries near him, and they all bow their heads.

Come *on*. Are they serious? "Don't you get it? We're in danger! We need to get off this bus!" I can see Kat, still on the other side of the prayer circle. Her eyes are uncertain, darting out the window toward the dark tracks and back to me. "Katy, *please!*" I can't get off the bus without her. The air feels heavy and sharp.

"I can't . . ." says Kat, looking helplessly at the sea of bodies and clasped hands blocking her from the door, from me. "I promised . . ."

"Let her through!" I scream, my voice rising hysterically. Is that a train whistle I hear? Pastor Shepherd's voice intensifies.

"Praise Jesus!" he says, his voice crescendoing to a wail.

"We call on you in Heaven's name to help us in our time of need!"

The growl of the ignition is slower now, deeper in tone. The battery wearing out? The engine flooding? I'm sure I can feel the tremble of an approaching train shaking the rails below the bus, and I shout desperately to Kat again, begging her to push through the group and get off the bus.

"Katy, please!"

She hesitates, looks at me helplessly.

Please!

I can see the headline: *Train Collides with Bus—Missionary Survivors Say It Was God's Will.*

I look out the back window and see headlights approaching. Pastor Shepherd points to them. "Hold on," he says, and a semitruck bumps into the back of the bus, pushing us off the tracks and down the hill. Michael pops the clutch, but the engine fails to catch; the bus jerks and shudders and rolls to a stop again. He cranks the starter, but there isn't any power left. Bump! The truck gives one more push and then veers around us, speeding off ahead. This time the engine catches, and everyone breathes a sigh of relief.

"Please sit down!" says Pastor Shepherd. He gives me a rather barbed look. "It's a good thing we weren't in the process of evacuating the bus when that truck bumped us," he says, his voice layered with smugness. "In moments of crisis, we must strive to make our decisions based on faith first."

"Tha-that's ridiculous." I'm so angry I'm stuttering. "You had no way of knowing the truck was coming. It could easily have been that train that got to us first." I point out the back window, where everyone can see the headlight of a train approaching the intersection from around the bend. "We could have been killed."

"It was not God's will for us to die there," he says. "We have a mission to complete."

This is bullshit. I storm past him to Kat, still frozen in

a half-standing position in her seat. I go to her, cling to her, hiding my sudden tears in her hair. "Why didn't you come with me?" I press the words right into her ear, my arms tight around her neck.

"I promised them," says Kat. "I can't leave."

"I can't stay." I pull back and look at her, searching her eyes. Pleading with her. I lean in and kiss her forehead; it lines up perfectly with my lips. I think it's the only time I've ever touched her first. And then I march to the front and demand for Michael to stop. I jump down those huge steps and stalk up the dark, unfamiliar road, back the way we came, not even looking at the bus as I pass it but listening—listening closely for the sound of footsteps behind me.

"Anna! Anna, come back!" Not Katy's voice, but *his*. Well, his voice may remind me of my father's, but he isn't going to sway me. "Anna, stop this nonsense! You can't just walk back to Wyoming!"

I don't look back. I keep walking, into the night, and eventually I hear the sound of the bus pulling away. There is no sign of Kat. My eyes sting, my shoes pinch, and I have no idea where I'm headed. The rhythmic slap of my rubber soles against the blacktop is all I hear, apart from a distant train whistle and the occasional low rumble of traffic, far away from this deserted road.

I have a gaping hole in the center of my chest, and I smile wryly as I recite my mantra. "I am empty and awake," I say, over and over, feeling more empty and less awake all the time.

When my legs finally give out, they take with them the last of my resolve, and I collapse in a frightened heap at the side of the road. What am I going to do, all alone? I don't even have my wallet anymore—no credit card, no cash. I can't go back to our car, even if I could somehow get back to our car. Because it's not *our* car; it's Kat's car. Kat. The hole in my chest threatens to cave in. How stupid am I? I think of her face, on the bus—how she hesitated. *I can't leave,* she said. So I left her. Tears, tears bringing with them snot and hysteria, and I shake my head frantically to make them stop. Empty and awake. Empty and awake.

I take out my cell and wonder what I could tell my father. I haven't told him about the car breaking down, or about getting sick, or heading to Mexico. "Hey, Dad, how's the weather? So I'm running away from a religious compound in Utah because a crazy minister wouldn't get a mechanic and relies on prayer to save us from oncoming trains. Can you come and get me now? Oh, by the way, I think I'm in love with a girl."

Wait, what? In love? *God*, these stupid tears.

Then there's the matter of my last text message, the one about how he *used* to be my hero. Kind of a shitty thing to say, but I needed him, and he was . . . gone—lost inside his own grief. It occurs to me that I haven't heard his voice— even the hoarse occasional whisper that passes for his voice since the fire—since we said good-bye in Sterling Creek. It feels like a decade has passed, but it's been only ten days.

I shove my phone back into my pocket and cover my face, pressing the heels of my hands into my eyes to stanch the flow. Empty and awake. No. I'm alone, that's what. And hungry. My stomach growls.

I'm not alone, though, not quite. Not according to my father or to Pastor Shepherd. When I was a kid, I prayed all the time—for things I wanted and things I hoped to avoid. I learned hundreds of prayers from my parents, but I haven't said a single one since my mother died. It's not like I haven't tried, but every time I think I *should*, the words won't come. My mind wanders. My heart doesn't believe.

"Well, this time I'm just going to talk, and see what happens." I say it out loud, just barely audible. Even so, the sound of my voice breaking into the silence startles me. I close my eyes. "Um, God? So it's been awhile." I pause. It's not like I need to pull out a bunch of excuses; after all, doesn't God know everything? So really, what's the point of prayer, then, if God already knows what's in my heart? "Yeah, I'm having a hard time, God, and I don't really know what I need to do next. Like, I don't know what to do in five minutes, and I don't know what to do next week, and pretty much I don't know what to do with the rest of my life." I open my eyes. This is ridiculous. Who am I even talking to? "Can you just . . . give me some kind of a sign that you exist?"

That's precisely when I hear it. The *slap slap slap* of feet. The feet are moving fast, much faster than my own exhausted pace, and hope leaps in my hollow chest. I wonder.

Slap slap slap.

I know.

"Thank you, God. Thank you for Katy," I say, breathless, and then I pick up my pack and run in the direction of those footsteps.

Hitchhiking is a lot less exciting than it sounds—at least, when there are no rapists or serial killers or cannibals. It's actually a lot like walking, except more frustrating because I keep expecting the cars to stop and put an end to this endless slog. Only they don't stop.

"I wonder how far we've gone so far."

"I wonder if we'd get more rides if we showed some skin." Kat pulls the straps of her tank top down and shimmies her shoulders in the dark.

"You are ridiculous."

"It's like my most endearing quality."

We hike on, the night's peace broken only by the familiar sound of our footsteps. The sky is clouding up, but a tiny bit of moonlight illuminates the road ahead—a dusty stretch of desolate land. Finally Kat breaks the silence. "So do we walk all night, or should we find a place to sleep?"

I wilt. How are we going to sleep out here? "We don't have our sleeping bags, or our tent, and there could be rattlesnakes and . . ." I can't go on without the risk of tears breaking loose.

"We could use our backpacks for pillows, and cover up with my jacket." Kat laughs. "I don't know, Anna babe, but it's going to be okay, if we just . . ." She stops and pulls me in for a hug, but I twist free.

"No, don't. Don't be nice to me. If you do, I'll end up sobbing."

"It will be okay." Kat's eyes plead with me, looking for forgiveness. "Are we . . . okay?"

I have no idea *what* we are.

"I'm hungry and tired and dirty and lonely and scared and a whole lot of other things I don't even want to begin thinking about." I look up. "And here's our ride," I say, holding out my arm, thumb extended.

Kat howls, jumps up and down, waves her arms frantically at what appears to be a bright blue-painted school bus.

She plants a sudden kiss on my lips as the bus pulls over just ahead of us. "I love you, Anna!" she sings, and then she turns and runs toward the open door of the bus, leaving me with the words, cut loose like a fish released, the one who bites again regardless of the result. I hook my fingers behind the straps of my backpack and run after Kat, after the shiny lure of her smile. Together, we step into the unknown, true dharma bums at last.

11

Thunder in the mountains—
the iron
Of my mother's love
—Jack Kerouac

When I was thirteen, I wanted to know what a tree looked like from the top, so I climbed an old, twisting cedar near the riverbank at the park.

"Annnnnaaaa!" cried my mother, a small blue figure below with crossed arms and an aura of fear. "That's far enough!" It really was, too. I knew this, but I tried to stand up, very slowly on shaking legs. The trunk of the tree tapered to a mere twig between my fingers, bending under my grasp. The river roared up at me as it churned around the rocks below. I held on and squeezed my eyes shut like a terrified kitten.

They didn't need to call the fire department or anything. Eventually, I pried loose each finger and slithered down onto a lower branch, and then another, until I was back on solid ground with my mother's arms wrapped so tightly around me that it made me feel dizzy and sick.

"Mom. Mom! I'm not a baby." I shrugged her arms off and looked around to check if anyone had seen. "I only wanted to see what a tree looks like from the top."

Her arms reached for me again, pinning my shoulders, crushing my head against her chest. "Anna, good grief. Trees look the same at the top as they do at the bottom. Branches and leaves." She tightened her hold. "Did you even think for an instant about how terrified I would be? You could have been killed."

*The next moment is one that I wish I could erase, even
though I hate the thought of erasing any memory of my mother.
"I wish I had fallen out of the tree," I said. I pushed my mother
away with finality. "Not everything in my life is about you."*

*I remember her face then, the way her tears seemed to halt
in their tracks, the way her eyes flashed with danger. "Someday
you'll understand," my mother muttered. "When you have a
daughter, you'll understand."*

If my mother were alive, she would have killed me dead
for getting on that bus. Maybe most mothers would. Four
boys, college-age with their dreadlocks and tie-dye and dirty
feet—guitars and drums stashed around the vehicle—greet
us with an enthusiastic cheer. I hesitate for only a second
before following Katy and squeezing in beside her on one of
the bench seats. A boy with a broad grin and beads woven
into his hair closes the door behind us, and we're off, moving fast, the sound of The Grateful Dead in our ears.

"Hey," says Kat, with her usual confident smile. "Where
you guys headed this evening?"

They all laugh, a nice friendly laughter; the whole bus
seems soaked in good humor, a giant rolling teapot steep-
ing in happiness. "We can go wherever you want us to go,
and back again," says the beaded boy. "We don't really have
a plan. We're here to meet real people and learn new things
and float the rivers and climb the mountains and smoke the
good Buddha, love." He grins even wider. "I'm Zane. This is
Seth, Frankie at the wheel, and Bo riding shotgun. And you,
my friends, are *on the bus.*"

"I'm Kat." No Katherine for this crowd. "Well, really
we're in quite a predicament." She nods. "Our car broke
down in Gillette, Wyoming, this little town way the hell out
in the middle of nowhere and so crazy far away from where
we are right now. We kind of got . . . abducted."

"Not abducted, not really," I say, finding my voice. I

smile at the two boys sitting on the bench across the little table. "We got abandoned once, and robbed, and then . . . I think . . . we were brainwashed." I laugh to show it's a joke, but I mean, it's pretty much true. I can't put my finger on it, but something about these boys, this bus—I feel strangely at ease. Maybe it's back to the freedom of anonymity, but I almost feel like I could tell them everything. I shake my head and stick my index finger in my mouth to keep myself from spilling all.

"Exactly," says Kat. "*Exactly exactly.*" She grins at me, and I know we're okay again. Happiness fills the void in my center.

"Gillette, huh?" The quiet boy with a shock of white blond hair—the one called Seth—pulls out an atlas and twists the shade of the little reading lamp toward the page. "Well, that's not so far." He hands the atlas to Zane. "We're heading up to Kalispell, but we've got lots of time. Festival's not till the Fourth."

"What kind of a festival?" says Kat. "Music?" She gestures at the instruments stashed about the bus. "Are you guys musicians?"

Seth runs a hand through his springy blond curls and ducks his head. "Strictly amateurs," he says.

"We're following this jam band on tour," says Zane. "Have you girls heard of Selective Silence? We're friends, sort of."

"Well, Zane and Seth have a crush on the lead singer, if that makes them friends," says Bo from the passenger seat.

"It's not a crush," says Zane, laughing. "It's a straight-up obsession."

"Is she hot?" Kat smiles, bemused.

Seth pulls out a zip-up binder full of photos, concert posters, ticket stubs, and such. He pushes it across the table, pointing at a photo of the band. The lead singer is tall and thin, with a piercingly interesting face framed by two thick, glossy braids. "The shaman," Seth whispers, tapping the photo. "We love the shaman."

I laugh, partly from his proximity, the clear gaze of adoration on his face. He leans in even closer. "So . . . Gillette?" he says.

"That would be awesome."

"We'll drive all night!" says Frankie from behind the wheel.

Kat pulls the album closer and peers at the singer's face—her gaze intense. "God, this face. It's so striking . . . it's almost painful."

"It's indescribable," says Seth, nodding vigorously. "And yeah, the shaman's for real. I mean, for real a mystic. You'll know it when you see the band perform. It's like they put the whole audience in a trance or something." He runs the edge of his thumb over his chin, where a little billy goat scruff is trying to grow. "There are stories . . ." he says.

"Stories about freaky shit. Talking to dead people, that kind of thing," says Zane. "The shaman plays this drum, and it's like, whoa . . . you can feel your heart rate changing, matching the beat, and then the shaman starts singing . . ."

"Minds are blown," Seth finishes.

"Totally."

"That's not all you want the shaman to blow," says Bo, laughing.

I blush, and Seth ducks his head and runs a hand through his curls. "It's not like that," he says.

"I want to meet the shaman." My desire surprises me. I haven't ever wanted to meet someone famous or important. Those hypothetical questions about meeting a famous person, living or dead? They make me nervous, contemplating fame. I know I would be tongue-tied and stupid. I'm afraid I would be boring and humorless. Still. What if . . .

"I bet we could get in to talk to the shaman at the festival," says Zane.

"Come on, you guys haven't really even met the shaman," says Bo, making a scoffing sound. "I mean, getting a signature on your tickets as the shaman walks by isn't meeting the shaman. Shaking hands in a line of fans isn't meeting the shaman." He laughs, dragging off his cigarette.

I pull the photo closer and peer at the shaman's face again. Freaky shit. I don't believe in that kind of thing, but . . . well, what would be the harm? "Do you think the shaman could talk to my dead mom?"

There's a tiny awkward moment, but then Seth takes my hand across the table, and he says, "Well, we can ask."

His eyes are calm and unwavering. I breathe in his strength and exhale my longing in a sigh.

"When is this festival? And where?"

"July Fourth. On somebody's land, up by Glacier National Park. Will you come?"

Katy and I exchange a look. I shrug.

"Why not?" says Kat, nodding. "Fourth of July, in Glacier. We'll meet you there."

"So what would you have the shaman tell your mom for you?" Seth slides my cardboard cup of coffee and my candy bar across the gas station counter, including them in his purchases.

I slide them back. "I don't know. It's stupid really. A big stupid cliché."

He puts his hand on top of mine, on top of my cup. "Stupid, how?"

I let him pay. "She died last year." I hold the door for him as he gathers his stuff into his pockets. "It was . . . so dumb. Some kids were playing with matches under the stairs one night, and when the fire accidentally got away from them, they ran instead of telling someone. My home, my parents' church, it all burned down. My dad and I got out, but she . . . didn't." We step out into the parking lot, but we linger there, not quite ready to rejoin the group.

"Oh, Anna, I'm so sorry." He says what everyone says, but he's totally sincere. "That's not even remotely stupid."

I shrug again, trying to stop there, leave it at that. Why am I telling him all this, letting this strange wandering boy hold these pieces of me?

I look away, but the words slip out anyway. "I thought . . . for a long time I worried that I had started the fire. Because I smoked in my room, and because we fought that night. But I know I put it out." I sip my coffee and wrap my free arm around myself, holding everything in close. "I know I put it out, but I was so relieved when two little boys confessed that they had started the fire. And then I felt like an awful person for being glad that they did it. Those poor kids, to have that kind of mistake eat away at you for the rest of your life."

"Anna." He stands closer, shifting slowly so that he has his arms around me. I can feel the squish of his purchases in his pockets. "I don't even know what to say."

I laugh to comfort him. "Don't worry, nobody does. People just sort of hover around me for a while and then get bored and wander away before they catch it."

"Catch what?" He tightens his arms; for a moment I am completely tucked into his embrace, and I feel okay with it, almost, in a way that's new and comfortable at the same time. Then he relaxes his arms—the embrace is over—but he doesn't step back, doesn't stop holding on to me.

"My bad luck." I lean in the tiniest bit, willing my body to uncoil, the spicy scent of his shirt against my cheek, the light rapid beat of his heart behind the ribs I can feel through his clothing.

"Anna," he says, and I look up. I think he's going to kiss me.

I pull away at the last instant. I don't know what to say, how to explain. "Sorry!" I disentangle myself from his arms, clumsy with coffee and apologies. My lungs feel funny, like I'm an amphibian learning to breathe out of the water. "I can't . . ." I turn and walk unsteadily across the parking lot toward the bus, parked under the gas station awning. I see

Kat waving from the doorway and quicken my pace. "Katy!" I call, and then I'm running.

Frankie drives all night, just as he said he would, and I sleep through most of it despite all the caffeine I consume. When we finally pull into Gillette, it's nine thirty in the morning, and we all pile out of the bus to stretch our legs and say our good-byes.

"But it's not really good-bye," says Seth, keeping his hands to himself but not his smile—that irresistible smile. "Anna, I'm happy we met. I feel . . . well, it's stupid." He runs both hands through his curls.

"It's not stupid." I scratch a mosquito bite on my knee to keep my hands from reaching for him. "I'm really glad you guys stopped for us. I . . . you're easy to talk to."

He nods, the curls bouncing in time. "Seriously, talking with you is amazing. Like I've known you all my life." He stops, looking away at last. "I wish . . . we could talk more."

"Well, there's always the festival, right?" I smile, both relieved and saddened to be free of the intensity of his smile.

He steps closer, takes my hands. "I know," he says, when I open my mouth to protest. "It's okay. I just . . . will you really come?"

I nod. "We'll be there. I want to see this shaman for sure." I see the look on his face and add quickly, "And you, too, of course. I mean, all of you." I nod again, feeling stupid, fastening my eyes on the bus, so bright and gleeful in the morning light. "Don't worry, Seth. We'll be there." I squeeze his hands with an air of finality and extricate mine from his grasp, walking purposefully toward our car—where Kat waits.

"Said your good-byes?" Kat asks, her voice bright and a little brittle.

I bite my lip, worrying about her tone, the layers of meaning. I glance back over my shoulder toward the bus and raise my hand to wave. "Are you all right?"

She nods and unlocks the door. "Everything's fine," she says. "Why don't you wait here, and I'll go explain to Leroy about why we're late and our money situation. We can get our bank stuff straightened out at the local branch."

I lean over to put my backpack on the floor, and I see it. "What the hell? Kat, look what's on the floor of the car."

Kat leans over me, squinting into the dim space next to the console. "Is that your wallet?"

I pick it up, sinking into the passenger seat to look through all of the compartments. "Everything's here, Katy, except the cash. My drivers' license, my ATM card, everything."

"Those sleazy bitches," says Kat, under her breath.

"Well, at least now we can pay for the car." I hand her the bank card and drop the wallet into my backpack. "I don't suppose there's much point in telling Leroy about his sister-in-law. Casey will just call us liars."

"Revenge," says Kat. "But I mean . . . it worked out, so that's sort of stupid. We'll stop and mail the money to Shaggy and then head out. I just want to get back on the road." She slips one foot out of her flip-flop and cracks her toes against the ground. "I . . . I'm glad it's just the two of us again," she says, without looking at me. She shoves her foot back into her shoe and turns away, heading into the garage.

The two of us. I watch her walk away, thinking about how much simpler things are when it's only Katy and me. Those people from Pastor Shepherd's church—I don't know whether to admire them for their faith or pity their foolishness. The way they cared for a raggedy homeless girl with the stomach flu simply because it was the right thing to do. The way they trusted that prayer could keep their old clunky bus running all the way to Mexico. What I do know is that their extremes help to put my father's faith into perspective, help me to remember his quieter, more sensible belief.

I pick up my phone. *God makes people do irrational things*, I type.

I set the phone down and pick up Kat's copy of *The Dharma Bums*, thumbing through it and letting the words wash over me. My first response to this book has been to roll my eyes and dismiss it—it seems so frustratingly zen, trying to make things clear by means of complications—but I admit it's growing on me. For a moment I wonder what Seth would think of it. I imagine him listening like Katy does while I read it out loud, but it feels like a betrayal. I push away the thought of his springy blond curls and magnetic smile. *The two of us.* So much simpler this way.

My cell phone chirps, and I check the screen. *So does love,* he says.

Kat opens the driver's side door and tosses me a chocolate bar. "Success!" she says, leaning in over the door. "Ready to go?"

I nod. *So does loss,* I text back.

Kat plugs in the music. "This song, this is my driving fast song," she says, pulling out of the lot. "So. What are we driving toward?" Her tone is brisk, uncharacteristically inaccessible. I feel a little hollow inside.

"I think I'd like to find someplace we can hunker down, stay in one place for a while, after all that craziness." I take out the map, unfolding it awkwardly in the confines of the passenger seat.

"What about our list?"

"List?"

"Yeah, our finding God's Love list. I mean, we can check off church and old people, right? Done and done." Kat laughs.

I dig out my journal and open to our list. "I'll add the shaman to the list. Or does that fall under music?" The map crumples across my lap.

"Sure, add the shaman. So what's left? Art? Nature?"

I nod, my eyes slipping over the remaining items. "And . . . some other things." I blush. "I mean, like, meditation." I turn my attention to the map.

"You got a plan?"

"We're right here. Let's go this way to Yellowstone. We'll find a little twin pine and learn to meditate. Then, when we're ready to move again, we'll go backpacking, deep in the woods." I smile at Kat's pained expression. "Oh, you'll see, Katy Kat. It will be lovely."

"You're the boss, Anna babe. Give me some directions."

"Okay, left turn up ahead." I point; the plan spools off bravely into the future.

"I think Yellowstone will be my exhibition opening," says Kat, pulling out onto the highway.

"Exhibition of what?"

"Of my artwork. I have a project in the works. I'm calling it *Good Lock.*"

I laugh, surprised. "What? Kat, you haven't mentioned a word about this!" Kat raises her eyebrows, bouncing them off the dark fringe of her hair, and then smiles lopsidedly. "You haven't asked."

"Well, I'm asking now. What is this exhibition?"

Kat shrugs. "The little keys I've been drawing. I'm going to put them in places they will be discovered someday. Their discovery will cause an impact, give their discoverers a little bump at that random moment in their life. A little impact—that's my exhibition. *Good Lock.*"

"But how is that an exhibition? It doesn't display your art; you never even know what happens to it. What if it just blows away in the wind?"

Kat shifts gears and settles back into her seat for the drive. "Exactly," she says. "But whatever. I open in Yellowstone."

12

Girls' footprints
in the sand
—Old mossy pile
—Jack Kerouac

*Our new apartment was on the other side of the railroad tracks
in a dilapidated old building stained red with the taconite dust
that blows off the trains passing by. Every day when I walked
home from school, I crossed a footbridge high above the tracks
and looked down on a row of cherry trees. In some ways, my
mother was right; a tree does look the same from the top as it
does from the bottom: same branches, starting as weighty limbs
and narrowing to the tiniest twigs; same leaves, quivering in the
slightest breeze or in the rush of the trains; same colors, same
rustling, same gentle sway. But from the earth, looking up, a
tree is hopeful; it might be touching the sky. From above, looking
down, you can see—it's stuck in the dust, just like us.*

"This isn't what I wanted." I stretch out full length on
the picnic table and close my notebook with a sigh. The
impatience, the restless boredom in my voice annoys me.
I scowl at the skinny lodgepole pines and wish I could pin-
point the source of my irritable mood.

"What do you mean?" Katy looks up from her sketchbook. Is she drawing more keys? So far Kat has "displayed"
many of her creations—tiny ornate skeleton keys—in a
variety of places. All of them are hidden where she hopes

someone will discover what she calls, "The Impact of Good Lock on an Otherwise Ordinary Moment."

"I mean . . . it's pretty and stuff, and I think I've started to get the hang of meditating, but . . ." I close my eyes against the brightness. "It doesn't seem like this is what I'm looking for, not yet." The trees rising up all around us are spindly and gawky—a forest of awkward adolescents recovering from a fire, like me. I feel myself drifting, remembering the time when I was a kid and I climbed that old cedar tree and freaked my mom out. The girl who dared. Where did she go?

Kat doesn't look away from her drawing, but she nods. "Maybe I'm ready to go backpacking."

I sit up, my eyes blinking away the sky. "Really?" I pull the road atlas out from the bottom of the small pile of books on the table, books I've been trying to occupy my mind with all afternoon. "What if we headed straight up to Glacier? We could set up a base camp, do a couple hikes, maybe one back-packing trip, and wait for the festival. For the boys."

"There are grizzly bears up there," says Kat. She frowns at the map.

"It's a rucksack revolution, Katy." I grin at her. "You started it." I want to feel what it's like to carry everything we need on our backs, to sit against a pine tree in the middle of absolutely nowhere and just become a dot of nothing in the universe.

Kat taps the end of her pencil against her bottom lip.

"What are you working on?"

She holds up her sketchbook, shrugging.

"It's me!"

"Maybe," she says. "It's a girl, anyway." The girl is stretched out along the edge of a sunny rock, her hands palm down against the rock like she is bracing herself for something. Her eyes are closed. Her hair falls over the cliff, billowing up around her face. Far below her, a suggestion of water—an ocean in the distance.

"It's totally me." I reach for the paper. "I want to crawl

right into this picture and stretch out like she is, in the sun."

Kat stares at me for a long moment, and then looks away, but not before I catch the flicker of sadness in her eyes. "Can I have it back?" she says, and I hand it over. She closes the sketchbook.

"Katy, what's wrong?" There's something about her face that scares me.

"It's fine." Her voice is dark, sulky. She gathers up her pencils and packs them away in her satchel.

"I . . . did I say something?" I've upset her somehow.

Kat shakes her head, but she won't look at me. "So are you going to show me what you were writing, then? Fair is fair." She lifts an eyebrow at me but then quickly sticks those silly sunglasses over her dark eyes.

"Katy, I . . ." I grip my notebook tightly. There is a long silence between us.

"Anna?" She pulls her bag closer to her and stares at the table.

"Yeah?"

"Can you pretend you didn't see that drawing?"

I shrug. "Okay. Why?"

"I can't explain." She pulls off her oversize sunglasses and fiddles nervously with the bright orange bows. "You're right; it's you in the sketch. But I kind of wish . . . I kind of wish it wasn't." She raises her eyes from the glasses to meet mine, the irises so dark in the shadow that they seem to blend into the black pupils. "Please, forget about it, okay?"

"I don't get it. It's a beautiful picture, and I totally love it."

Kat nods. "Me, too. But I don't want to think about it anymore."

We spend the next three days holed up in a cute little Montana campground about halfway between East and West Glacier, and I can tell that this is the wilderness I am seeking. There are some small trails through the woods, and we do a few practice hikes to get used to wearing the big packs that I bought before we left.

In the meadows, tall, creamy flowers bloom on thick heavy stalks. Bear grass, says Melvin, our eccentric campground host. It's easily as tall as my waist, sometimes taller. Melvin says we'll need to fight through it, that it grows so thick it obscures the trail. It has a sweet, fresh smell in the sun.

Tonight we leave the packs behind, tramping happily through the woods just as the sun sinks low enough to send long golden beams of light through the soft green filter of the forest canopy. I pick up a long stick as I walk, enjoying the feel of the sturdy branch in my hand.

"I think I'm actually happy," I say, wielding the stick like a sword. I spin in the trail to face Kat, who raises her own walking stick to meet mine.

"A duel to the death?" Kat says, giggling.

I laugh, too, and we spar for a moment playfully until Kat gently presses the tip of her stick into my chest. "On your knees and beg for mercy."

Oh, god. This feels silly and dangerous at the same time. I kneel. I look up at Kat, beautiful and fierce standing there with the setting sun in her hair and her face so stern. Only her eyes are full of mirth. I stare.

"Close your eyes, prisoner."

I giggle stupidly, my heart leaping against the point of her stick.

"Close your eyes. And *stop* laughing."

I try to obey, shaking a little.

Katy moves her makeshift lance to my neck, pressing gently. "Close 'em."

I close my eyes, serious at last. There is a long silence, and I feel genuinely vulnerable for a moment, as though Kat really does have a sword to my neck. Then I feel the stick come down and gently touch each of my shoulders.

"I . . . dub . . . thee . . . mine," says Kat softly. "Sealed with a kiss." The stick falls to the forest floor behind her. She kneels down in front of me and touches my face with both hands. It's all I can do to stay here, to be here, to hold still.

I squeeze my eyes shut, but I can feel Kat's breath lightly playing on my neck, just below my right ear, and a shudder runs through me. I can't do this. I want this. I want her. Heat. Breath. I gasp at the touch of Kat's mouth on my earlobe, warm kisses trailing down along my throat.

"Oh," I say. "*Oh.*" Kat's lips find mine, and I can no longer think; everything is a blurry sea of tongues and hands, breath and skin. I press myself closer to her, marveling at the power of the longing I feel, a force almost palpable.

"Anna . . ." Kat's breath flutters in my ear, small bird wings.

I pull away. Take a deep, shuddery breath. Touch my fingers to my lips. I can hear her breathing, but neither of us says anything. I open my eyes to find Kat looking at me.

"Hi," she whispers, still out of breath.

"Hi."

I shrug, feeling shy. "Um, wow."

"Are you okay . . . with this?" says Kat. Her hand on my arm.

I don't know. I shake my head, shrug, nod. "I don't know," I say, and I let myself lean in again, finding her mouth. This time I keep a part of myself back, a part to tell me when to stop.

Her hand curls around the back of my neck, fingers twining through my hair.

I'm losing myself again, like I'm a ball of yarn; I can feel myself tangling up in her. It's a tempting feeling—playful but panicky. I'm no good at knots. "I . . . I can't. . . ."

"I know," whispers Kat. "It's okay."

I look into her eyes. "I *want* to."

"I know. I'm not . . . ready yet, either."

I nod. "I want to, though."

"Me, too." Kat laughs and picks at the bark of the stick that now lies discarded on the trail.

I scoot closer. "So . . ." I can't say it.

"What?" Kat doesn't look up.

I squirm. "So are we like . . ."

"Girlfriends?"

"Lesbians?" I don't know why this is a whisper word. I can handle being gay, but like . . . I'm not crazy about a label that instantly makes people think about my sex life.

Kat shrugs. "It doesn't seem to be a big deal to me that you're a girl, I guess. I just . . . like *you* best."

Relief. Leave it to Kat to say just the right thing. I nod. "Me, too."

As we turn to hike back to our camp, Kat tucks one of her good lock keys into the branches of a little shrub near the spot, and even though it breaks the rules of leaving no trace, I can't help but smile at the thought of its discovery.

Preparing for our very first backpacking trip takes the better part of a day; I feel almost back in control with my clipboard and my checklists, standing on the bench of the picnic table surveying the gear we have spread about the camp. "I couldn't see spending the money on a water purifier when we can just boil water." I frown at the two stoves. "Unfortunately that means carrying more fuel."

"You can put it in my pack," says Kat.

"And I'm not entirely sure that our sleeping bags are going to be warm enough without all of our other blankets."

"Well, we can snuggle together for warmth." Kat winks, and I, of course, feel my face get hot. This whole thing— whatever it is between us—has changed the way we sleep together. We've shared a bed at countless sleepovers since we were twelve, but lately the distance between us has become somehow precarious. Locked in our separate bags, we sleep in little cocoons of steamy breath and unwritten rules.

"What else, what am I forgetting?" I run my eyes up and down the list, but I can't identify what's escaping me.

"Let's go get our backcountry permit." Kat scratches a mosquito bite on the inside of her wrist. "Look where the little fucker got me. Itches like mad." She holds up her swollen arm. Since reaching Glacier, Kat has discovered that she has an allergic reaction to mosquito bites; they swell up into quarter-sized lumps. "It's hard to be all zen and shit when you want to claw all the skin off your arm."

Kat isn't much interested in Kerouac-style meditation. She can't see any value in sitting still and doing nothing for so long when she can get herself to that empty state a lot faster through her painting.

As for me, I've been sort of meditating in the mornings and evenings since we got to Devil's Creek. The first day I tried to just sit still and think nothing, to let my mind go empty, but the more I tried to stop thinking, the more thoughts I had.

Now I'm trying something different; I repeat the first line of the prayer my mother cross-stitched and hung on the wall. "Lord, make me an instrument of thy peace." I sent my dad a text about this almost-prayer. *I pray each morning in the woods, but it's Mom I'm talking to.* His answer came back with record speed. *I'm certain your prayers make her sing.*

I breathe slowly, trying to picture the words dropping down into the deep well inside me, trying to imagine my mother singing. Hoping my father will sing again, too.

"I guess it's as good a time as any," I say, referring to the permits. "Maybe we can get some dinner in East Glacier?"

We pack up and head to the main ranger station, where we fill out the paperwork, and a ranger makes us watch a short video about grizzly bears. It's pretty intense. We buy some little bells to hang from our packs and a couple of bigger bells to carry. Learning about the bears reminds me of the time I had my wisdom teeth out, how my mom and I had to sign all these forms that basically said we understood that I might not ever wake up from the procedure. We joked about it, but we signed our names, one beside the other, her loopy *A*'s mirroring my own.

"Should we buy some of that super-powered pepper spray?" says Kat.

I startle, realizing I've been lost in my head. "Um, it seems like that would piss them off. Maybe we should just try to be calm and stuff?"

Kat laughs, glancing over her shoulder as she folds a Good Lock card into a guidebook about wildflowers and replaces the book on the shelf. "Okay, Anna babe, but I'm not sure I'm going to be thinking super rationally when I'm staring down a thousand pounds of steaming, rancid-smelling bear. You know?"

She puts her arm around my waist, drawing me close as we stand in front of an interpretive display about the grizzly bear. She slips her fingers beneath the waistband of my jeans, sliding her hand over my tattoo. She leans in close and whispers, her breath heavy in my ear. "Danger can be exciting," she says.

"Katy, stop," I say, pulling away. I look around, embarrassed. My knees are wobbling.

"I'll stop," says Kat, grinning. "For *now*."

And suddenly I forget everything I've learned about bears.

Driving out of the park on the Two Medicine Road, just after crossing the boundary into the Blackfeet Indian Reservation, I see a sign advertising two-dollar showers. "Katy, pull over!" We haven't had a shower since the Shepherds' home, haven't even cleaned up with running water since the sponge bath at the church, after I was sick. For the past week, we've been taking "baths" with a tub of baby wipes inside the tent. The thought of hot, steamy water and clean hair is pure bliss.

Kat turns the car down a winding road, following signs to a quiet campground tucked against the banks of Two Medicine Creek, where we purchase two showers and two candy bars. We stand outside in the dusty parking lot, holding our towels and the key to a small wooden door marked GALS.

Kat frowns. "I feel kind of weird, buying a shower. Like some kind of transient."

"Well, we *are* transients, Katy."

"Yeah, I guess." She kicks at a clump of dirt on the trail. "So. Should we go shower?"

Kat cracks her toes. "Yeah." A pause. "Separately, huh?"

Insta-blush. Why am I such a prude? "Yeah. You want to go first?"

We peek in and find a dressing room and a shower stall. "You can come in," says Kat. I sit on a small metal folding chair while she undresses; it's weird now to see her naked, and I look away. How stupid is this? We've been naked around each other a million times in the past six years. Kat steps into the shower and I look into the silver metal mirror nailed to one wall.

I stare myself down. What the hell? Why is every thought in my head about sex these days? I remember how I thought about hooking up with Shaggy, and why? Because he was nice to me? Because I didn't love him? And then there's Seth . . . even now the thought of Seth's smile, the feel of his heart beating against my cheek sends a thrill over me that embarrasses me and excites me and seriously, *What the hell?* I shake my head, looking away, undressing for my own shower.

I unbutton my jeans, sliding my hands over my hips, my fingers pausing on the spot under my tattoo where Kat's fingers had lingered. I can almost feel her hand there. My head spins.

"It's just sex," I say out loud, to myself, to my reflection. One hand travels lower, pressing hard. It's just sex. No big deal. Nothing to be ashamed of. In the room next to me, Kat turns off the shower, and I hear a satisfied sigh. I wonder—an idle thought—what would happen if I kept this up, if I were to let Katy walk in while I'm . . . my breathing falters at the image, and I hurriedly pull my hand away and start undressing matter-of-factly, ignoring the waves of heat and steam and wet. I wrap my towel tightly around myself just as Kat emerges, also safely tucked into her own fluffy towel.

Kat smiles. "I had this sudden feeling that there was like a camera in here or something," she says. "I hate it when I get that feeling, like someone's watching me."

I laugh, a little shaky but not noticeably so, I hope. "Yeah, ew, especially in the shower." I take a step closer. "Looks like the water was hot."

We have a slightly awkward moment passing each other between the two rooms, and then I close the little curtain and hang up my towel on the hook in the corner. I'm so shaky and weak that I wish I could sit down or even lean on something, but a glance at the cinder-block walls tells me that's not the best idea. Instead I take a couple of deep breaths and shake my head to clear it. Seriously, this is getting out of hand. I turn on the water, and it is still hot— scaldingly so—and for a moment I'm able to lose myself in the bliss of the water beating against me, washing away the grime.

"I'm filthy," I say, under my breath. Shame settles over me like a familiar refrain, the kind of song you don't really like but can't stop singing. What would my father say? What would he do, if he knew that while I professed to be seeking God and praying to my mother I was really getting tattoos and doing drugs and thinking about sex all the time? I lather my hair roughly, my fingernails raking across my scalp with sharp little digs of guilt and shame and fear.

We wake to the sound of raindrops on the tent, running down the skylight in long wavering lines. "It's raining," says Kat.

"Your powers of observation are amazing."

"We still going?"

I roll on to my side, curling up in my sleeping bag. "It's not supposed to last more than a few hours." I can barely get the words out between yawns. "We already got our permit."

Kat groans. "But I'm so comfy here."

"I'll make us some coffee." I sit up, unzipping my bag. "You go ahead and take it slow." I pull my rain shell from the bottom of the tent and zip it up. It really is dismal out there, but I'm determined.

Kat burrows back underneath the covers. "Sounds good," she murmurs sleepily.

I emerge from the tent into a gray drizzle. The day is warm despite the rain, and I can imagine the way the heat will hang on us once this rain dries up. I boil water for coffee, using a little bit to brush my teeth first, spitting into the fire pit. The raindrops make little smoky puffs as they hit the ashes, and I lean my head back in my hood. The rain rolls off my face.

When the coffee is ready, I unzip the tent and hand in a steaming cup. "Oatmeal?" I lean into the tent, dripping on her. "Or I could make eggs? We'll be stuck with oatmeal on the trail."

Kat sits up, her dark hair tousled like a sleepy child. She looks hopeful. "Would you really make me eggs? With some cheese on them?"

I nod, sipping my coffee. I kind of want to kiss her, but there's a line I can't cross, initiative I can't take. Can't, can't . . . I can't even touch her. I sit back on my heels, under the vestibule. "I'll make fried potatoes, too." I will cook for her instead.

"That would totally get me out of bed," she says.

"Well, good. 'Cause you're in charge of packing up the tent." I smile and stand up, heading over to get the cooler out of the backseat of the car.

An hour later, the rain is still falling, though it's just on the heavy side of sprinkling, really. I've got the dishes washed up, and everything is packed for the trip, distributed between the two huge backpacks.

"Are you ready?"

"I guess," she says. "I don't really know how you get ready to walk seventeen miles into a grizzly-bear-infested wilderness with only the shit you can carry on your back, but if you think this is going to help us find God, well, who am I to argue?"

I smile. "All right, then. Let's go."

Nine hours later, give or take, Kat and I lean against a tree in the Park Creek campsite cooking area, sharing a foam mat to keep our butts dry. She sighs. "So that was like eight miles, then?"

"Well, more like seven, actually."

"And tomorrow we're doing ten?"

"It will be easier, I promise." I'm full of shit. "I mean, maybe it won't rain."

"Or it could freeze, and my boots will be two solid chunks of ice."

"At least we didn't run into any bears." We spent most of the hike singing loudly.

"Yet."

"Yeah. I guess that's why we cook over here and sleep somewhere . . . else?" I nod toward one of the little trails leading away from the cooking area.

Kat breathes out a long shuddery sigh. "Why are we doing this, really?"

"We're finding proof of God, remember?" The words come easily, but I hear how empty they are. "Nature, you know. It's on the list."

"I know that, but what do we expect to find, exactly? What is this place going to show us about God's love?" She waves her hand aimlessly at the natural world around us.

I don't have an answer to that. I mean, are we seriously looking for God to be lounging against a tree, speaking in tongues or something? Do I expect the water in my plastic canteen to transform into wine? "Maybe we can understand God better out here, away from all the distractions. Maybe here in the wilderness, I can focus on my meditation. Maybe God will speak to me."

Kat stretches out full length on the ground, her spine crackling. "This isn't like the Old Testament times, though, Anna babe. And you're not Moses, wandering the desert." She tries to rub her own back. "Couldn't God just send out an e-mail? Start a blog?" Kat laughs. "It's okay, Anna babe, I'll stop bitching now. I'm just tired."

My smile is as weary as hers. "No, you're right. It's silly. I just . . . I mean, okay. Think of what our bodies have done today. Isn't that pretty amazing? And, like, look at this." I pluck a tiny purple flower from the grass beside me. "Everything is so perfect and amazing. I don't know why I can't accept this—this little flower, or my own body, or gravity, or I don't know, a grizzly bear—as proof that there's a God."

Kat takes the flower. "What do you think would be different, if you could? How do you think faith would change you?"

"Oh, I don't know." Maybe it wouldn't. The whole question is depressing. I stand up and stretch, rubbing my fingers over my hips, which feel hot and sore. "My hip bones are piercing through my skin." I run my fingers over my tattoo, which is completely healed.

"Ha, my hips are fine." Kat folds down the top edge of her pants and pats her own rounded hips. "I knew these curves were good for something! Too bad it's something I despise with every fiber of my being!" She laughs.

"That's not fair. Give it a chance." For once, I don't even think about it; I reach out and run my fingers over Kat's hips, tugging her closer. I think of that evening we sparred on the trail, the longing, and I wonder, Is this it? "Hey, did you bring your gun?" My fingers freeze as though they may encounter deadly metal at any moment. I can barely suppress a shudder at the thought.

"Are you kidding?" says Kat. "That thing is heavy. Hell, no."

"Good," I say. "That *thing* makes me nervous."

"Having your hands in my pants makes me nervous."

Yeah, no kidding. I manage a laugh. "No way. Katherine the Invincible? Scared of an innocent like me?"

"Maybe a little." She pulls away. "Grab that mat, let's go check out the bedroom."

"Scandalous." My heart is fluttering. Is this happening? "You think our packs are okay just lying here?"

Kat rolls her eyes. "Um, hello? We're eight miles into the woods. Nobody's going to steal them." She fishes her sleeping bag from the bottom compartment of her backpack and nods toward the nearest trail.

We meander through the woods, finding the little wilderness outhouse and three tent sites. "I like that one back there the best," says Katy. "It's the most private."

Privacy. Eight miles into the woods. My mouth is dry.

"It's okay," she says softly. She leads the way to a little grassy hollow and spreads out the foam mat and sleeping bag. "Sit with me," she says, patting the mat beside her. "I'll roll a joint."

I hesitate. This is scary. There's something in Katy's eyes, some determination that simultaneously thrills and terrifies me. I look around the clearing, at the beauty of the rain-glazed foliage. Time seems to stretch out and lengthen like the sleeves on an old sweater tucked around my fingers and wrapped around my chest, for protection. I wait, uncertain.

"You should take off your boots, Anna." Kat doesn't look up from the Baggie and her project. "And sit down already." One hand pats the foam beside her. So close.

My chest. It's exploding. I obey, unlacing the wet hikers and extracting my tired feet. I sit on the edge of the wide foam mat and wiggle my toes in my new pink wool socks. "Wow, they're dry. That's amazing."

Kat smiles. "Here, can you light this so I can take mine

off? I'm totally going barefoot. I don't care if it's muddy. My feet feel like they've been serving some hard time in those boots." She peels off her socks and wiggles her toes, the nails now painted a deep red. "Feel nature, little toes!" She kicks her feet through the weeds, laughing. Raindrops bounce this way and that off the tall, wet grass and sparkle in the hint of sun. "You got that thing lit yet?"

I look down at the joint. "I don't know how, Kat. I've only ever seen you do this. Once." I sit cross-legged, my feet still snug in their pink socks.

"Ah, well, it's time you learned then," says Kat, and just like that she's . . . in my lap, basically. Her hands are up underneath my shirt, and then, well, more than her hands. Oh, god. I'm still struggling to light the joint as Kat's mouth travels over my stomach and ribs, moving up gradually . . .

"Got it," I gasp, just as Katy unhooks the clasp of my bra and then . . . "*Oh.*"

Kat sits up and pulls her own shirt over her head, and then her sports bra. I feel the smoke turning a lazy spiral inside me; I can tell already that whatever part of me pulled away from this the other night on the trail—that part is all curled up inside me, sleeping blissfully. In its place, a dizzying hunger.

Katy pulls me down beside her on the mat, both of us on our sides, face-to-face. Our eyes meet.

"I think I'm good, probably," I say, waving off the joint. I'm stuttering, stupid. "I mean, I'm . . . yeah, I'm good." Without intention, my hands and then my mouth move closer, and I smile into her skin when I hear the hitch in her breathing. The heat of our bodies is a stark contrast to the chill of the air.

"Anna, are you sure about this?" Kat's voice sounds tight, strained, and I can feel the weight of the longing she is holding at bay, equal to or greater than my own.

Am I sure? A pause. "Yes, I'm sure." The words are barely audible, but Katy nods and kisses me, and once again,

I feel myself unwinding, weaving—a merging of heat and heartbeats. I can't breathe.

"*Katy.*" My whole body twists under the tension of her tongue.

"I don't know what I'm doing," I say. For a moment I am so lost, the dancer in the back row who hasn't learned the choreography. Then Kat's fingers touch my face, twine into my hair; I smile, hold her eyes for just a moment, and the distance between knowing and not knowing seems to disappear.

13

A bubble, a shadow—
woop—
The lightning flash
—Jack Kerouac

*I don't know why it's such a big deal—losing your virginity.
Aren't there a million first times in life? And even in sex?*

*I thought of my first time as an awkward-but-necessary
hurdle that I was anxious to clear. My lingering virginity was
an obvious and uncomfortable liability—like eczema or something—and I wished I could just be rid of it. Maybe it's awful
to even admit this, but I didn't want this first time to be about
feelings; I definitely didn't want it to be about love.*

*Love. Talk about terrifying. But this—this first time with
Katy—well. So much for everything I thought I wanted.*

> *it could be our history, the secrets shared*
> *and those we keep silent. it could be our together-trek*
> *in the mud, bonding like soldiers.*

> *Or maybe,*
> *it's the bear.*

"Did you hear something?"

I lift my head. "I can hear your heartbeat."

Kat struggles to sit up, spilling me off to one side. I protest as I land in the damp grass.

"Shhh," hisses Kat. "I'm serious. I hear something."

Kat picks up her pants and gets one leg through, but stops when we both hear the noise. "I swear to god, somebody's messing with our stuff," she says, jumping up.

"That sounded like . . . our cooking kit, maybe?" I scramble to my feet and follow after Katy, who is already hopping down the path, struggling to get her other leg into the purple yoga pants as she goes.

"Kat, wait!" I whisper-shout. My wool socks squish into the mud on the trail, water seeping between my toes. *Ick, ick, ick.* Out in the open now, no longer huddled with Kat under the sleeping bag, it's chilly out here, and goose bumps rise all over me. I hug my arms around my upper body as I stumble after Kat toward the cooking area. "Kat!" I call a little louder, but she doesn't listen, too intent on following the distinct banging sounds coming from up ahead. What if it's another group of campers, just arrived? What if the banging is their own pots and pans as they cook up something for dinner? What are they going to say when two half-naked girls burst in on their food preparations?

Lost in this panicky thought stream, I run right into the back of Kat, who has stopped short on the edge of the cooking area, her pants forgotten in a tangle around one foot. "What the . . . ?" My whisper trails off as the huge shaggy brown head swings up in a casual swivel, turning away from the shredded pack in front of it and focusing its watery brown eyes on us, frozen in fear and shock at the edge of the clearing.

The bear is enormous. Its dark, shaggy fur hangs heavy and matted over its haunches, rolling in a giant ruff around its neck, smeared with rain and mud and other things. It looks nothing like bears do in family movies, where a clever dog will bare his teeth protectively and the bear will turn tail and run. This bear is solid; the rank smell of him permeates the clearing, establishing his jurisdiction. This is his home, and we have trespassed.

"What do we do?" Kat whispers from the side of her mouth. "What did that ranger guy say?"

I think back to the interpretive sign at the ranger station, but all I can remember is Kat's hand slipping into my jeans. I blush, a stupid thing to think right now. The bear moves his head back and forth, still looking at us with his tiny dark eyes.

"I don't remember." The bear swings its head back over to the backpack and takes a swipe at it with one huge claw, shredding the nylon and scattering a bunch of clothing across the log bench behind it. "Holy shit, we're dead." I clutch Katy's arms, trying to pull her backward, but Kat resists.

"No, I'm pretty sure he can't see us if we don't move," she says in a stage whisper.

The bear, satisfied with his display of power, turns back to us, his head shifting from side to side rhythmically. He moves up onto two legs—a giant. Kat, no longer so sure of her plan to remain motionless, turns as though to run, but I catch her and hold her back. "No," I whisper, remembering something from the sign or from our conversation with the ranger. "You were right. He's having trouble seeing us. That's why they stand up like that."

We're standing in the shadow of the trees; the bear is in the small clearing made by the fire ring and benches. The late afternoon sun, which has been fighting the rain clouds for the last couple of hours, filters down into the clearing at a low angle—not terribly bright, but it's possible that it's shining right into the bear's eyes.

"We're supposed to back away from it." The details are coming to me, but not fast enough. I remember something else, how bears will do a fake charge, how you shouldn't run, no matter what. The bear swings its head back and forth, making grunting sounds, and I know it's going to come at us. "Katy, don't move."

Strangely, I find that the terror coursing through my

system as the bear charges—its body undulating in awe-in-spiring ripples—only makes everything come into a clearer focus. Instead of seeing my life flash before my eyes or freez-ing in panic, it's as though everything slows down; every de-tail is sharp, every sense acute. I step in front of Katy, stand-ing as tall and straight as I can.

The bear runs toward me, fast. I can see the moisture on his muzzle, can practically count his long yellow teeth. I hear the breath puffing out of his nostrils in agitated snorts, and it takes every bit of my will power to keep from scream-ing. At what feels like the last possible second, the bear veers off course and stops, whirling around with amazing agility.

Kat's arms are clasped around my waist, her face buried in my hair. I hold still, trying to watch the bear, but I keep my eyes averted, hoping he won't charge again, fearing that he will. What if we can't stand still for another pass? I know if we run, the bear will attack us. Newspaper headlines come, unbidden, to my mind. *Hikers Found Naked, Mauled.* Humiliating. The bear lopes toward us again, this time a little slower in his approach, but still terrifying. *It's just a bluff,* I tell myself, squeezing Katy's hands. *He'll turn to the side again.* But what if he doesn't?

The bear veers, grunting fiercely, so close this time I can feel the ground tremble, the heat and the deadly weight of him, and I squeeze my eyes closed. As though out of re-flex, a prayer springs to my lips, but I don't pray to any God; I pray to the bear.

Please, Bear. We respect you and we're sorry for invading your home. We're leaving, now, and we hope you will accept our apologies and forgive us our trespasses. Please, Bear. Amen.

Out loud, I keep my voice low and monotone, holding my arms out somewhat from my body and keeping my eyes averted. "Please, Bear. I am Anna. This is Katy. We're only passing through. We'll be gone before you know it."

The bear stands about fifteen feet from us, on all fours, facing away. I walk backward, talking steadily, pushing Katy back behind me. "We're leaving now, Bear, no worries. We were dumb to leave our packs out like that, and I hope you won't come back here now and mess with people just because we were so stupid." I move back another step or two, and the bear stands up on its hind legs once again.

Katy makes a strangled sound, pressing her face hard into my back. I need something to distract it, something we can leave behind to slow it down, in case it decides to pursue us. I look down and see Kat's purple yoga pants, still tangled around one ankle and covered with mud. "Kick your pants into the trail," I say. "Please, Bear, we mean no harm. Just let us go."

The bear swings its head from side to side. Oh, god, if we can make it through this I'll . . . oh, who knows what I'll do, but something impressive. Something important. "Please, Bear. You have no use for us." Kat wiggles her foot out of her purple pants, and I shove them forward on the trail with a slow movement, pushing Katy back another couple steps. Now we're well into the cover of trees, and I hope with every fiber of my being that the bear will lose interest in us

We step away—now twenty-five feet away, now thirty. The bear drops back down onto four legs, and I stop. "Wait a minute." My mouth is dry. *Please, Bear. Please, Bear.* "If he charges again, don't move. If he attacks you, play dead. Curl up in a ball and cover your neck. Don't make a sound."

She whimpers, and I feel her trembling behind me.

The bear retreats, and I hear the sound of nylon tearing as he turns his attention back to our packs.

"Are we still alive?" Kat asks, when we finally get back to the sleeping mat. "Did we actually escape the freaky psycho-bear?"

"Hey," I say, defending the bear. "It's not his fault. We were idiots, you know. That bear could end up hurting some other campers, and it's all our fault for leaving those packs like that. Now I don't know what we're going to do, or how we're going to get ourselves and all our junk back to the car tonight."

Kat shakes her head. "No way, Anna. I'm not going back there. I'll cut straight through these woods. I'll climb over these huge logs and scale the cliffs and whatever it takes just to not go back anywhere near that freaking bear." She pulls at the edges of the sleeping bag as though trying to wrap it so tightly around her that she can disappear. "I don't care about 'leaving no trace.' I want to get out of here like yesterday. I've had it with nature, grizzly bear style."

I nod. "That's okay. I'll get the stuff myself. It's actually probably better if only one of us goes. Anyway, if I get attacked by the bear for some reason, you'll be able to go for help and at least they'll know where to start looking for me."

Kat rolls her eyes. "Way to go, Anna. Make me feel all guilty. Now of course I'm going to help you since you're so unbelievably idiotic. It's not like I can just leave you to be eaten by that monster."

"I'm not getting eaten. I'm going to wait until it leaves. Then I'll go and grab the packs."

"How about we just run in the opposite direction until we get to the car? We can lock ourselves in and call the rangers from our cell phone to let them know we don't want all our shit back because we're halfway to, like, Los Angeles or something." She shudders. "Somewhere without wildlife, anyway."

I laugh. "I thought you said danger is exciting." I can't believe I'm being so coy. I don't even blush.

She laughs, but it's a shaky one. "Not standing naked in front of a bear the size of the free world as he contemplates whether he thinks it's worth it to reach over and snap your neck with his massive fucking claws." She lowers her voice. "Did you *see* those claws, Anna?"

"I think we're safe." I honestly have no idea if we are or not.

"Maybe we should make some noise?"

"You're right. There could be another one."

Kat lunges toward me and grips my arm. A tiny whimper

escapes her. "Anna babe, will you promise me something?"

"What is it?"

"If we get out of this alive, will you promise me that we don't have to go out in the wilderness again? At least not with bears?"

"Come on, you have to admit it was amazing to see him like that, so powerful. And I mean, if that isn't God, then I don't know what is."

Kat's eyes are skeptical, but they soften as she reaches for my hand. "Thanks for keeping everything together back there, Anna babe." Her voice is barely audible. "I sort of freaked out, didn't I?"

"You did fine. We both did what we could." I shake my head. "I've only ever seen you scared like once or twice, you know. You see me break down every other minute."

"Oh, come on, Anna. You're like Indiana Jones or something." She leans in close, her breath tickling my ear.

"I don't go looking for danger," I say, but I have a hard time forming the sentence, and an even harder time getting the breath to say it.

Kat laughs. "The world is a dangerous place, I guess," she says, her lips brushing against my neck. "I'm just glad you've got my back."

By the time we decide it's safe to make a grab for our stuff, the sun has already sunk low; it touches the peaks of the range of mountains to one side, and the light angling through the trees is fading fast. We discuss the logistics of two exhausted people moving a gigantic heavy pile of ripped-up equipment out of the woods. In the dark.

We approach the food area singing loudly, holding hands, but the bear appears to be gone. Remnants of packaging and shredded nylon litter the entire area, and we scramble around the site, cleaning up.

"We have to make *sure* there isn't any food left around here," I say, but the light is fading fast.

Both of the packs are useless, so we load all the gear onto the middle of the sleeping bag and lash the ends to a big stick. When we finish, it's almost dark.

"I'll go ahead since I have the headlamp."

Kat nods. "I'm just glad to have pants on again."

I take a look around the little camp, saddened by the fact that our stay here is cut short. I thought maybe we'd find enlightenment in the wilderness; instead we're facing another grueling hike in the dark, with this awkward burden on a makeshift pole. All I really want is to eat some dinner and get some sleep.

"This is going to suck," says Kat.

I start down the trail—the dark, muddy expanse of it. "Yeah, pretty much." My legs tremble, my shoulder aches, and my stomach growls. I shake the bear bells with one hand while gripping the pole on my shoulder with the other. I stumble under the burden, so far from divine.

The dark trail seems endless, but at last we reach the car, bruised and sore and covered in mud, just as the sun is making an appearance in the east. We collapse on the gravel of the parking lot, barely noticing the rocks beneath us.

"I think," says Kat, so weary that the act of forming words is almost beyond her reach. "I think that was the worst night of my entire life."

I nod, my hand closing tight around hers. "Me, too," I say, and then all at once the falseness of saying this rushes over me as the memory of the *real* worst night of my life looms in horrifying detail across my exhausted brain. For the first time since we left Minnesota I'm once again right there on the edge—the edge of Anna and a vast chasm of emptiness and sorrow.

No, not really, I want to say. *Actually it was much worse when my mom died.* I long to say these words and jump into that abyss, to feel myself split apart into all my separate atoms.

I can't say it, though, so instead I squeeze Katy's fingers until I think I might break them in half and press my other hand against the backs of my eyes, hard.

"I know," she says. "I know." Kat extracts her hand from my grip and stands up, unlocking the car and pulling a hunk of cheese out of the cooler along with a tube of crackers from the grocery bags. She makes me three little sandwiches.

"You'll feel better with some food in you." She hands over the crackers, and I nibble a little, wishing my stomach felt less queasy.

"I'll feel better when I pull the tent out of the stuff sack to find that it isn't completely ruined." I lean back against the side of the car. For the first time I notice the rocks digging into my butt and the back of my legs. "I suppose we should survey the damage, huh?"

"Eat first," says Kat, handing me three more cracker sandwiches. "And maybe we could just spend an hour or so napping in the car?" We stuff the tattered remains of our things into the trunk and recline in the front seats.

I wake just once in the next four hours, long enough to turn away from the sun coming in through the driver's side window and fall back to sleep curled up on my side. When I surface again, the temperature inside the car is sweltering, even though we left the windows rolled down halfway. My body aches in places I can't even name, and the back of my throat feels parched and scratchy.

I lean over and fish around in the cooler for the bottle of orange juice I purchased in East Glacier, knowing that we would want something cool and sweet after our trip. My mouth feels furry, and I can smell myself. Disgusting.

"It's five thousand degrees in here," says Kat, her eyes still closed.

I hand her the bottle of cold juice. "This helps."

Kat holds the bottle up against her forehead. "Can we just go swimming or something?"

Swimming does sound good. "We should probably figure out if our tent is ruined first. If we have somewhere to sleep that isn't this bitch of a car, then we can ask Melvin about someplace to go swimming. At least we'd smell better afterward."

Kat opens her eyes and takes a swig of juice. "We stink," she pronounces. "Like terror and sex."

Heat floods my cheeks. "Katy . . ."

She squeezes my knee. "I love making you blush, Anna babe." She sticks out her tongue at me. "This dharma bum business is hard work."

"I guess the path to enlightenment is never easy."

"Yeah." Katy laughs. "But I didn't count on a bear."

14

Drunk as a hoot owl,
writing letters
by thunderstorm.
—Jack Kerouac

I'm still not sure if I'm getting closer to figuring out God's love. One minute I can see God in everything—in Katy, in prayers of desperation, even in the grizzly bear. Other times it seems this trip is showing me that there is nothing personal at all about God—that if he exists, he is indifferent to our actions and inactions.

Or possibly it's like Kerouac was saying, and nothing is real except the illusion of reality. Nothing but the void, calling to me. Maybe, like Jack, I should just drink myself silly over these zen verses and revel in every contradiction, certain that underneath all the nonsense the truth lies glittering.

I'm too rational for that, though. I want to capture evidence of God—of his hypothetical love—and pin it down in a spreadsheet, rows and columns neat and orderly. I want to find the secret algorithm, assign it a symbol like the figure eight of infinity. I want to file it in a folder labeled FAITH and close the drawer, no more questions. No more doubt.

The tent is salvageable. It's not easy, but Melvin the campground host comes by with his cheerful yellow cap and his satiny old-man jacket snapped up tight to his chin even as the two of us are sweating in our skirts and halter tops.

"Well, now, you gals look like you could use a tube of some of that tent goop, seal that thing back up." We tell him about the bear, and he nods, then chuckles amiably. "Bad news, bears," he says. "I'll be right back."

We inspect the damage, which is considerable, but not as bad as we feared. My sleeping bag is dead; high-tech acrylic fill spills out from at least a dozen rips. The big camping backpacks are ruined, but I can't imagine ever convincing Kat to use one again, anyway.

Melvin strolls back into camp, bearing two different tubes of seam sealer and tent repair glue. He also has some strips of patching material and two ice-cold sodas.

I crack open the can of pop and read the directions on the back of one of the tubes. "Melvin, you are a savior." He's actually kind of a weirdo, but thanks to him, we may have a place to sleep.

He waves his hand bashfully and ambles away, while we set to work, sweating and hoping.

Finally, Kat sighs. "You want to find a restaurant and get something to eat?"

My stomach growls. "I don't know, Katy, I'm so stinky and yucky."

Kat slams the car door and tackles me in a hug—the kind of hug that prior to the last twenty-four hours I would have called a bear hug. "You are dirty and delicious," she whispers into my hair.

My breath gets trapped somewhere in my poorly functioning lungs, and I sound like a strangled parrot. I pull away. "Showers," I say. "Let's get clean and then find a place to eat."

I pick up my phone from the picnic table and see there's a voice-mail message. "Seth and the guys," I say as I listen, only realizing afterward how I turned away from Kat, like it was a secret. Like it was something to hide.

"They're here," I say, hanging up the phone. "They want to meet us for dinner at that little restaurant up the road."

"When?"

"Right now. Showers first, though." My filthiness bothers me now more than ever.

"Well, let's go then," says Kat, and she tosses me the car keys. Shower and food. Impending heaven. With a side of boys.

An hour later, we're showered and seated in a big pine booth, heaping plates of burgers and waffle fries in front of us. Above our heads hangs a huge bearskin, and I keep sneaking nervous glances at it. I'm a traitor to the bear on the mountain who spared my life, sitting here below the pelt of his dead brother. My guilt weighs more than my burger and sinks to the bottom of my stomach. Please, Bear, don't go back there. Don't get yourself destroyed.

Beside me, Katy talks and laughs brightly, telling stories about our travels, talking about her art "exhibition," all wit and charm. She sparkles under the attention of the four boys. I lean back against the wooden booth and let the conversation flow around me.

Seth breaks in, and his smile is for me alone. "How long have you been up here?"

I tilt my head to one side and think. "A few days, I guess. We were going to go backpacking. Well, we *did* go backpacking, but . . . a grizzly ate all our stuff, so we had to hike back out."

The table falls quiet; all eyes are on me, attentive and eager to hear the story. "It's kind of embarrassing, actually," I stammer, the words faltering under their gaze. "I mean, we were stupid."

There is a chorus of questions, and my face gets hot. There is no way I can tell this story as it really happened. "We left our packs on the ground in the cooking area, and . . . um, we went back to the tent site for a while . . ."

I must look like such an idiot. Salvage this, Anna. Tell the story. I take a breath. "While we were hanging out, a bear got into our packs and destroyed all of our stuff. It was scary."

Lame, Anna.

Katy laughs. "Anna leaves out the part where this huge freaking bear charges like right at us, all stinking and hot and snorting and crazy-eyed, and she jumps in front of me and stares down the beast like she's made of awesome. *Twice* that thing charged at us, and twice Anna stood her ground, while I was a blubbering mess."

Her dark blue eyes shine with admiration as she tells it, and she throws an impulsive arm around my neck and squeezes tightly.

"She talked to it, too, and this monster-bear looked right into her soul. He must have decided she was like his long-lost bear sister or something because he left us alone." She smiles and shoots me a wicked look, and I see what's coming. "Oh, and did I mention we were both completely naked at the time?"

"Katy!" I duck my head, but I can hear Seth laughing and it's okay. Everything's okay.

"Naked Bear Warrior Princesses!" says Zane, and a cheer rises up all around us. Nobody asks why we were naked; nobody cares. I smile and exhale.

I barely notice when Seth slides his arm around me. "She must be quite a trip to be around all the time," he says, nodding at Kat, who is telling another story, one in which I play no part.

I nod. "Katy? Yeah, she's awesome."

"You guys been friends long?"

Friends. Yes, we've been friends for a long time. "Yeah, ages and ages. Kat knows me better than anyone else on earth." My heart skips a little when I say it, and I squeeze her hand under the table. She slides her finger lightly across the palm of my hand and up the inside of my wrist, tracing designs on my skin; my breath catches in my throat.

"We're on a pilgrimage," I blurt. What a thing to say.

Seth moves his arm across my upper back and then lets it linger there, his hand on the back of my neck. It almost feels possessive, and I bristle a little even as I feel myself melting under the heat of his skin. He smells good—fresh and clean, with just a hint of something musky and dark.

"A pilgrimage? Awesome. Where are you going?"

I squirm under the dueling attentions of Katy and Seth's hands, though both of them seem unaware of the other. "Well, I guess we don't really know yet, do we, Kat?"

Kat turns away from the rapt eyes of Zane. "We don't know what?"

"Where we're headed after we see the shaman."

"Oh, yeah," says Kat, nodding back at the others. "We're using bibliomancy to determine our course."

That's my word, my idea. I frown.

"Get the book, babe," says Kat, pulling her hand away and holding it out. "I'll flip and you choose, and we'll decide this right here and now."

I can still feel the thrill of Kat's touch; the absence of it fills me with an almost palpable yearning, while Seth's hand is heavy on the back of my neck. His soft, ocean-colored eyes search for mine.

"What book are you using?" His fingers drift upward, twining into my hair, leaving a path of heat in their wake.

"Kerouac. *The Dharma Bums*." The words catch in my throat. "We're searching . . ." My eyes are trapped by his; I can't look away. "For God, I guess." I feel my face getting warm, and I pull away, ducking down gratefully to grab my pack from under the table, removing the book from its pocket.

"You know, acid can be a great way to have a spiritual experience, if you're open to that kind of thing," says Seth, running his hand through his own hair—the hand left empty by my sudden movement. "I mean, I don't know if you would be interested in tripping, but if you were . . ."

"I have to use the restroom," Kat says. "Anna?" Her eyes are full of secret meaning, and I nod.

Seth slides out of my end of the booth, while Zane and

the two other boys clamber out of their end to let Katy scoot out. The restroom is a single occupancy, but she drags me in behind her anyway.

"What's up, Katy Kat?" My tone is nonchalant, but I can still feel the weight of Seth's hand on my neck, can still feel the way the two of them were touching me at the same time, tugging me in opposite directions.

Kat leans against the wall, her eyes downcast. Her dark hair is shiny and wavy, fresh from the shower, and I want to touch her. I want to. I take a step closer, but Kat doesn't look up. I can't.

"It's those boys," says Kat. "They want to sleep with us."

"Boys are like that, I guess."

"Well?" She looks up at me finally, her eyes full of misery. "Do we want to sleep with them?"

I think for a minute. In a way, yes, I want to go out there and lean into this tow-headed boy, breathe in his musky smell, and see where things lead. I like him. I'm . . . *attracted* to him.

"You and I could just be best friends, I guess," says Kat, still looking at the floor. She sighs. "Oh, Anna, I don't know what I want. This is so messed up."

I reach for her; I tuck a dark strand of her hair behind one ear, lean in to kiss her gently. She's tense, coiled tightly, as if to spring. Or to run away.

She squishes her face up close to mine, her nose touching my nose. "I don't want to share."

"Okay." I can't focus. We're too close.

"But what about this acid business?"

I shake my head, even though it's on our list. "I don't think it's a good idea."

Kat bites her lip. "I'm not sure. It could be really cool, but what if we trip with them and it turns into this big seduction ploy and we fall for it and everything tumbles down and falls apart and we don't even have each other anymore?"

"That wouldn't happen." Would it?

"But do you really love me, Anna? Do you? You never tell me anything." She takes a breath and then slaps both hands over her mouth. Her eyes are wide above her fingers, which slowly part to form a small gap through which she whispers. "Oh, god. Forget I ever said anything so lame in my life."

I laugh, sorry to find humor in her pain, but relieved, too. "So we're agreed—no acid. And Katy. I'm not going to drop you and sleep with the first pretty hippie boy who happens to pick me up on a psychedelic bus."

In her eyes, a sliver of hope. "You *do* love me. More than this Seth character?"

Why does this have to be so complicated? "I like him."

"Oh, fine. But do I get you to myself or what?" She slides her hands into my pockets, tugging my skirt down over my hip bones. Her thumb traces the outline of my tattoo.

"Katy!" My knees threaten to buckle. "We should go back. We've been in here forever; they're going to wonder what the hell we're doing."

"Let them wonder," she says, but she unlocks the door.

The boys barely seem to notice our return. They are in the middle of a spirited conversation about haircuts with the clean-cut bartender and a guy at the bar with a strange mullet.

"Yeah, I never get a haircut!" Bo says, shaking his head of thick black dreadlocks at the man. "Scary shit happens in the barber shop."

The boys laugh uproariously. We pay for our food and make our way back out to the parking lot, where I stand in wonder with my head tilted back. There are so many stars I can't help but contemplate infinity.

"You two staying over at Devil's Creek, then?" says Seth. His hand on the small of my back startles me, and I slip away, out of his grasp.

Zane opens the driver's door of the bus and fiddles with his keys. "We could maybe join you tonight, have a fire or something?"

We mill around a bit in uncertain groupings—the boys orbiting nearby but tripped up by our closeness, by Kat's arm linked in mine. Kat smiles at Zane and shrugs. "Sure, you guys are welcome to hang out." She winks at me. "But, you know..." She nods to Seth and Zane, "I mean, Anna and I . . ." She raises her eyebrows.

Seth nods slowly, comprehension dawning. "It's cool, Kat. We get it."

Zane climbs in behind the wheel, looking a little flustered. "Yeah, okay. Got it."

Kat laughs and sidles up to him. "Of course we still want you to come over," she says, pulling his hand toward her and writing on it with my purple pen. "That's our campsite. We'll meet you there." I'm the only one who sees her slip a Good Lock key behind the front seat.

"What if they never find it?" I ask on the ride back to the campground.

"That's the point, babe. You're not the only one trying to have faith."

At Devil's Creek, Bo and Frankie go off to buy a couple of bundles of firewood from Melvin, while Kat shows Zane and Seth how we fixed the tent. I sit on the picnic table and write in my journal, trying to get down the day's events before they swirl out of my memory forever.

"You writing a book or something?" says Seth. He leans over my shoulder, and I move my arm a bit so he can't see.

I scrutinize his tone for any hint of mocking but find only curiosity and interest. "I don't really know. I just write. I always have. I write down what happens, and I write down my thoughts, and I write things that are made up, pieces of stories, I guess." I close my notebook before he can ask to see it.

"You could write a book about your traveling, about you and Kat. Your adventures and stuff. Like that bear, I mean. That's a good story." He smiles, warm and inviting.

A tiny part of me would like for what he says to be true.

"What about you? What's your story?"

It's his turn to shrug. "We're just guys, you know. We don't have much of a story. Well, me and Zane knew each other from high school, and Bo and Frankie we met out in Oregon. We worked all winter together at this little brew pub on the coast. We planned to work there this summer, too, but then Zane got his bus running again, and we heard about this band called Selective Silence, and the pub business was slow, so we took off for a ramble. We're just . . . on the bus, I guess."

He shrugs in an entirely different way than I do. A way that seems humble and shy. I wonder about him. What is his family like? Is he going to go to college? What does he dream of? "Do you think it's silly, this pilgrimage thing?" I blurt out. The question surprises me. He doesn't speak right away, and more words tumble out. "I mean, you don't have to answer that. I don't even know what *I* think of it."

He nods. "No, it's cool. I guess...I think it's a good idea to examine your beliefs. I went through this pretty heavy paganism period. I was way into that shit." He shrugs again. "My mom is Wiccan. My little brother has become a born-again Christian or something. I don't know, really, but he's always going on about me accepting Jesus as my personal savior." He flashes me a vaguely apologetic look. "It makes me feel like I'm watching the home shopping network, you know? Now, for a limited time only, Jesus! Call now, and we'll throw in the whole Trinity!"

I smile. "My dad's a minister," I say, and then I want to take it back. *Nice*, Anna. Now he'll feel embarrassed.

"So you know where I'm coming from," he says, smiling. "At least on some level." He folds his hands on the table in front of him. His fingers are slender, like a pianist's. "I think I'm an atheist, but I'm not brave enough to say so all the time. In case I'm wrong, you know."

I know. I stuff my journal back into my backpack and turn to him, my knees touching his under the table. "I'm glad we're here. I'm glad you're here. I'm just . . . glad." Oh god, I'm such a dork.

We set up the comfy camp chairs around the fire, and Bo drags the picnic table closer while Frankie and Zane build up a good blaze. "Thanks for forcing me to abandon those missionaries, Anna," says Kat, who sits cross-legged in the green chair. She gestures around our circle. "It's like everything happens for a reason or something like that."

"Anna, do you have your book? You could choose where we all go next," says Seth from his spot beside me.

"It's right here." I dig through my pack in the firelight, searching for the book, but it's not in its usual place. My hands become more frantic as I experience a sick sense of déjà vu. "Guys, did I take the book out in the restaurant?" I remember leaning down under the table to take it out, and then . . . what? What happened next?

"I don't know," says Seth. "You and Katy went to the restroom, and then when you came back, I can't remember. Didn't we just pay and leave?"

"The waitress had already cleared the table when they got back," says Zane, "because she asked if we thought the girls were done, and we had her wrap up their leftovers. Remember?"

This is so uncool. That book is our guide. "We didn't get the leftovers, either," I say, racking my brain. Bo hands me a joint, and I hit it without really thinking; then I regret it as the spiraling haze makes its way through my core, wrapping itself around my anxiety like a coiling serpent.

"Well, let's go back and get it!" says Zane. "I'm sure they wouldn't throw it away!"

"We don't all have to go back," says Seth. "Maybe Anna and I could go, and the rest of you stay here." He stops and shrugs. "I mean, or I could go myself, if that would be better, or . . ." He trails off.

I stand up. I want the book back, in my hands. I want my brain back, without this fuzzy spiral. I want . . . *Katy*. I turn to her, take her hand across the distance between our chairs. "I'm sorry, Kat. I'm such an idiot. I'll get the book back."

She smiles, but there's something sad or wistful about her eyes. "It's okay, Anna babe. Go with Seth. We'll be all right here."

I gather my backpack to my chest. Everything about this moment seems crucial, as though a huge tragedy is lurking in the wings, waiting for us to get caught without our talisman.

Seth and I climb into Katy's car, and I shove my backpack into the space between the seats. As I shift into reverse, ready to steer around the big blue bus, my elbow knocks the pack into the backseat.

"Shit." I reach around to scoop up the stuff behind the passenger seat and shove everything back into my bag. It's totally random junk—a tampon, my cell phone, pens and pencils, a tube of chapstick.

"You're really worried about this book, aren't you?" Seth's proximity startles me; I can actually feel his breath on my cheek. I pull back into the driver's seat, and he shifts over so that he's also sitting up straight. I can hear the soft sighs of his breathing, and it makes me sort of panicky.

"Yeah, the book. It's like . . . the reason we went on this trip, see. We did this paper on social change, and Kat's dad told us all about the beat poets, and we started reading this book together . . ." I'm rattling on, but then he leans in closer and lightly kisses my cheek, or really my neck, just below my ear. The tip of his tongue grazes my earlobe, and I pull away. My face burns.

"I'm sorry," he says quickly, putting his hands up. "I don't know why I kissed you, it's just . . ." He laughs nervously. "You don't *seem* like a lesbian."

"I'm not a lesbian," I say. "Or, I mean, maybe I am. I don't know, I guess I think that's like calling myself a cat person when I've never owned a dog, you know?" We're quiet for a minute, and then I clear my throat. "I like you, too, though. And . . . you know, if it weren't for Katy . . ." I don't know what else to say. How stupid is this? Shouldn't I know, one way or the other? Shouldn't I *be* one way or the other? How do people manage to make things work out so that they only ever fall for people in one chromosomal category— or do they just ignore it when it doesn't work that way?

He nods in the darkness; I can't see him, but I feel the movement.

"I get it," he says. Then, after a long pause, "I've thought about being bi, too."

Bi. Another label, this one with a whole different set of connotations. Greedy, indecisive, sex maniac. Enough of this. I'm sick of analyzing my sex life.

"Ugh, I wish I hadn't smoked that joint Bo passed around. Everything's all blurry in my head."

There's another silence as both of us try to think back over the evening, and in the middle of the silence, I hear a strange sound—a sound like somebody calling my name from a great distance. "Did you hear that?"

"Hear what?" We sit quietly for a moment, listening carefully over the sound of the engine, and then it comes again, a tiny little voice, shouting.

"Anna!"

"What the . . ." I look in the rearview mirror nervously. "You can hear that, right?"

"Um, yeah, I heard something." He fishes around in the backseat. "It's coming from . . . here!" He pulls my cell phone out of the front pocket of my backpack and hands it to me.

"Anna, are you there?" shouts the tiny voice. My father's voice. Coming out of the phone. I must have accidentally speed-dialed him when I was gathering up the stuff that fell on the floor. Which means that my dad . . .

"Oh, god." I stab frantically at the End button, terminating the call. "Oh my god, I just called my dad and then talked about . . . what did we talk about?"

Suddenly the phone rings in my hand, and I punch the Off button, panicking. "Tell me what we talked about!" I'm practically screaming.

Seth points out the window. "Um, you just missed the diner," he says.

"Goddamn it!" I pull off on a dark side road, but instead of turning around and heading back, I drive all the way in, through the trees, to a little brown gate. I sit there with my head resting on the steering wheel. "Tell me I did not just talk about having sex with Katy and smoking weed while on the phone with my father."

Seth pats my arm. "Maybe he didn't hear that part."

"What am I going to do, though? If I call him back, it'll be so awkward. But if I *don't* call him back, he'll probably call the police, search-and-rescue teams, oh *god*." I whimper. What has happened to my life? Everything's out of control.

"Look, let's go back to the restaurant, find your book, and then we'll worry about it. He's not going to get the search-and-rescue team after us *this* fast, is he?"

I sigh. "Probably not." I lean back against my seat and turn to Seth, who is vaguely illuminated by the dashboard lights. "I really did say something about me and Katy, didn't I?"

Seth frowns. "Damn. I think *I* did, actually. I think I said you didn't seem like a lesbian."

Hopeless. My father is probably right this instant having a heart attack either because he believes his only daughter is a sexual deviant or because he believes his only daughter is in mortal danger. "Can you drive?" I'm so shaky.

"Sure," he says, and opens his door. We walk around the outside of the car and meet right in front, in the path of the headlights. For a second I feel pinned here, between the car and this gate, trapped and lost. Without really thinking about what I'm doing, I step in close and lean against Seth, my face in his chest. I'm lost. I'm empty and aimless, so light and insubstantial that I'm sure I'll scatter, piece by ir-retrievable piece, into the wind.

"I need to get Katy's book." He puts his arms around me awkwardly. "I'm supposed to be the one who keeps it all together."

I breathe in his smell, anchor myself on his heartbeat. This is so different from holding Kat—his body thin and roped with wiry muscles. I look up at that unruly hair that gives him a boyish look even without his charming smile.

It's not a decision. It just happens. I stretch up with my head tilted back to kiss him. My heart quickens as his arms tighten around me.

Seth tastes different, too; his tongue moves in my mouth differently. I kiss him hungrily, as though I can pull some substance from his body, some solidity to fill this desperate vacancy in me, to keep me here. He presses me even closer, and my hand drifts to his jeans with a will of its own, coax-ing a surprised gasp out of him. I've never touched a boy like this.

"Whoa," he says, breathing hard. I slide my hand inside his pants. Who is doing this? Another Anna—a crazy, des-perate girl who has completely lost her mind. A traitorous wreck of a girl. The girl who dares? Not a girl who cares. But I don't stop.

"Oh, wow, Anna. *Oh.*" Seth's breathing is ragged, and I feel somehow powerful, knowing it's me he wants. Knowing that I control how much of me he gets.

I look up at him, at his face illuminated by the head-lights. He smiles, kind and sincere. And puzzled. I don't have an answer for him. I have nothing. Another Anna's fingers work the button out of its loop, separate the two halves of his zipper. "I'm sorry," I whisper, ducking down. I'm sorry for him because I don't love him.

And I'm sorry for Katy because I do. Love her.

Seth gasps again, puts his hand on my chin, lifting my face up to look at him.

"You're beautiful," he says, his voice a raspy whisper. "I . . . I'm not sure about this."

"Come away from the headlights," I say, and I pull him into the shadows.

When we return, book in hand, Kat knows something is wrong right away. I can't very well tell her all of what's wrong, so I launch into an abbreviated version of the accidental dialing. "What should I do? Should I call him, or pretend like nothing happened and hope he doesn't send out a search party?"

She squeezes my hand tightly. "Your dad is going to freak out, isn't he?"

I step away from her, a single step. I stink of boy. I've ruined everything, and why? I fucked up; that's the only answer—I'm sick or something, sabotaging everything we have as soon as it gets a little serious. As soon as it gets a little real.

"Text him," says Kat. "Just say, 'Oops, my pocket dialed ya! Everything's fine!' Then turn your phone off right away and deal with the fallout later." She's so positive that everything will work out, so hopeful. But I'm miserable.

Okay, I can do this. Assume that he didn't hear anything, send him a brightly cheerful and innocent text message that will let him know I'm okay. I turn on the phone. New voice mail. Oh, god. Slowly, I bring the phone up to my ear.

"Anna? Anna, this is dad. Um. Your phone called me, I think. I was just checking to make sure you're all right. I heard . . . a boy. And . . . well, I think maybe we should talk. I'm worried about you, Anna. Call me. Please."

"Damn it, he totally heard." I hand the phone to Kat, and she holds it up to her ear. "Tell me what to do."

"Well, I'd say he sounds more concerned than angry," she says, handing it back. "And wow, that was like, the most I've heard him say in forever."

Zane sidles over, grinning. "Dudes, I have an awesome plan for the evening."

I smile at Zane and nod, distracted by a thought. "Wait, he *does* sound concerned, doesn't he?" And it's true. Not only is my dad actually stringing multiple words together, but the tone! I listen to the message again, my eyes getting wider. "His *voice!*"

I push the phone toward Kat. "Listen!" I can barely contain myself. "It's his old voice again, isn't it?" The voice of my childhood.

"It's close," says Kat, smiling.

"What's going on?" says Seth. He looks back and forth between us, his charming mouth twisting into a puzzled grin. "Anna, you look so happy."

"We're gonna drop some acid," says Zane. "That should make everyone happy."

"I *am* happy," I say. I could almost grab Seth and Zane and Kat—throw my arms around all of them and just *squeeze*. "I'm going to call my dad!" I put the phone up to my ear and listen to the message one more time. His golden voice, the voice that would mesmerize an entire congregation . . . I can't help myself. I twirl in a circle.

"Do you think that's a good idea?" says Kat. She puts a hand on my arm to steady me, but I spin away. Sure, it's not going to be easy talking to him. He's upset, but even *that* is an improvement over silence. Isn't it?

"It's always a good idea," says Zane. He pulls a tin of mints from his pocket and pops one into his mouth, then passes them around. I take a mint and laugh.

"This is crazy," I say, and I hold the phone to Zane's ear, as if it will mean anything to him. "My father's voice—listen!" Zane listens obediently, raising his eyebrows at Kat.

She smiles and shakes her head. "Anna's dad has had a hard time since her mom died. Hey, thanks," she says, taking a mint and passing the tin to Seth. "This is the first time he's really spoken much since the fire." She reaches for *The*

Dharma Bums, still clutched in my free hand. "I'm so glad you got this back, Anna babe. Now we can figure out where we're going." She flips through the pages rapidly. "Here, Anna, pick a spot."

I dial my dad's number. I feel certain that everything will be fine, now that we've got the book back, now that my dad has his voice back, now that I know that being with Seth isn't what I really want. I put the phone up to my ear and stick my finger into the book.

"Um, Zane?" says Seth. He hands the mints back.

"Hey, Dad," I say. "Yeah, I got your message."

For a while it's hard to focus on his actual words. I'm entranced by his voice. "Anna?" he says. "I'm worried about you, baby."

Katy points to the spot on the page next to my finger and shows it to Zane. He reads out loud.

"'. . . finally northern Washington on the farm of a friend in the Nooksack Valley . . .'"

"Wow," says Zane. "That's really weird that you actually chose the exact name of a place."

My father keeps talking—my attention divides down the center into two boxes, like a split-screen movie. "I know things haven't been easy," my dad says inside his box. "I wasn't there for you, Anna. I didn't think about how vulnerable you were, and then when this trip came up . . . well, I trusted Kat. She's always been a good friend, even without being a believer . . ."

In the other box, Zane is still reading the names of real places in northern Washington. "'. . . The names like *Nooksack* and *Mount Baker National Forest* . . .'"

I shift my attention, letting my father's words sink in. Wait, is he blaming Kat for all this? Because she's not a believer? "It's not that I blame Katy, not entirely," he says, his voice undulating into the rhythm of one of his sermons. "Our world is immoral, and I know that influence is hard to resist, especially when you're young . . ."

"Dad, it's not like that, okay? This is not about me being led astray by the world." I lower my voice, and in the other box, everyone looks away, although of course they're listening, too. "I'm not *vulnerable*."

"I'm still disappointed in you, Anna. The drugs, the . . . *experimenting* . . . but I blame myself, primarily. I wasn't able to give you the kind of guidance you needed." He goes on, and even though I'm listening to my father speak to me about my sex life—even as he trivializes everything I've started to accept about myself and my feelings for Kat, as he uses words like *misguided* and *naive* to describe my state of mind—I'm still amazed to hear him talking at all. It hurts—I feel terrible for disappointing him—but beneath that is so much relief that he even has the capacity again to be disappointed.

"I'm sorry," I say, but I'm not sure if I'm sorry for real or if I'm only sorry that he overheard.

"I want you to be happy, that's all," my dad says. "You'll think about coming back home, like I said?"

"Okay, Dad. I'll think about it."

"I love you, no matter what." He never says that—only my mom said that.

But I can't say it back. I hang up, feeling strangely light-headed. "Hey, guys," I say, and it's like every emotion in the universe collides in a lump in the back of my throat. The boys exchange a look and go off to busy themselves with the fire.

"Kerouac says we're going to the Nooksack Valley!" says Kat. She touches the side of my face, sweeps her thumb gently across the little spill of tears on my cheek, and I lean into her hand and close my eyes.

"He heard everything," I say, the words sticking to the lump.

"Oh, babe." She puts her other arm around me and draws me in closer.

"It's okay, I think. Or it will be." I whisper into her hair.

There's no way I'm going to tell her that my dad thinks she's corrupting me. "He's disappointed, I guess." I take a deep breath and pull back so I can look her in the eyes.

"Does he hate me now?" She bites her bottom lip, and I know how much it would hurt her to know. I feel another twinge of guilt about what happened with Seth.

"Of course not, Katy. He loves you like a second daughter." I sigh. "I wonder how he found his voice back."

Kat squeezes my hand. "The same way you did."

"Am I different?" I think maybe yes, but maybe no.

"*So* different," says Kat. "Don't you remember when I had to do your homework for you because you were such a zombie you couldn't remember the numbers from the math problem long enough to copy them into your notebook? Every day it's like you're waking up, like I see a little more of who you used to be." She grins. "Maybe your dad just needed a little waking up, too."

The fire flickers, and we all settle in quietly to watch the flames. Frankie produces a big jug of red wine, and we pass it around in a nice, comfortable quiet.

"Acid is so awesome . . ." It's Zane who speaks at last, breaking our companionable silence.

Kat laughs. "Well, you guys can do all the acid you'd like, but count us out."

"Why?" says Zane. He and Seth exchange a quick look.

Kat twists her hair for a moment. "Okay. Well, you know how we're doing this dharma bum thing, right?"

Zane nods. I watch the firelight dance in Katy's eyes. Sitting here, warm and happy, I feel like all the pieces of the puzzle are already in place. It doesn't matter to me, at this moment, whether or not God is real. It doesn't matter what happened with Seth, or the situation with my dad, or any of it. And Katy is beautiful. I want to kiss her, right now, in the flickering warm light from the fire. In my mind I entertain thoughts that would make me blush if I weren't already flushed from the fire and the wine.

"It's like . . . everything is so perfect right now, with you guys, like you are perfect little dharma bums yourselves, right down to that jug of wine. And I don't want it to change." Kat draws her feet up into the chair, wraps her arms around her knees. "Plus, it's time for us to move on. I can feel it. We're headed up to northern Washington, to the Nooksack River. We've been here too long."

She feels exactly the same as I do. I close my eyes.

"I am empty and awake," I say aloud, and the words fall like drops of water, like pearls off a string broken loose on the dance floor, hitting the floor one by one and rolling, rolling across the room, seeking the unexplored corners where lovers are twining and shy girls sit curled around themselves waiting for the pearls to arrive, one by one, into their empty hands.

I open my eyes again, and the campfire wavers in front of me. Everyone is silent, staring into the flames.

"Um, so, Kat? Anna?" It's Zane, breaking the silence again. He sounds nervous.

I smile. The smile grows and spreads across my face, and I wonder when was the last time I smiled like this, so wide it almost aches.

Kat is smiling, too. "What is it, Zane?" Her words come out like a song.

"Are you guys okay?" he asks.

We both nod, and Zane looks relieved.

"It's just . . . there was acid in those mints we all ate. I thought . . . I thought you knew. I mean, I had just said that we were going to trip, and nobody said anything really, so I handed it out, and you all took some, and . . . I really wasn't trying to be a jerk, I promise." He looks pained.

Kat looks thoughtful for a moment. "Well, I did kind of wonder why suddenly everything seemed sort of . . . *deep*." She laughs.

"*Meaningful*," I say softly. My smile remains.

"Is this your first trip?" Seth says.

I roll my head to one side slowly, thinking about the question. "I wonder what it would be like to spend your whole life like this," I say. "I mean, I don't think I'd want to, but I wonder if this is how the shaman feels?"

"Well? Is it your first trip?" Seth is talking. To me.

"What?" I'm vaguely annoyed that he's asking me this question again and again. Shouldn't he just know the answer? Katy knows. I turn to Kat and give her a grateful smile, but she's turned away from me, in deep conversation with Zane. Inside my brain, I hear a little click—a switch is thrown, and like a train car following the tracks, I feel myself veer off to one side and plummet downward, underground. I sink into my chair and cross my arms across my chest, trying to hold in the feelings.

"I asked you if you had tripped before." Seth doesn't seem to realize that he has said the same thing like fifty million times.

"Look at them over there," I say, my voice dark. "Looks like they're about to hop into bed together." Seth chuckles nervously. I scowl.

The chair I felt blissfully at one with a few moments ago has now become a prison—a torture device designed to keep me a captive to this vision of betrayal. The weight of my own treachery dwindles as my mood plummets—in my heart I was always true to her, I'm sure of it.

Kat is laughing at something Zane is saying; I can't hear them above the noise of blood pumping in my ears. The fire at my feet suddenly shifts and grows, looming ominously with its fiery tongues, and the sulfurous light it casts on Zane's face makes me draw back in horror and amazement.

"He looks like a demonic lion." I don't intend for anyone to hear, but then I realize that I'm actually making a scene, that those words were louder than I meant them to be. Still, I'm unable to stop myself from screaming when Zane's wild mane of hair seems to grow thick and lustrous around his face—thick, unwieldy yellow hair with tongues of fire interwoven.

Everyone stares at me. "Anna?" Kat leans closer, and I squeeze my eyes shut in case this grotesque vision transforms Katy's beauty into something evil as well.

"I can't look at you, Katy Kat! I can't bear it!" I cover my eyes tightly with my hands.

Arms wrap around me; voices croon into my ears.

"Hush, hush, hush . . ."

"It's okay, it's okay . . ."

"It's beautiful . . ."

"It's okay, it's beautiful, hush, hush, hush . . ."

Their soothing refrain melts into a swishing sound—wind fluttering through poplar leaves, and Katy's lips brush lightly across my fingers pressed tightly against my eyelids; all of the molecules shuffle back into their proper order again, and I dare to look up at Kat.

Her face is as radiant as ever, and although her eyes are black holes and the edges of her face glow with a tiny corona, the hideous phantasmagorical scene of a moment ago appears to be gone.

"I'm okay," I say. My voice is a thin little wisp. I feel stupid. The bad trip girl, the one who freaked out and thought the sky was falling.

I force a laugh. "You totally looked like the devil," I say to Zane. "Like a cross between the devil and a lion." Saying it out loud seems to steal the power away from the image, but I notice the dark shadows from the firelight that gather underneath his eyes and in his hair, and I shiver a little.

He smiles, but he shakes his mane a little and says, "Whoa. What if I *am* the devil and a lion?" and then he roars and dances. He paws at the air and stalks like a lion creeping through the veldt, and I shiver at the predatory look in his eyes. I feel myself unraveling again, the edges of my sanity nothing but ragged loops of string, getting shorter and shorter.

"STOP!" I cover my eyes again.

"Let's go for a walk, Anna," says Kat, and I peel myself up from my chair to follow her through the darkness. She leads and I stumble behind, fixing my eyes on the beam of her flashlight, which sweeps ahead of us and draws the dark in close around us. I reach out one hand and get a fistful of her shirt.

Kat laughs. "WHOOO! WHOOO!" she hoots. "Do you remember that owl, when we were kids?"

"I wanna go now, Katy. Can we? I want to get away from that lion creep who is trying to take you away from me."

"Me? You think Zane is taking *me* away? What about you and Seth?"

The ground beneath my feet is moving; I'm sure of it. She doesn't know. She can't know. No. The ground isn't moving, not exactly. It's more like . . . like I can feel the movement of the earth itself, like the slow rotation of the planet is suddenly accelerated. Or maybe I've actually slowed down in time enough that the movement of rotation and orbit just *feels* fast. I stop in the middle of the small dirt path and lie down, pressing my ear to the soil. The sounds that greet my ear are so ancient, so massive, I know I must be listening to the formation of rocks, the slow trickling of underground rivers, the blind squirmings of creatures far below the surface.

"I can hear the metamorphosis."

Kat stops in the trail and turns, shining her light on me. "You can hear *what*?"

"The metamorphosis. Of the rocks. Of the earth." I roll over onto my back. "Of myself."

Kat sits, cross-legged, near my head. "Are you going to turn into a big grasshopper or something?"

"Seriously, Katy, there are things I need to say."

"Yeah." I can hear her breathing, and then she whispers, "There are things I need to hear."

I don't know how long I lie there without speaking, but

I'm fairly certain it's long enough for us to become sedimentary rock formations here on the trail. I want to tell her, mainly because I want her to reassure me. I want to tell her because I want to tell her everything, but I can't. These secrets could start with a trickle, but what if they become a torrent and crack us apart?

The earth spins. Magma cools, crystallizes. "You were right," I say.

"Damn straight I was." Kat's fingers weave into my hair, deftly combing and twining it into a thin braid. The sensation of each strand knitting together is so astonishing that I fall completely out of the world to ponder it.

"Right about what?" she says, when it becomes apparent that I'm not going to elaborate.

"Right about . . . everything." I close my eyes to enjoy the sparklers and sunbursts on my eyelids. Pleasant images, but just little empty distractions. "You're so smart, Katy Kat."

"You're really tripping hard, aren't you?"

"That's what I'm talking about." I feel the words slide back into place. "You were right about the acid. We totally should not have done this." Tears escape my eyes.

"Are you okay?" Kat leans down and kisses my forehead lightly, just a brush of lips and breath and love, and I can see the kiss through my eyelids—a burst of light peach and rose.

"No, that's what I'm saying. It's too much, too much to handle too soon." I roll over onto my side. "It's just . . . a lot of a lotness."

"A lot of a lotness?"

"You know. A lot of a lot. Ness."

"And God? Are you learning anything from this trip?"

I think for a long time, while she continues to braid my hair. "It's not working out that way." My words sound like they're coming out at the wrong speed. "But the lot of a lotness is sending me inside myself instead, and Katy . . . "
I wait for the words to revolve slowly toward me. "It's . . .

awfully . . . ugly . . . in . . . there." I sit up so Kat can reach the hair on the back of my head, her fingers twining and twining until my whole head is transformed, and then I turn to her and slowly smile, wearing a crown of coils.

Kat studies me with her dark eyes. "We should probably stay away from the boys for a while, hey?"

I nod, but I don't trust myself to open my mouth.

"All right." She stands up, then bends to haul me to my feet as well. "Let's go try to get a little sleep. It's going to get better, Anna babe. Ugliness is just a preface to true beauty."

I squeeze her hand and stumble after her toward the tent. I want to believe her.

15

You'd be surprised
how little I knew
Even up to yesterday
—Jack Kerouac

The hours pass, but not in any kind of real sleep. I turn and turn under the blanket, but I can't escape from this dream. Or not even a dream—more like an endless loop of film playing over and over—

> *my mother's face, lightly*
> *freckled, laughing soundlessly,*
> *her head thrown back.*

> *camera follows her eyes up*
> *to a green scarf spiraling*
> *into the dark blue sky.*

> *begin again.*

"You said we could ask him." I shiver in the night air and cross my arms over my chest. "I keep dreaming about her, and I'm sure it won't stop until I ask him."

"Well, but Anna, it's four in the morning. We can't just knock on the shaman's door and demand a meeting. I mean, can't you wait until the festival?" Seth and the rest of the guys are still hanging around the fire, which has settled into a comfortable bed of glowing coals. Zane sits, wrapped from his chin to his toes in a fuzzy red wool blanket, his eyes glued to the embers in front of him. He looks as though he hasn't moved a muscle in the last six hours.

Seth tries to lead me toward a chair by the fire. He holds one hand on the small of my back, and I hate it. "You're still tripping, Anna. You don't really need to see the shaman right *now*."

I shake my head, twisting away from his hands. I'm *not* still tripping. I suppose the acid isn't completely gone from my system, but my head is clear. "This is not about the drugs. This is about my mother," I say. His nearness petrifies me. I can't stay for the festival. I need to get far away from Seth before I ruin everything. My stomach clenches, and I take another step away. If it's not already too late, that is. "Seriously, Seth. Can we . . . can we please go?"

Zane shakes his mane of wild hair. "Anna, dude, sit down, please. Nobody is in any condition to drive right now."

I don't sit down; I can't sit down. I circle the fire, walking around the outside of the ring of chairs. Around and around, my brain circling relentlessly around the idea, the same way that green scarf had spiraled up into a sky the color of Katy's eyes.

"We could walk there, to the land where they're holding the festival," says Bo. "The waitress at the restaurant said the band has been there since midweek, hanging out, drumming and stuff."

"Wait, are we close?" I stop circling. "Can we walk to the shaman?"

"Sure," says Bo, "but it's kind of far. The road is just past the place we had dinner."

My face burns at the thought of that road. How was I to know that was the shaman's front yard? I shake my head. It doesn't matter; Seth doesn't matter.

Seth tries to talk me out of it. "It's a long walk," he says. "The shaman might not even be there, and besides, it's the middle of the night. What if the shaman won't see us?" He puts his hand on me again. "You're not thinking clearly, Anna babe." There's something ugly about his mouth when he's telling me no.

"Don't call me that." My voice is too sharp. "I'm sorry." I lure him away from the circle, start him toward the road so the rest of them will follow—disentangle themselves from their chairs like ancient, heroic trees extricating their roots from the soil and migrating. I take Seth's hand and squeeze. "Katy's the only one allowed to call me that." I laugh, and so does Seth, and it's okay for a moment, even though I can see the dark bubble of sadness that wells up in him when I take my hand away. This whole situation is sad. I need to be gone.

"Come on, you guys! Let's go see the shaman!" I traipse along the edge of the road with my ragged entourage, following the pale path of the pavement in starlight. We walk for what feels like forever, all of us quiet and soaked in wonder, full of whispered revelations and small observations.

It takes my breath away when we hear the drums. I know the boys talked earlier about the drumming, but I hadn't really expected it to be so powerful. I can feel my heart adjusting its rhythm to match the beat. Our steps fall into the measure as well, and even my thoughts shift into a meter that's like poetry, like song.

We slip past the little brown gate, following a well-worn footpath I hadn't noticed until now. Seth and I exchange a glance as we pass the place, but there's no room in this rapid rhythm for shame or sadness. There's a bounce in our steps, even before we hear the shaman's voice—an indescribable voice that shifts up the scale in eerie arpeggios and draws me, draws us all, toward it.

Up ahead there is a clearing, and in that old pasture-land we can see a little tent city—shelters in all shapes and colors, lights softly glowing in some of them. At the edge of the field, they've set up a small, circular stage. It is lit by a ring of tiki torches and some scattered candle-lamps. Around the stage, about fifteen or twenty people are sitting, cross-legged, on camping mats or sprawling on blankets and rugs. Along the periphery, more people are dancing—whirling their bodies in time to the drums, following the winding syllables of the shaman's voice.

The music is unending—a jam that keeps reinventing itself, reemerging in a new form. Sometimes the shaman sings; sometimes only drums. We sit together on the grass and listen. As we sit there, my head straightens out entirely—the lingering remainders of the acid melt away—leaving me with a feeling like the moment just after unpacking a suitcase, when everything is exactly where it belongs for once. I notice the precise moment the shaman disappears from the stage.

"Follow me," I whisper to Katy. The boys are oblivious. Bo and Frankie are dancing near the edge of the woods, and both Seth and Zane are completely entranced.

"Are you sure we shouldn't tell them?" Kat's voice is worried, but she hurries after me toward the dark woods. "Where are we going, anyway?"

"Into the woods," I say. "The shaman is waiting."

A thin layer of nerves buzzes along the surface of my skin as I approach the black edge of the forest, but my eyes are open wide; the darkness gives way a little at a time, reluctantly falling into shadows and shades of gray. I pick out an opening in the woods and find a trail, an uncertain smudge of charcoal in the inky blackness ahead of us.

Kat grips my arm. "Anna, no way." She pulls me back. "Please, don't make me go down that trail, not in the dark." Her voice cracks. "Can we at least bring the boys? Safety in numbers?" Her fingernails dig into my skin.

I hesitate, but there is a force compelling me, and I shake my head. "No. No boys." I step into the forest.

"Well, I'm with you," says Kat, twining her fingers into

mine and pulling me back for a moment, for a kiss that's like the bright color of bear grass in the sun. "You're not going anywhere without me."

Something in her tone makes me scared that she knows what happened with Seth. My chest contracts; my lungs feel as though the air has been vacuumed out of them. Around me the darkness is thick and strangling. I turn back to the trail without speaking, but I keep a tight grip on Katy's hand.

The trail is long enough to keep the Shaman's brightly painted teepee hidden from sight during the daylight, but once we round the last bend, we can see it glowing in the darkness, a curiously bright cone of canvas in a circle of flickering torches. Music still permeates the air. Even the torches seem to burn with the same rhythm.

"This is creepy," whispers Kat.

I hear singing coming from inside the tent—much softer, but the same singing we heard onstage. As before, the voice draws me. I approach the door flap and wonder how to knock. This thought makes me laugh, overcome with my own absurdity.

From within the teepee, the singing dissolves into an answering laugh. "Come in, then!" says a voice. "Don't be lurking outside my door."

My fingers grapple with the edge of the flap, and Katy and I duck inside.

"Wow, it's roomy," says Kat. She turns to the figure seated along the opposite side of the circular room on what appears to be a small futon. "Um, hi," she says, tugging me forward a little. "You must be the shaman. I'm Kat, and this is Anna."

The shaman's face is pleasant, joyful even. "A pleasure." That soft, strangely resonant voice again. The shaman's hands move lightly across the head of a small ceramic drum. The sound is soft and soothing. I breathe in time.

Kat twists her hair into pigtails as she talks. "Look,

I'm not sure how this works, or whatever, I mean, I know we're probably supposed to bring you tobacco or something or at least have an appointment, but we just . . . Anna had a dream about her mother. She wants to talk to her in the spirit world."

The shaman laughs softly. "No, she doesn't." A soft rhythm of taps on the drumhead, a ringing sound as thumbs strike the ceramic edge.

"What?" Kat's fingers stop their twisting. "She doesn't what?"

"She doesn't want to talk to her mother in the spirit world." The shaman's eyes study Kat for a moment and then shift once again to me. The effect is instantly sobering. A hand beckons me closer before returning to the drum. "Why are you here, Anna?"

I swallow, my throat dry. "I . . . I saw her scarf. She was laughing. I *miss* her."

The shaman's eyelids lower, a protracted blink. "I can feel your urgency, Anna. I can feel you seeking." Shadows falling across cheekbones. Eyes opening; for a moment they appear transparent. "Here." The shaman holds something out to me, a green shimmer tucked into a brown hand, a hand glowing with a warm light.

I reach out, take the piece of fabric, recognize it at once. "Where did you get this?"

The shaman's hands beckon upward, drum falling silent. "It came spiraling down out of the sky one day." In the quiet of the tent, the musical voice is honey seeping out of the comb, full and heavy and ambercolored. The sound fills the room, slows it all down.

I lift it to my nose and inhale the soft hints of jasmine from my mother's throat. It's impossible. A miracle?

"Can you prove that God exists?" The words are pulled from me.

The shaman laughs, a throaty chuckle.

"We've been looking everywhere," I say. "We made a

list. We need proof." I turn to Katy, realizing the truth as I do. "*I* need proof," I say.

The shaman's eyes grow suddenly fierce—dark and sharp like obsidian. "If you want to find proof of God's love, you can't go checking off a list, chasing after all these *things*, all these experiences you think will present evidence for you one way or the other. If you want proof, Anna, *you* have to be the proof. If you open up, you will not lose everything. You will find it."

My brain stalls. The honey of the shaman's voice has filled the teepee, slowed everything down until it stops. "This is my mother's scarf," I whisper.

"It's a shadow to comfort you."

"It smells like her."

"You won't stay for the festival, will you." It's not a question.

"I can't," I say.

"Be open," says the shaman. "You know what love is." A raised hand. Eyes close. We are dismissed.

The morning lingers on into early afternoon before we get moving. Seth heats water over the fire, and I watch him through my eyelashes, thinking about how weird it is to meet people like this, to get close to them, and then . . . they're gone. Will we ever see them again?

"Are you sure you won't stay for the festival?" says Seth, his voice soft in my ear.

I move away from him, feeling complicated. "Yeah, I can't . . . I can't stay here anymore." I can't be so close to him, is what it is. I can't look at him without getting confused. "Wanderlust, you know?" I look at him then, at that charming smile. I could almost kiss him, and the thought of that hurts on several levels.

He nods. "I'll miss you," he says.

"I'm sorry," I say.

That's it for good-byes, and it feels all right. The

shaman's words are tucked into a pocket inside me, mostly untouched. I wave at Seth through the open window as I back out of the spot, and he blows me a kiss. Kat squeezes my hand and turns up the music so that the sound drowns out the space of our leaving.

16

Useless, useless,
the heavy rain
Driving into the sea.
—Jack Kerouac

I worry the shaman's words like a hangnail while I drive, push-
ing into the setting sun, fleeing from a boy with a perfect smile
and the memory of Another Anna. No matter how fast I drive,
how many times I twist and tumble the words, I can't seem to
move forward.

A shadow to comfort me. Be open. You know what love is.

I know nothing.

"Campground!" Katy points at a brown sign with a
white silhouette of a tent.

At last. We've been driving forever, and I had just about
resigned myself to sleeping in the car.

"It's *free*, too!" Kat happily clutches her bag on her lap
and slides her feet into her sandals.

"Well, I sure wouldn't pay for it." Even in the dark, I can
see that the place is nothing more than a dusty field with a
little circle drive and some carved-up picnic tables scattered
around. Nasty words are spray-painted on the side of the outhouse. I stand with a hand on the trunk, watching the litter
tumble across the ground.

"It's windy," says Kat, her arms full of the blankets Melvin gave us to replace our wrecked sleeping bags. "And it
smells like rain."

All of the sites are on a slope, so all night we fight to keep from sliding into each other. I wake up while it's still gray dawn and chilly, blinking back feverish dreams of Seth and demon lions and a million kinds of betrayal. Suddenly a cold, wet drop of liquid hits me, right between the eyes. And then another. I sit up, the cold water driving the dreams out of my head. It's fucking raining. In our tent.

"Oh, no *way*." Every seam we gooped is leaking, while the bottom of the tent has proven waterproof enough to keep all the rainwater from running back out again, turning our tent into a lopsided kiddie pool. Kat and I are tangled in a damp jumble against the downhill wall of the tent, along with most of our stuff. "Hey, Katy? We've got a problem."

"So I've discovered." She sits up beside me, shivering. "My sketchbook," she says, and I can tell it's not good by her tone.

"Oh." She holds up the ruined pages and tries for a smile, but it's clear how miserable she is.

"Katy, I'm so sorry."

"Check the book," she says, and I pull *The Dharma Bums* out of the front pocket of my backpack. It's completely waterlogged, as is my notebook.

"I'll make coffee," I whisper. She doesn't respond. I lift the zipper on the soggy tent and step out into a muddy stream. The rain is letting up, but the damage is done. We're cold, wet, and homeless.

A few hours ago I would have given anything to stop driving, but now the road is once again my sanctuary, and I pack up the dripping camp with a melancholy resignation.

"What do we do?" My voice is tiny and uncertain. Kat and I sip coffee and stare at the smoldering log we tried to light on fire to warm us. I'm supposed to be the one who knows the answer to questions like that, the one who takes charge. But it's too much—our tent ruined, all our stuff soaking wet. We stand there, silent in our private miseries.

"Pack it up," says Kat. Her voice is tired and flat. "Nothing to stick around here for." She's right, but where should we go? We climb back into the car, and I peel the pages of the sopping wet book back until I find the passage about Mount Baker and the Nooksack River. Kat drives, which sets me on edge. The atmosphere in the car is not happy conversation or comfortable silence but a strained, desperate kind of heaviness that is only made worse by the gray sky and drizzling rain. I lean back against the headrest, my mood turning—disintegrating from sad to sullen to surly.

"We're going to need a new tent." I scowl. I have no energy for civility. "And that means no more money for anything fun."

"Well, you're the one who just *had* to go find yourself in the wilderness." Kat exits off the highway and pulls into the parking lot of a discount store.

"And *you're* the one who dragged me away from the cooking area before I had a chance to store the packs properly."

"You weren't exactly hard to convince." We glare at each other in the parked car.

Kat looks away first. "Are you coming in?" she says, her words clipped. It's clear she expects me to, but I just shrug and turn toward the window. I spent three weeks picking out the perfect tent for this trip; I don't want to go in there and pick out a cheap replacement.

Kat slams the driver's door and stalks off across the lot.

Of course I should sprint after her, but I'm stuck here, pinned by the weight of everything I can't say to her. I stab at the radio, trying to find a station that will come in clear, but all I can get is a trashy-loud morning show deejay yapping about some big reality radio show contest, and how the deadline is Friday the thirteenth.

Friday the thirteenth. Might as well be today, for all our luck. How could it get any worse? A wry laugh slips out. *Friday the thirteenth.* The thirteenth of July. My eighteenth birthday.

It's too much. The stupid tears take hold of me, pressing

all the space out of my throat until I'm forced to gasp, and with that gasp comes a shudder, and I let it go, rocking back and forth in the seat, crying until I'm spent.

There's a rapid knock on the driver's side door, and I look up, startled. It's Kat, holding a big cardboard box and a smaller plastic bag. I reach over and open the door for her.

"Anna, seriously, it's not the end of the world." Kat frowns at me. "You're making a scene."

I shake my head. "It's my birthday. It's almost my eighteenth birthday, and look at me! I'm pathetic. I'm . . ." My voice catches. I don't say the rest of it, of course—*I'm a horrible person who betrayed your trust and messed around with Seth. My dad thinks I'm misguided and thinks you're a bad influence.* "I miss my mom," I say instead.

Kat sighs. "Anna babe, of course you do. I miss her, too, if you really want to know. Now come on. Pull yourself together. We'll totally do something fun for your birthday." Her voice is still on the chilly side, but I allow her words to comfort me.

"Can we go to the ocean?" I sniffle.

She nods. "That's pretty much where we're headed."

"I'd like that." I wipe my eyes with a napkin I find in the glove compartment. "God, I'm sorry I'm such a mess, Katy." I pause, empty of excuses but feeling the need to explain anyway. "It just feels like one thing after another, you know?"

I'm about to ask about the new tent, about whether she found a new sketch pad, but my phone beeps. A text message. My father? The thought makes my stomach plummet, and I wonder what happened to my joy about his recovery. It seems to have been replaced with the realization of his disappointment in me. I rummage around in my backpack until I find my phone. "It's from Seth." I read the text, and it's so sweet it kind of makes me ache inside.

"Well? What does it say?" Kat raises her eyebrows.

I read the text again. It's no big deal, really. He says hi, and he says he's thinking about me, that he hopes everything will work out the way that will make me most happy. It's that part, though, that makes me shove the phone into my pocket. Whatever will make me happy. As if I know what that is.

"Um, he just says hi and hopes we're doing okay." It's not a lie, but I still feel a twinge of guilt and another twinge of annoyance at Kat for being nosy. I shouldn't have to share every detail of my life with her. Or feel bad if I don't. As soon as this thought occurs to me, I see how stupid I'm being, how irrational, but I can't shake the feeling even so.

I reach out for Kat's hand; it feels so far away and unfamiliar, like I have no right to reach for it. "Look, Katy, thanks for taking care of getting us a new tent. I'm sorry I kind of panicked. I feel so out of control, and . . ." I have no excuse.

"I know, I'm the same," says Kat, but she isn't. Then she smiles brightly. "Well, I got this tent for half price, and I bought you a new notebook, too. We'll find a campground somewhere in this Mount Baker area, set up some clotheslines, and hope our blankets will be dry by night." She shakes her head. "And if they're not, well, I don't know what we'll do."

My smile is weak. "I don't know, either. But Katy?"

"Yeah?"

"Can I drive?"

"Oh my god, thank you, yes." She pushes the keys into my hands.

I settle into the driver's seat and watch Katy climb into the passenger seat, the bump of her orange satchel against her legs. Who would have thought, a year ago, that this is where I would be, a week shy of my eighteenth birthday? A girl with a dead mom. A disappointment to my father. A thousand miles from home. Recovering from an acid trip. In love with a girl? And no longer able to put into words my reason for being here, in this car—on this journey.

About six hours later, we pull into the Mount Baker National Forest and find a little woodsy campsite hidden in the deep, mossy forest. Even in the midst of my gloomy mood, I'm entranced by the beauty of the place—the strong snowy dome of Mount Baker rising up in picturesque splendor, the trees standing ancient and wise in their thick, hanging coats of Spanish moss, the birds shrieking like insane toddlers. We string the clothesline that Kat bought around the trees and hang all our wet gear to dry. Kat moves with a sense of purpose around the camp, gathering wood for a fire, but I feel paralyzed. I sit at the picnic table with my damaged notebook and trace over the places where the ink smeared.

I read a story once about some aboriginal people in Australia who wished themselves dead. Like, they lay down on the rocks or the sand or whatever and just said, "Okay, that's enough." And their hearts stopped. For months after the fire, I tried to die like that, but it wouldn't work. My heart is stubborn, I guess. Or, more likely, my will is weak.

I mean, I know that sounds melodramatic. It's not that I wanted to die because my mom died. At least, it's not that simple. Everyone's mom dies eventually; I know that, while it sucks, it's not an insurmountable loss. It was everything else that was too much. I had to go to school, and I had to find a way to make all the sounds coming at me all day form themselves into words that I could copy down into notebooks and memorize. I had to put food into my body and dig out my winter boots when it got cold. And I could have managed, if that were all. But on top of that, people expected me to talk to them; they wanted to know what was next for me, what my plans were. Thinking about my nonexistent plans was what made me will my heart to stop beating.

This dark feeling looms over me again, and for the moment I try to push away the realization that despite the distraction of our stupid little road trip, I still have no plans, no path into the future. I take out my phone, tap out a message to my father.

What do I do next? I type, and I wonder if he has gone back to the church. I think about what Kat said, about how she misses my mother, too, and it occurs to me that the church was grieving the same as us—they lost not only my mother but their spiritual leader as well. They offered us so much. Cards, money, open arms. Dozens of heavy glass casserole pans full of "hot dish." They waited for us, gave us time to come back.

Will he go to them now? Will he persuade them to pray for me, for his lost sheep? The phone jumps in my hand, the soft beep that says I have an incoming text.

Come home, Anna, like I said on the phone. We can move forward together.

Kat stops on her way to the fire ring with a bundle of wood from the car, and raises an eyebrow. "Texting Seth?"

I tilt the phone toward me. "Oh. No. I will, though, you know. To reply to that message he sent earlier." I slide my finger across the screen while I continue to explain. "I'll tell him we're at Mount Baker. Keep in touch. You know."

Kat smiles, but her eyes are less than happy. "Hey," she says softly.

"Hey."

"Is this birthday thing a serious deal? Are you going to be okay?"

I shrug. "I mean, it's hard to think about my dad all alone, worried about me, asking me to come back home . . ."

"He wants you to come back home? You didn't tell me that."

"I know." I clear my throat. "He thinks we're making a mistake. He says . . . that sometimes this kind of thing happens, that people get confused and think . . ." I can't finish. I can't stand here, with Katy, and tell her this is meaningless.

"I *love* you, Anna." Kat's voice is soft but confident, no room for doubt. "I'm not a stupid phase, okay?"

I know; I know it's true. The words. They're right there in my mouth, but I can't say them. I want to tell her; I want to tell her everything that's inside me, but I can still hear my father's voice, the voice of my childhood, asking me to come home.

Kat sends me to the campground host for two more bundles of wood, and when I return, she's cleaning her gun. "You don't have to watch, but if I don't wipe it down now, it will rust." She doesn't look up.

Headlines chase across my brain: *Girl Shot While Cleaning Gun, Fatal Firearms Accident in Local Campground.* "I don't like it," I say.

"That isn't news to me." She holds the gun up in front of her and polishes it with a little gray rag.

I walk all the way around to the opposite side of the iron fire ring and drop the bundles of wood on the ground. "I don't even like the *idea* of it."

Kat sighs and looks up at me, through the dancing flames. "Look, Anna, I have this gun to defend myself. I shouldn't have to sit here and defend myself from *you*." She stuffs the rag into a small zipper bag and flips open the little spinny thing on the side of the gun—the place where you put the bullets. "Just come here and I'll show you."

"No way." I'm not getting any closer. "I told you, I don't *like* it." I take another step back. "I really wish you'd get rid of it, Katy. When I look at that thing, all I can see is a tragedy." All I can think about is losing her.

"It's not even loaded. I promise, Anna." She holds it out to me and spins the little chamber to show me it's empty.

"I don't care. Get rid of it, Kat. *Please.*"

"Fine, I was done, anyway." She sets the gun down on the picnic table while she seals the plastic bag, then stashes both in her satchel. "There. It's gone. Happy?"

"I meant get *rid* of it. For good." I'm not happy, and it's only partly because of the stupid gun. I stir the fire with a long stick, ducking backward as a shower of sparks flies up toward my face.

"Not gonna happen, Anna babe. It's all I have left of my

grandpa, you know? This gun is a part of practically every memory I have of him—holstered right at eye level when I was a little kid, or sometimes his entire belt would be curled up on top of the television cabinet, out of reach and so forbidden." She taps her toe against the long cardboard box on the ground next to the table. "So. Should we put this cheapo tent up and see if it can keep us dry?"

I shrug. "Might as well, even though the bedding will probably be wet going in." I'm tired of bickering. I'm tired of everything.

The rain incident not only ruined our things; it made us grumpy and short-tempered. Maybe it's because we aren't feeling well—both of us wake with scratchy throats and dull headaches—and maybe it's because it's hard to be homeless, even with a new tent. In any case, the mood lingers through several sticky, humid days of recuperating and lounging around camp.

"A motel room," says Kat, "with laundry facilities." She takes a bite of eggs and points her fork at me. "It could be your birthday present, babe. A shower, clean clothes, and a real bed."

I pull the map of Washington out of the gigantic plastic zipper-bag marked MAPS. The bag bulges with our gathered geographies—an intricately folded collection of lines and squiggles and paths traced in yellow highlighter. I spread the map out on the picnic table and smooth my hand across it. "We could camp at this little state park on the coast south of Bellingham and play in the ocean. Maybe get a motel on the peninsula."

Kat studies the map. "Ooh, look, we could drive down to the peninsula here and then take a ferry over to Victoria. It's touristy, but it's supposed to be really beautiful."

"I've never been on a ferry. Or, like, on anything that went over the ocean."

"What does Jack say?"

I dig through my bag for *The Dharma Bums*, relieved when I find it. "Here, you choose this time." I hold the book in front of me, thinking about my birthday as the pages float by. Kat lets the whole book flap past without choosing a place.

"I'm nervous," says Kat. "This is a big responsibility." She laughs, and I flip back through the book again, more slowly. "I hope I don't pick something stupid."

At last, after two more passes through the book, she closes her eyes and plants her finger on a page. "I don't know why this is such a big deal," she says, giggling. "But it totally is."

It's a big deal, and Kerouac's talking about chocolate. I read, "'For some reason or other, a Hershey bar would save my soul right now.'" I raise my eyebrows at Kat.

And for a little while, we only need to worry about dessert.

What I Want for My Eighteenth Birthday

- *To go back in time and stop messing up everything that matters most (or to find a way to fix all these broken pieces . . .)*
- *To see my mom (even one last hug!)*
- *To make my dad happy (even if I don't go straight home?)*
- *To taste the ocean (is it really salty?)*
- *To have the courage (for all of this)*
- *To make a plan (a path into the future)*
- *To take a long shower (HOT!)*
- *To sleep in a real bed (I'll share with Katy . . .) (But not with a bear!!!)*

17

Those birds sitting
out there on the fence—
They're all going to die.
—Jack Kerouac

Two Birthday Haiku from Larabee Beach:

Midmorning sun,
tiny scuttling crabs slip
from shadow to shadow.

Plump purple starfish squish
into impossible angles.
Waves crash, littered with kelp.

I'm alone up here at the top of the sandstone cliffs, thinking about Kerouac and his writing, how it has grown on me. Even the parts that used to make me roll my eyes. I flip through a few pages of my notebook, and I'm surprised by how much poetry I've been writing—how much easier it comes to me now.

When I run out of words, I stare out over the ocean, the raw force that has sculpted these rough rocks beneath me—formed them into a work of beauty, entirely unique.

I wonder if it hurts, being carved out like this, one grain of sand at a time. I wonder if the rocks realize that for every part of themselves they lose, they gain something beautiful.

I'm eighteen years old. An adult. I lean back against the passenger seat and gaze at the ocean shore passing by my window. Of course there's nothing new to feel; my birthday is just a number on the calendar—and a supposedly bad luck number at that. I laugh.

"What?" says Kat. She drives with one bare foot up on the dash, which makes me nervous. She reaches into the box of doughnuts between us and pulls out a powdered sugar-coated pastry, which she eats with both hands, using her knees to steer. God, I hate when she does that.

"What are you thinking about?" she says.

I tear my eyes off the road ahead and look at her. "My birthday. My bad luck birthday."

Kat laughs, two pale smudges of sugar at the corners of her mouth. "It's going to be awesome, Anna. I mean, it already is, isn't it? We got to hang out on the beach, you touched a starfish . . . and it's only getting better! Next up— Vancouver. Something important is going to happen there."

"Maybe. I don't know. Birthdays always seem sort of anticlimactic, you know?" I flip through the last few entries in my journal, trying to distract myself from her driving. I remember what Seth said about writing a book and wonder if anyone would ever want to read anything like this.

"Do you feel eighteen?"

I shrug. "I feel older, actually. Way older." Will I ever catch up to how old I really feel?

"Reincarnation, baby. You're totally an old soul."

"I don't know. I mean, when Jack is talking about reincarnation, it sounds like the most natural thing ever, like of *course* we have lots of lifetimes. Of *course* it's going to take us a few lifetimes to get there, to nirvana or whatever." I watch the ocean out my window, the endless rolling waves. "But . . . then I think about souls, and how complicated it would all get to keep track of, and it just seems absurd."

"Anna, *look*. I don't need any more proof than that right there to know that there has got to be a God. *That* is pure divinity." She points at the sun, the clouds filtering the light into long, radiant fingers. "Or if there isn't a God, does it even matter?"

"Beauty is truth?" I could believe that.

"Truth, beauty," says Kat. "And I need ten dollars for the ferry."

By the time we get to Port Angeles, there's only one more ferry sailing to Victoria that will allow us to get back that same night. It will leave us with approximately forty-five minutes on the island and will cost us close to thirty dollars each way.

"No way." Birthday or not, I'm not spending sixty bucks for us to spend less than an hour in Canada. That's not even enough time to get something to eat. As if we could afford it.

"We're going." Kat stands firm at the ticket booth. "This is my gift to you, and you're going to accept it. I want us to do something different, something completely out of character. We can act like tourists." She pouts comically, and it makes me ache to see how cute she is with her lip stuck out like that.

"Katy . . ." I don't want to go. Everything feels dark and wrong somehow. "What are we even going to do there?"

"Most of the shops are open late," says the girl behind the ticket booth. She taps her black-painted nails against a stack of brightly colored brochures. "Or if you're not really into shopping, you could go see the wax museum, which is awesome, very spooky, in my opinion. Or for your birthday, well, I don't know how you feel about this kind of thing, but—" She smiles like a conspirator and leans in close to us through the window. "Last time I was there I got my fortune told by a palm reader, and it was *so amazing*. Like *everything* she said was completely true. It was crazy."

"Anna babe, let's do it!" Kat jumps up and down while she pays for our tickets.

"A palm reader?" I wrinkle my nose. "Probably a scam,"

I say, but my voice betrays my curiosity. Katy and I went through a big palmistry phase once, devouring a fat book on the subject that Kat found in her dad's bookshelves, poring over our futures and pasts in the lines wavering across our splayed hands until we felt certain of our grand destinies. I haven't even glanced at my palms since my mother died. Still, my birthday list includes a plan for the future, so . . . why not?

"Totally not a scam," says the girl, handing us our boarding passes. "It's weird because she doesn't seem like a real fortune-teller, but you have to go. Her name is Renata, and she, like, freaked me out. Look for the neon hand; you can see it from the pier."

The sky has darkened considerably, and once we're on board, the wind off the water is biting cold. I'm happy to have my coat and a knit hat to keep my ears warm, but even so, when the rain starts pelting us, we head inside to the cafeteria.

As we stand in line to pay for food, the ferry pitches so violently that I actually have to grab hold of a post to keep from falling over, and even the crew member who takes our money gets wide-eyed and says, "Whoa, it's never been this rough before!"

"Well, that's comforting," says Kat, as the room lurches back and forth.

We squeeze our way along the passage toward some tables and chairs. "Kat, what's going on? Why is it so crazy?" I peer out the little window. "Look at the waves. How long is this ride?"

She shakes her head. "Like an hour and a half? It will be okay, Anna. These ferries go back and forth in all kinds of weather."

"But they sometimes sink, you know. I've read about it." I look at the carton of chocolate milk on my tray—the poppy seed muffin and the foil-wrapped pat of butter—and I feel vaguely ill. "What if we sink?"

"We're not going to sink, Anna."

"But we could."

"We could do a lot of things, Anna. I mean, if something bad is going to happen, then it's going to happen whether or not we worry about it beforehand." But she doesn't touch her food, either; instead she twists her hair into pigtails and breathes in through her nose and blows out slowly from her pursed lips.

I push my tray away and fold my hands in front of me. I look like I'm praying, but I'm only thinking. "Are you ever scared of dying?"

Kat tips her head. "I was scared when the grizzly was about to maul us."

"He wasn't going to maul us. He was so beautiful." I was afraid then, too, but not for myself. "I think I'm more afraid of other people dying," I say. *Like you*, I don't say. "The thought of my own death never used to bother me, but lately it's starting to. I think it's all this uncertainty about . . . what comes next." I open my hands. "I feel unfinished."

"I'm okay with dying," says Kat after a small pause, "but I'm a baby about pain, so I hope it's quick."

I shudder. "Like that stupid gun." Up until Kat pulled that pistol on those guys in Sage Creek, I had never even seen one in real life, not even a hunting rifle. "A gun is like an accident waiting to happen." Like playing with fire.

Kat rolls her eyes. "I told you, Anna. I'm a good shot. My grandpa was a *police officer*. He taught me excellent gun safety before he passed away."

I'm not convinced, and worse, now I'm angry, on top of being afraid. We sit for a while in a tense, strained silence, and still the boat heaves and rocks; even the crew walks around gripping the rails and looking mildly concerned. Kat opens a book but doesn't turn pages. I take my journal out, and it sits on my lap, unopened. The sky is nearly black.

"We shouldn't have come." I can't help it. My stomach roils.

"Shut up."

"Don't be mad, Katy Kat." I'm making everything worse. "I'm not trying to be a pain in the ass. I'm just scared. And . . . it's my birthday!" The ferry rolls underneath us, and I smile a grim smile while gripping the edge of the table. "And if we die, I really don't want to die with you mad at me."

Kat sighs. Her face twists into a dark frown. "I can never stay mad at you, Anna babe. Even if I want to."

That doesn't make me feel better. I want to make things better between us somehow, but I can't figure out how to get back to the way it was before. Like when we first started driving, the way it felt so good to be solid and real. Now I feel like I'm suffocating.

"I think I'll feel better up on the deck," I say, standing up. "Fresh air, you know?" Maybe if I can see the ocean, feel the rain on my face, it will be okay. "You coming?"

Kat lifts an eyebrow. "Apparently." She throws her food into the garbage can and follows me outside.

We cling to the rails running along the side of the cabin. The ferry pitches back and forth, and I clench my index finger between my front teeth and bite down, hard. The sky and the ocean are all one flat wash of gray—a fine spray of mist in the air underneath the lash of fat raindrops and bitter wind. I can't breathe. Wasn't this supposed to be fun?

"Shakespeare died on his birthday!" I have to shout over the wind and the rain.

"You're not going to die, Anna!" says Kat. Still, I see the way her hands grip the rail for the rest of the trip. The ferry shudders under the barrage of waves.

At last we reach the dock in Victoria, and I sway, still wobbly from the rough ride. We pass through customs quickly with a wave of our passports, but the well-dressed woman in line ahead of us turns back and rolls her eyes. "It takes like five seconds to get into Canada," she says, "but of course going back home takes forever. I always end up getting my stuff searched. Seriously, do I *look* like a terrorist?"

I shake my head and smile, but it's one more thing to worry about. My hand presses tight against the pocket where I keep our passports. Katy's already walking toward a neon hand in a window up ahead.

I hang back, uncertain, pulling my arms tight across my chest. Victoria is still covered in a smothering murk, and the sky looks threatening. All the Americans seem to be here for the shopping; they move in droves, loaded with bags, clambering with all their heavy packages into the tiny carriages pulled by athletic boys and girls on bicycles.

"Anna, come *on*." Katy doubles back for me and tugs on my hand. "I have some questions about the future," she says, lacing her fingers through mine.

I worry about the answers.

I expect the fortune-teller's shop to be dimly lit and mysterious, but it's bright, clean, and modern—not a scrap of moody fabric or archaic symbolism to be found. A young woman wearing a dark tailored suit and red high-heeled shoes stands beside an empty, glass-fronted counter that looks like it might have been a bakery case as recently as this morning.

"Hello!" The woman smiles brightly, setting down her pencil on top of the counter and extending her hand. "I'm Renata. What can I do for you two?" She has a light accent that I can't identify. Her dark hair is pulled back and knotted in a professional-looking configuration at the nape of her neck, but stray curls escape in reckless spirals around her neck and ears.

Kat nods to her, businesslike. "You read palms, then?"

"Yes, I read palms, the Tarot, tea leaves, some aura work. . . ." The woman ticks the items off on her fingers quickly, like a waitress naming salad dressings. There is nothing about her that feels the least bit mysterious or occult.

I smile nervously. At times like these, my voice seems to retreat, a tiny seed hidden away in the center of a prickly casing. "Um, how much is it?"

Renata waves her hand dismissively, her fingers laced with glinting stones. "Fifteen dollars American is fine," she says. "For each of you, of course."

Kat gives me a look, and I hand her a twenty. Too much, too much. I clear my throat, shifting my weight from one foot to the other. The bright lights are dazzling. "Should I, um, show you my palm?"

"Oh. Have a seat. I'll be right over."

The only seating is a little round table with four metal chairs, like you might find in an ice cream parlor. Renata moves to one of the chairs and perches on the edge, smiling serenely. I drag my right hand away from its grip on my backpack and hold it out to the unlikely psychic, who takes a cursory glance.

"You are a very logical person," Renata says, looking into my eyes. "You think things through carefully." She keeps the same passive smile on her face, her eyes never straying from mine. "Even when things get very difficult, and they have been very difficult already, you keep yourself together, all your feelings locked away, sometimes to the point of making yourself seem inaccessible to others." She turns to Kat. "You see this reserve in her, right?"

"Well, sure," Kat says. "But, I mean, anyone can see that."

Is that true? Am I really so guarded that a perfect stranger can pin me down with one look? I stare at my hand, which is still sitting faceup on the table, my fingers curled in now as though they are hiding something precious. I raise my eyes again to meet Renata's. "Don't listen to her. She thinks just because she's known me forever that she knows everything about me."

Renata laughs, a surprisingly deep and mirthful laugh, and her whole face crinkles up. "That's exactly what I'm talking about, hon." She takes my hand, smoothing out my fingers and looking seriously at my palm. "Hmm," she says, and lets go. "Time for my cheaters, sorry. Be right back."

She crosses the room, her heels clicking on the tile floor, and disappears into a doorway behind the glass counter.

"This is lame," says Kat. Her face is dark and moody, her eyes glaring after the retreating psychic. "She's not really reading your palm. She's just saying stupid things based on how you look and how you act. That's not palmistry." Kat leans back, tipping the chair until her back rests against the front window of the shop. "Ask her some questions, Anna babe. Ask her why you have like seven billion islands on your line of intellect. Ask her why your Fate line splits in half on your right hand and into three directions on your left." She leans forward, jabbing a finger into my palm.

I hear the sound of Renata's shoes returning and look up to see her emerge from the back room. There is a bead curtain in the doorway, the only thing in the entire shop that looks like you'd expect from a fortune-telling shop, but it's almost comical when the well-dressed and coifed Renata slips through it, now with a pair of red-framed reading glasses perched on her nose.

"All right, then, hon, where was I?" She takes my hand once more, peers down at it briefly through her glasses, and then looks back up. "I see that you are going to take a journey with someone very close to you." She pauses, checking in with my eyes for some signal that she is correct. I keep my face as neutral as I can. "Across water," adds Renata.

"Well, *obviously!*" Kat says, the words exploding out of her. "I mean, it's pretty clear we're Americans, and of course we care about each other; Anna just basically told you we've known each other half our lives. How else are we going to get off this island without taking a journey across water?" Kat grabs my hand and jerks it open.

"What do you think about this, huh? What do you say about these islands? Sorrows, right? Are they in the past or the present? Why does her Fate line split like this? And why does she have like a thousand crazy lines wandering all over the place right there?" Kat speaks quickly, urgently. "Will she ever be happy again, Renata? Answer me that and I'll believe you know what you're talking about."

Renata blinks, removes her glasses, and sets them carefully on the table. She folds her hands in front of her. "All right," she says, and the smile she has been holding on her face slips away. She nods, looking thoughtful. "All right," she says again. "I'm still getting the hang of when to tell it like I see it." She puts her glasses back on and beckons to Kat. "Let me see your hand."

"Another fifteen bucks?" says Kat. "I don't think so."

Renata shakes her head. "No charge, just let me see your hand. A special—two for the price of one."

Kat is silent as she extends her hand.

"Well, now," Renata says, peering closely at Kat's palm, examining each of her fingers. "Creative. Willful. A sort of fiery passion that sometimes gets you into trouble."

"All of which I've shown you since walking in here," says Kat, her tone flat.

Renata nods, bites her lip, and sits back in her chair. "Anna?"

I nod, extending my hand again.

"And . . . ?"

"Katherine," says Kat.

"Anna and Katherine." She studies our hands, side by side, for a long time. "So, okay," she says at last. "This is what I see."

We lean in, our heads bent over our palms.

"Both of you are strong—*intense* might be the right word for it."

Kat listens, her face guarded.

Renata looks at me first. "Obviously I can't tell exactly what happened, but I know something awful is in your past, something that causes you tremendous sorrow, and especially today, for some reason. The pain gets in the way of your trust." She runs her fingers lightly across several lines in my palm.

"I can see by these little feathery marks here, by the way this line splits into two at the end, that you're artistic—maybe a writer, an actor, or a dancer. Looking carefully, this split could almost be divided into three, which denotes brilliance, genius. So I would guess that you are very talented.

"However, the way this line falters—can you see it? How it splits into so many directions?"

I nod. "Wandering, like Kat said."

"You're at a very interesting point right now, Anna. It's not like your whole life is going to come down to a single decision—one way leading to good and the other to ruin—life isn't generally that dramatic." Renata tucks several renegade curls back into her bun, but they escape again the moment she removes her hand.

"I see this as more of a . . . road map. You have any number of paths ahead of you." She folds my hand tightly closed around the crazy lines on my palm. "I suppose you want to know about love?"

Do I? I look at Katy, who is staring at her own palm. What good would it do me to know? And what harm? I shake my head no.

"I do," says Kat. "Tell me."

Renata nods. "You, Katherine, are a beacon for love. You *exude* love; you bleed passion and desire and a sort of earnest hope in the goodness of people around you. This you strive to hide beneath a veneer of cynicism." She frowns, biting her lip again. "Of course, with this comes potential for pain, as well. For rejection and loss." Her voice softens even more. "You know this. You're familiar with this. You will always be the one who loves more, the one who shares more of herself."

Kat makes a face. "Well, doesn't that just sound delightful?"

Renata inclines her head. "It's not all bad. One thing about loving so completely is that you will experience a great deal of happiness in your life. Sometimes those who are more reserved miss out on that kind of joy."

I squirm.

Renata studies the two of us closely, her hands fluttering around her ears, fidgeting with the curls. "I don't . . . I don't usually claim to be a psychic. Not exactly," she says. "I mean, not in the typical way." She glances around her as though someone might overhear her secrets. "I'm a scholar, a gatherer of mystic knowledge, with a bit of intuition and a lot of reading." She pauses; her brows knit in concentration. "But I feel . . . intuitively I sense . . . and your auras maybe . . ." She trails off, biting her lip, as if we will allow her to leave it at that.

"You sense *what*?" My patience for this whole thing is wearing thin.

"I feel like the two of you should be very . . . *cautious* in the next few days. There's a strong bond between the two of you, and I sense that there is something, perhaps something outside of you, but also maybe within you? Something that threatens this bond."

The door of the shop opens, the little bell jangling, and Renata starts, sits up straighter, tucking in several tendrils of her hair and removing the red glasses. She smiles brightly at the small group of tourists who enter, all curious and nervous whispers. "I'll be right with you!" she says.

We stand, but Kat is pensive, her eyes narrowed. "You should stop fighting it," she says to Renata. "Your hair. Let it go free. I think I might actually believe you if you did."

Kat slides a tiny card underneath the edge of a sign on the wall near the door, a skeleton key with an intricate border of vines twining along the edge. I take one last glance at the shop, at Renata smiling at her new customers, and then we exit and wander along the crowded sidewalks, working our way back to the ferry docks in an uncomfortable silence.

I think even Katy regrets coming here. We board the ferry back to Port Angeles with heavy steps. I can't believe we're spending four times as long on the ship as we did on the island. And all we get out of it is this heavy awkward feeling hanging between us. We have to wrestle Renata's words aside just to catch a glimpse of each other.

"Well?" I break the silence at last. We've been on the ferry for an hour without really speaking beyond the utilitarian necessities, and now we've stepped outside for some fresh air and to take a look at the ocean. It's still cold, but the sky has finally cleared. A few stars are even visible. "Thanks for taking me out for my birthday."

She snorts. "Some present."

"Katy, I don't know how to make things better, make things the way they were. I feel like nothing is ever going to be right between us again. Like what Renata said was true, and it's already happened."

"Well, it *has* happened, Anna." I have to lean in close to hear her. "It happens and it happens and it happens."

What is she talking about? Does she know about Seth? Should I try to explain it? Is there even an explanation? "I'm sorry," I say.

Katy looks at me for a moment, and her face is hard to read. "It's not something you can apologize for," she says. "It's the way you are. Renata was right; I'm always going to be the one who loves more." Her eyes shift away, looking out over the channel, squinting into the mist. She leans against the rail. "You have no clue what I need from you."

I open my mouth, but it's hard to find the words. "So tell me," I say at last.

"Tell you. You think I don't tell you? You're all locked up tight, Anna, and what am I supposed to say? Your mom died. How can I be mad at you when you're dealing with that?" She keeps focusing on the water, on the slightly darker gray line far across the water that is Port Angeles.

I move a step closer and hang my arms over the rail, too, so that our elbows are just touching. "So is this about the palm reading?" I know it isn't, but I think we could get over it, if we pretend it is.

"No. Well, yes. Sort of." A bitter laugh, and then Kat

sighs. "Look, Anna, what do you want from this—from *us*?"

"From *us*?"

"*Is* there an us? Or are we just some kind of fucked-up friendship that includes occasional sex?" She glares at me, her dark eyes shining with tears. "I need to know, Anna, what you actually feel. Not what you think you should feel, and not what your dad says you feel. *You*, Anna. You're like a door slamming in my face. I don't need to know everything; I don't need a lifelong commitment or anything, but still, I'd like to know if you think of me as a friend or . . . as *more*. Because if this is just . . . experimenting, well then, okay. But I need to figure it out for myself. In my head." She looks away. "In my heart."

My stomach flops. I open my mouth, totally prepared to promise myself to Katy forever, to pledge my love—to say yes, "*Hell yes!* There is an "us"! There's so much "us" it makes my heart skip beats just thinking about it." The words won't hop the fence, though; they slouch on the other side with downcast eyes, kicking stones. I'm left wordless, openmouthed, at a loss.

"Fuck it, Anna. I know how it is. You're . . . it's like you're broken or something. I get it, but I mean, it's getting old, you know?"

I don't know. I *do* know. I shake my head. Renata's words spiral through my brain. *Something that threatens this bond.* . . . I know what that something is, and I have to confess. I open my mouth, but she speaks first, and my words hang there, on the brink.

"You can't spend the rest of your life running away from any kind of real emotional connection. So your mom died, Anna. I'm sorry, okay? But you have to *get over it*."

What? I try to make sense of what Katy just said, to make it line up with the words that are poised on my tongue—the words that slip out now, in my stupor.

"It didn't mean anything," I say. "The thing with Seth, I'm so sorry."

Her head snaps up. "The *thing*? With Seth?"

A tsunami of pain. My chest splits open, my lungs collapse into ruins, avalanches of oxygen spill out into the sea.

Oh, god. "I'm sorry, Katy, so so sorry."

"You know what? *I give up.*" She could have shouted the words out to sea and had them echo off the distant shore, and they would not have resonated as loudly as they do right now, a mere whisper. "Forget this."

I feel the force of the words like a physical blow, like when I was a little kid and I jumped off the peak of the henhouse at my grandparents' farm, the way the impact of the ground against my chest knocked the wind from me and left me unable even to gasp, to cry out. Just emptiness inside me, and the inability to draw in a breath to fill that space.

This is what it means to be stricken, I think, stupidly.

Katy's eyes hold mine for just a moment longer, but it feels like eons—her bleak gaze of accusation. Of condemnation. Of loss. And then she walks away.

"No!" My voice stops her. "We're not going to forget this." I flounder. I need words, but really, what is there to say? She's right.

She doesn't turn back, doesn't look at me, but she stops leaving. This is my chance.

"You're right, okay? I know I'm everything you said. Broken." I draw a shaky breath. "But how am I supposed to get over it without you? You're what holds me together, Katy. You're the only one. Not Seth. That . . . it didn't mean anything."

But it's not enough. Kat whirls around to face me, but it's not like on television, not like in a romance novel. She does not run into my arms while the music swells. She does not cry and tell me she forgives me. She spits on the deck of the ship.

"Shut up," she says, in a voice I've never heard—a bitter voice, jagged like broken glass. "I can't believe I kissed that mouth, the same mouth . . ." She doesn't finish. "Do you even realize how easy it would have been to fix this? Do you even know what I wanted from you?"

I'm crying. I open my mouth to speak, but there's nothing there.

"I'll tell you what I didn't want, Anna. I didn't want some messed-up confession, some pathetic revelation about how you lied to me, how you held my hand and told me I was more important to you than those stupid boys and then ran off with one and . . ." She laughs. It scares me. "Your big confession? It doesn't make anything better. It doesn't make *you* any better. All it does is prove my point once and for all. You'll do *anything* to escape your feelings. I thought maybe this trip would help you. I wanted my best friend back, you know? But you're too afraid to let her out."

I close my mouth. Empty, empty.

"I've always loved you, Anna." She puts her stupid orange sunglasses on, though the sky is dark. "You don't even see me. You only see your own reflection."

"Excuse me, ladies. Is everything all right back here? The guy wears a uniform and a severe-looking mustache. His jacket says BORDER PATROL. I'm still crying, mutely, and the sight of him makes me freeze, petrified with terror. Kat glares at him.

"Everything's fine," she says. "Or it will be, as soon as we can get off this boat."

What does she think will happen then? Is she just going to leave me? I deserve to be left. Everything she says is true.

The guy gives us both a stern look. "We're almost there. We'll be heading into customs in about ten minutes, but it looks like it might take a little longer than normal this evening. Nothing to worry about, but security has been tightened at all our borders."

Kat smiles at him. She is perfectly composed. "Thank you, Officer. Have a good night, now." He does not smile back, but he nods and steps back inside.

I try to catch her eye, remembering. *What about the gun?* "Katy—"

She holds up one hand. "Not speaking," she says.

The headlines scroll across my brain. *Teenager Held on Charges of Terrorism. Girl Gunslinger Captured at Border: Authorities Call It a Victory for Homeland Security.* "But Kat—"

"Anna, shut the fuck up before I say something I can't take back."

I look up. We're quickly approaching the shore. She can't go through customs with that gun or she'll be in so much trouble. I don't know what to do.

I have to do something. I lunge toward her, reaching for her orange satchel.

"Anna, what the—"

I catch hold of her arm and pull, but Katy tugs back, and we struggle back and forth a few times. She grabs a chunk of my hair, and her elbow smashes into my cheekbone, but I blink away the tears and keep clawing for the bag. "The gun!" My fingers close on velvet, and I yank the bag toward me, but I'm thrown off balance by the movement of the ferry.

"There's no gun!" She jerks the bag out of my hands. "I left it in the—" The velvet satchel flies over the rail and hits the water. It floats for a moment, and then the waves drag it slowly under the surface—a bright orange sunken treasure.

"Car," says Kat.

What I Cannot Say

only this—I was looking
for evidence of unconditional love,
but what I found was you.

standing on the ferry deck
your dark hair a fury in the wind—
Are you lost to me?

18

The taste
of rain
—Why kneel?
—Jack Kerouac

I thought I could find faith without choosing something to believe, which is sort of like thinking that I could keep what I had with Katy while trying out something new with Seth. Like we thought we could be dharma bums while we carried a cell phone. Or a gun.

Kat wants me to say that I love her, and of course I do. Do I love her the most? All I know is that the emptiness I feel when she will not look at me is so solid and heavy I can almost hold it in my hands, like a weapon. I carry it, wishing it would crush me, knowing its weight is my fault.

The beach is littered with drift logs—giant tree remnants bleached smooth by water and sun, charred by beach bonfires. We climb over several of them until we find a limb that is so wide and flat that the two of us can lie side by side on our backs on top of it, looking up at the stars and listening to the roar of the waves rolling in.

"I could kill you," says Kat.

"Well, you still have a gun." I slide my eyes cautiously in her direction, hoping she understands how absolutely horrible I really feel. About everything. Hoping she knows it's my stupid idea of a joke.

She doesn't look at me. "Homicidal Katherine is not ready for humor," she says.

Homicidal Katherine has not spoken to me since the customs officials took a brief, bored glance at our passports and waved us into America, along with the rest of the passengers on the ferry from Victoria. I had every expectation that Kat would unload my belongings on the asphalt of the parking lot and squeal out of town without a backward look. Instead she hands me the car keys in absolute silence, crawls into the passenger seat, and falls asleep. Or at least, she pretends to be asleep.

You can cry while driving but only a little because you have to be able to see the road. I listen to music and let the road carry me away—no maps, no Kerouac—as though I can erase the whole business with a few hundred miles in any direction. I'm sorry I threw her bag overboard. I'm sorry for everything that led up to that moment, and I'm sorry that in the end it was an unnecessary loss. If they had searched her and found a gun in her possession—a concealed weapon, unregistered, loaded—who knows what could have happened. Maybe they wouldn't have let her back into the country. Maybe they would have thrown her in jail. I had to make a decision, and if there's anything I've learned from this trip—from Katy, actually—it's that avoiding a difficult decision doesn't make it go away. Still, I should probably talk to her next time instead of throwing her stuff into the ocean.

My tears are drying up, the way tears will, even though the empty hole remains. My phone chirps. I find a sign for the beach and pull into the parking lot to blow my nose and see who messaged me. I'm relieved to see it isn't Seth.

Happy Birthday to my daughter, all grown up. You know your heart, just like your mother did. All of my love to you, and to Katy, as ever. Dad.

So is that true? Do I know my own heart? Can I find my way into the future? I look at Kat, who pretends to wake up. She won't look at me, but she quirks one eyebrow up as she gazes out the dark windshield, the way she does when she's about to tease me but isn't sure if she should.

I sit there for a minute, my fingers poised over the keyboard, and I think about what to say, what to do. How to face at least one of my fears. At last I start to type. *Trying to let my heart lead instead of my fear. Do me a favor? Save all those college applications. Love and thanks, Anna.* I hit Send and then get out of the car and walk toward the sound of the ocean, hoping she will follow.

"So do you want to talk?" I kind of don't know what else to say, but I guess it's what comes next.

Kat sighs, swinging her legs off one side of the log, facing the ocean. Ahead of us, the moonlit surf rolls in and in, crashing into the infinite expanse of stones—stones smoothed and sorted by shape and size in the pounding and pounding of the waves.

Kat hops off the log. "I'm super pissed at you, Anna, and I can't see that changing anytime soon. But I know why you did it."

I sit up, awkwardly twisting a pocket of emptiness in my hands. "Do you mean . . ." Her satchel? Seth? More than that?

She faces me, looking me in the eye for the first time since she walked away from me on the ship. It's dark, but the little moon carves out her face in shadows and silvery highlights, and I can tell that she is scowling at me. "I mean everything, okay? I know. I understand. I just wish for one second you would have thought about me, about what I'm feeling. We agreed on some things. And I *love* you, Anna."

There's a little pause, and then she brushes her hair back from her forehead with both hands and twists it almost violently around all her fingers, looking back out to sea. "I don't need you to say you love me back. I don't even need you to know if you do. I just need you to be open with me." She drops her hands and makes a gagging sound of disgust.

"God. Could I sound any stupider?"

"No, I—I'm glad we're talking." After all this, I still can't do anything but stand here and stutter like an idiot.

She rolls her eyes a little, a smile tugging at the corners of her mouth, and her hand fills the empty space in mine as she drags me up off the log. "I know you love me, Anna babe. It's like my art exhibition. The impact of the Good Lock key exists, even if it's unspoken. Even if it's hypothetical."

I can't talk because of these stupid tears. She leads me toward the water's edge and doesn't stop when she gets there; she wades right in, shoes and all. The water is so cold that my feet are almost instantly numb, but I don't care. It has to be past midnight. The only thing I need to feel is the relief that this terrible birthday is over. I pull her close to me, so close not even the sea can separate us.

We walk back to the car in dripping silence, still holding hands. The salt smell in the air permeates our clothes and our hair, filling the car. "We never did sleep in a bed or get our laundry done."

"I know." Kat sighs.

"I'm just glad my birthday's over." I roll down the window, leaning my head out to see the stars. "Do you remember Sage Creek, when you said you wanted to stay up all night? To see the moon kiss the morning star?"

She smiles. "That feels like a million years ago."

It does, too. "What if it's all just words, Katy? What if all of this"—I gesture helplessly—"is only running away? Maybe we should just give up and go back home." I pull the green scarf the shaman gave me from my hair and press it up to my nose, searching for the scent of jasmine, but the smell of my mother is gone—replaced with the ocean and Katy and me.

Kat tilts her head to one side, thinking. "I think we've come too far for that. We can't go back now, or we'll always be wondering what was going to happen next. Maybe we're about to make the biggest discovery of all."

"Maybe. But what if we don't make it?" Everything seems so fragile right now.

"That's life, Anna. It's uncertain. You can be a good person, or you can be completely flawed. You can be on the road without a destination or you can stay in your bed all day long. You still never know what's going to happen next."

I look closely at the scarf in my hands, noticing for the first time the wandering lines embroidered into the silk fabric with gold thread. "This isn't my mother's scarf," I say. For a moment I'm caught in a wave—a riptide of loss—as though she's being torn from me all over again. I clench the imposter, the silk tight in my fists. *Be open*, the shaman said. *You know what love is.* Outside the car, the sound of the ocean is softer, soothing, the sound of a mother hushing her infant. *A shadow to comfort you.* I miss her, but it's okay; I know what love is.

"Let's move," I say, reaching for *The Dharma Bums*.

I flip the rain-warped pages of the book, and there it is. My mouth falls open. The most beautiful Good Lock key of all—Celtic knots winding delicately and intricately around a tiny glittering ruby that Kat has pasted in the center. My birthstone.

"Art should change things," she whispers. "Open something up inside."

I read from the place marked by my key. "'That night I went to sleep in my bag by the rosebush and rued the sudden cold darkness that had fallen over the shack. It reminded me of the early chapters in the life of Buddha, when he decides to leave the Palace, leaving his mourning wife and child and his poor father . . . and embarks on a mournful journey through the forest to find the truth forever.'" I close the book, my heart so full. I press my Good Lock key tightly against my chest.

"Oh, but that's a sad part, when the dharma bums split up and go off all alone," I say. I'm afraid, thinking about the meaning of the passage. Are Katy and I supposed to go our separate ways?

The thought tears me apart, atoms splitting. She takes my hand.

Kat takes the book from me and opens it back up, flipping a little until she finds the page again. She softly reads the next part out loud, the quote from Ashvhaghosha, "'Like as the birds that gather in the trees of afternoon . . . then at nightfall vanish all away, so are the separations of the world.'"

"But I don't want to separate from you, Katy." I mean it. "Not ever."

Separations. The word slices my thoughts into the wounds of separations I've already tasted. The fissure of my mother's absence still trying to knit itself into a shiny scar. Her auburn hair, her flashing eyes, her singing voice. The loss of my father—his crumbling into red dust and his fragile new faith waiting for me at the end of the long road home. And now the thought of losing Katy.

Be open. I reach for Katy, whisper into her ocean-heavy hair—all the words inside me. We hold each other with all we have, our arms and our hearts, trusting in their strength even as we know they're not always enough.

I pull away gently and reach into my backpack for the notebook I've guarded so close all this time, opening it up to the finding God's Love list. The shaman was right—I can't chase after a checklist of experiences to prove God's love, or I'll miss the chance to prove myself. Taking a deep breath, I tear them out, each list, paging through the journal until I come to the very last one—What I Cannot Say. This one I place on top before handing them to Katy.

She takes them, holds the pages for a moment against her chest before folding them into the Kerouac book, smiling gently as she looks at the page. "'A mournful journey through the forest to find the truth forever,'" she says, reading again from the book. She starts the car. "We can take that journey later. Right now, I could go for some pie. Some pie and a big cup of coffee. You with me?"

I nod, closing my eyes. "I'm with you," I say, and I rest my head on Katy's shoulder. Like my father said, I do know my own heart. The strong, sure heart of a girl who both cares and dares. For the first time on this journey I am perfectly content here in the passenger seat—my destination both known and unknown, my future both full of promise and empty of expectations.

Acknowledgments

This book has been an amazing journey, and I'm so thankful for the tremendous help and encouragement I've received along the way—all of it seeming to come at precisely the moment when, without the assistance, I surely would have given up.

Thank you to my very honest early readers—to David, who lets me talk each problem through until I find the answer, and doesn't say a word when the answer I reach is the one he suggested from the beginning. To Rae Mariz, Amy Danziger Ross, Brianna Privett, Amanda Thrasher, Bethany Griffin, Cat Hellisen, Cai Young, Jenny Pinther, April Castillo, Ryan Gebhart, and Andrew Carmichael, who read and often reread drafts. Each of you gave me exactly what I needed to push my book further.

Thank you to Tami Lewis Brown, for letting me read her terrific thesis on the road trip novel and for empathizing with the overwhelming feeling of tackling editorial revisions for the first time.

Huge thanks to the musers—I am in debt to you all. Writing without you might be possible, but it would be so much more painful. Thanks for inspiring me, amusing me, and talking me off the ledge. Thanks for query letter wrangling and plot brainstorming and ridiculous amounts of hand-holding.

Thank you to my family—for feeding me and snuggling me and putting up with me. Also for going to bed early and letting me write.

Thank you so incredibly much to my extraordinary agent, Sarah Davies—for the surprise phone call from London two days before Christmas, for her thoughtful reading and her brilliant strategizing, and for always making me feel as though my dream coming true is the most important part of her job.

And finally, so many thanks to all the people at Marshall Cavendish, and extra special thanks to my editor, Melanie Kroupa, whose careful questioning forced me to search out the heart of Anna's story and to make every word of her journey my very best work.

Elissa Janine Hoole has a
longstanding love of road trips and Beat writers, but it was
a summer-long ramble out West that inspired this debut
novel, when she and her husband set off across the country
with a backpack full of Kerouac books. Now settled in her
home in northern Minnesota, Elissa teaches middle school
English and writes until midnight, sipping cold coffee and
ignoring the laundry.

She still suffers from acute wanderlust from time to time,
but road trips now involve a mini-van and a chorus of "Are
we there yet?" from two small dharma bums-in-training.